# VICIOUS LIES

BASTARDS OF BOULDER COVE: *BOOK TWO*

*USA TODAY* BESTSELLING AUTHOR

## RACHEL LEIGH

*"In a world full of lies, the most dangerous ones are those we tell ourselves."*

**- Diana B. Henriques**

B C
BOULDER COVE ACADEMY

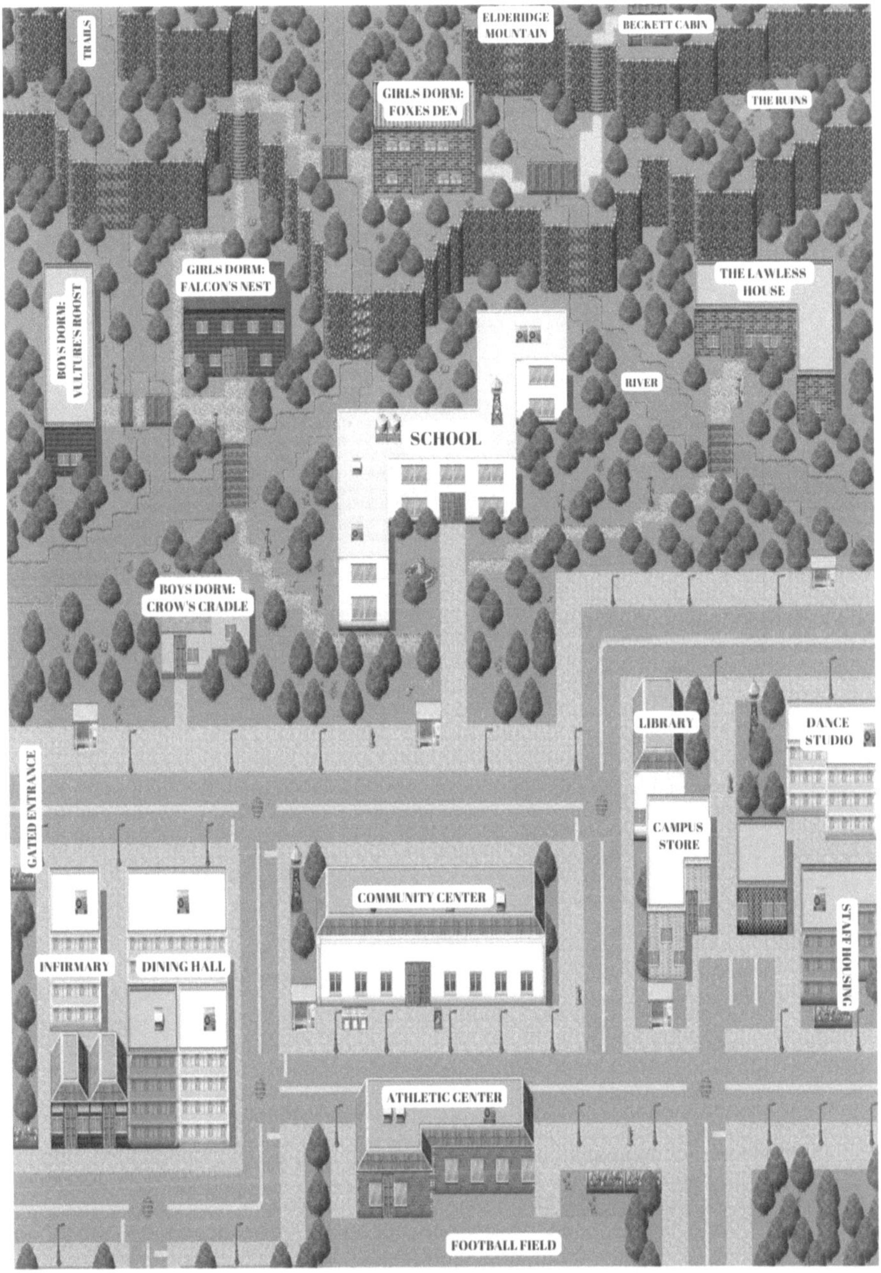

TRAILS
ELDERIDGE MOUNTAIN
BECKETT CABIN
GIRLS DORM: FOXES DEN
THE RUINS
GIRLS DORM: FALCON'S NEST
THE LAWLESS HOUSE
BOYS DORM: VULTURE'S ROOST
RIVER
SCHOOL
BOYS DORM: CROW'S CRADLE
LIBRARY
DANCE STUDIO
GATED ENTRANCE
CAMPUS STORE
COMMUNITY CENTER
STAFF HOUSING
INFIRMARY
DINING HALL
ATHLETIC CENTER
FOOTBALL FIELD

# PLAYLIST

**LISTEN ON SPOTIFY**

HUNGER STRIKE BY TEMPLE OF THE DOG

I AIN'T WORRIED BY ONEREPUBLIC

OPEN YOUR EYES BY STAND

SO GOOD BY HALSEY

BAD DAY BY FUEL

WASTING MY TIME BY DEFAULT

RUNNING AWAY BY HOOBASTANK

DARKEST HOUR BY ANDREA RUSSETT

EVER THE SAME BY ROB THOMAS

CHASING CARS BY SNOW PATROL

PINK VENOM BY BLACKPINK

ECHO BY TRAPT

FALLS ON ME BY FUEL

LOVELY BY BILLIE EILLISH, KHALID

DARE YOU TO MOVE BY SWITCHFOOT

CAGES BY MAGGIE LINDEMANN

HOLD ME WHILE YOU WAIT BY LEWIS CAPALDI

NIGHTMARE BY HALSEY

BLURRY BY PUDDLE OF MUD

ANGELS DIE TOO BY MAYDAY PARADE

BETTER THAN ME BY HINDER

Torn by Creed

Call Me by Shinedown

Love You From A Distance by Ashely Kutcher

Collide by Howie Day

While You're At It by Jessie Murph

Nothing by The Script

I Will Follow You Into The Dark by Death Cab For Cutie

**CHECK OUT THE PINTEREST BOARD**

## *Bastards of Boulder Cove Glossary*

**BCA:** Boulder Cove Academy

**BCU:** Boulder Cove University

**Chapters:** Groups within The Blue Bloods Secret Society

**The Gathering:** Student gathering to inform, promote ranks, and celebrate achievements

**Ceremony:** An occasion held where ranks are promoted, or demoted

**The Ruins:** Area of the BCA Property where social events are held

**The Tunnels:** An underground passage that runs beneath BCA property

**Eldridge Mountain:** Highest point in Boulder Cove

**The Elders:** Members of age who have advanced knowledge of The Society, typically the predecessors of current BCA students

**The President:** Oversee The Society as a whole

**The Chairman:** Oversee an individual chapter

**The Lawless:** Oversee the students at BCA

**Ladder of Hierarchy:** A system in which students are ranked according to their level of authority.

**Rook:** Lowest rank in the ladder of hierarchy

**Punk:** Middle rank in the ladder of hierarchy

**Ace:** Top rank in the ladder of hierarchy

**The Ladder Games:** Games to achieve rank

**The Lawless House:** Where The Lawless members live

**The Square:** Small gathering area in front of the academy's main buildings

**Foxes Den:** Girl's dormitory

**Falcon's Nest:** Girl's dormitory

**Vulture's Roost:** Boy's dormitory

**Crow's Cradle:** Boy's dormitory

**The Guardian:** Watchman and protector of society members

**Initiation:** An act of admittance as a leading member that takes place after graduating BCA, after which secrets of The Society are then revealed

# PROLOGUE
## SCAR

Fourteen Years Old

Have you ever looked up at the moon and thought about how the entire world, every single person, shares the same one? In this expansive world, we only have one moon and somewhere out there, other people are looking at it at this exact moment.

I look at it, talking to a nonexistent person in my head. Are you lonely, too? Are you hiding away from the world, while knowing you can't go far because we're all together under this one sky?

I overthink too much. It's just not fair that something so beautiful has to be shared with some who don't deserve it.

Damn those boys for existing in my world.

I stop walking on the trail on the backside of our property, the flashlight of my phone pointed at the old treehouse my dad had built for me when I was eight years old. I told him I needed a place to escape, because we all do at some point. Three days later, he brought me back here and surprised me with the most amazing treehouse. Okay, it's not that great, but it is to me, then and now. That small space positioned between two large oak trees was my sanctuary when I needed to get away from the noise of the world. And right now, I need it more than ever.

Moving my feet again, I head for the ladder. Since the full moon is offering enough light, I shut the flashlight off on my phone and stuff it in the back pocket of my jeans.

The wood is weathered, so I take care as I climb up, trying to avoid splinters in my hands. Mom's already spent too many nights pulling those pesky things out of my fingers. I smile at the thought. So much time spent on such a mundane task. It's those small acts that prove how much someone loves you. Even if right now I'm feeling all alone, deep down, I know I never am because I'll always have my parents.

When I reach the top, I press my palms to the hard surface and crawl over to the battery-operated lantern, hoping the batteries still work. When I flip the switch and nothing happens, I breathe out a sigh of frustration.

I stand up to pull my phone out of my pocket, but the base of my skull meets a two-by-four. "Ouch," I bellow, rubbing the sore spot on my head. It seems I've grown a few inches since the last time I was up here. Once I've got the flashlight on, I shine it around the small space. My eyes land on the 'no boys allowed' graffiti and I chuckle, even though someone did trespass and put an X through it with black spray paint. It's comical that the words even existed because there were never any boys who tried to invite themselves up. Not even Crew, Jagger, or Neo. Nope. They don't give a damn about me or this place. No matter how hard I try, I'm always on the outside looking in—except when I'm in this treehouse. Here, I'm on the inside looking out. I'm safe here. My thoughts are safe here.

Which is exactly why I let it all come out. Every tear, every sniffle, and every whimper as I cry into the palms of my hands. I cry until my throat burns and my chest collapses.

I'm running the back of my hand over my nose when I hear the crunching of leaves outside. My heart gallops in my chest, body frozen.

I finally call out, "Hello?"

Rubbing the palm of my hand on my jeans, I get onto my knees. Pressing my hands to the sides of the open space, I stick my head out.

*Must be a squirrel.*

I drop down on my butt and swallow the lump in my throat. More leaves crunch, and I find myself scooting away from the opening, instead of moving forward to look again.

That's definitely not an animal. At least, not a small one.

Instead of hollering out again, I shut off the light on my phone and I keep quiet. With my knees tucked to my chest, I hug my legs tightly. I'll just wait it out. Whatever, or whoever, it is will eventually go away.

My breaths are shallow, eyes wide, when, suddenly, the sound draws closer, and closer, and even closer.

Every bone in my body rattles when I hear someone coming up the ladder. The creaking of each wooden rung sends my heart into my throat.

Scooting farther away from the opening, my back bonds to the boarded wall.

"Who's there?" I choke out, licking my dry lips and drawing in a shaky breath.

A head pops up in the opening, and in a knee-jerk reaction, I move forward, stretch my leg out, and push the toe of my tennis shoe into the intruder's forehead.

"What in the world, Scar?" A guy's voice rings into the small space.

I gasp. "Jagger?"

"Yeah. It's me." He pushes himself up, and I reclaim my spot against the far wall.

"How'd you know I was here? Better yet, *why* are you here? Shouldn't you be at the movies with 'everyone who's anyone'?" I air quote the words used by Neo earlier, when he was pleading his case to Maddie on why she should go with them instead of roller skating with me.

"Gimme a minute." He drops down against the opening and rubs his forehead, babying the spot where I kicked him, if you'd even call it that.

"Oh, come on. Don't act like I hurt you. I was merely tapping your forehead. Didn't even put any force behind it."

"It didn't hurt at all." He picks at his forehead and I'm unsure why. "But you had gum on the bottom of your shoe."

I fight back laughter. "Oh. Well, it serves you right for invading my space."

"Your space?" He squints. "Since when?"

"Seriously?" I glare. "Since my dad had it built for me on *our* property."

Jagger laughs, running his sticky fingers on a floorboard while trying to wipe the gum off. "What are you talking about? This is my family's property."

"Shut up." I laugh, though it's not the least bit funny. Sure, the Coles' family property butts up to ours, but we've got over twenty acres, and there's no way my dad would build *my* treehouse on the wrong property.

"You're wrong, baby Scar." He tips his chin confidently.

"Last year I walked our property lines with my dad and my uncle and this treehouse is, in fact, on Cole land."

I run my hand down my face, watching him carefully to see if he's joking, but he looks dead serious.

Finally, he laughs. "I'm just messing with you. It's on your property, but you haven't been out here in ages, so I sort of took over it."

"You can't do that," I spit out. "This is private property."

He drops down, legs bent and hands dangling over his knees. "Oh yeah? You gonna tell your daddy on me?"

"Maybe I will."

He pulls a pack of gum out of his jacket pocket, unwraps it slowly while watching me, then pops it in his mouth. Rolling the wrapper between his fingers, he says, "Why are you here anyways?"

My response is immediate. "None of your business."

"Why were you crying?"

*He heard that?* "Again. None of your business."

"Is it because you weren't invited to the movies?"

"Stop!" I shout. "Quit asking me so many questions."

"Well, for what it's worth, no one went. My sister got a flat and couldn't drive us. By the time we'd have found another ride, the movie would be over."

Oddly enough, that makes me feel better. Neo begged Maddie—or forced, rather—to go with them and I wasn't invited, so here I am. Alone. Well, at least, I was.

"So where's Maddie then?"

He shrugs his shoulders. "I dunno. I think they all went to Crew's house."

"Why didn't you go?" It's not very often that Jagger and I talk, and it's a bit uncomfortable. He's at least three feet away, but it feels closer. Almost too close. Like there isn't enough room for both of us in here and my lungs are having trouble taking in air.

"Needed to recharge my batteries." He slaps his hands to either side of him onto the old wooden floorboards. "And this is where I do that. We all need an escape from time to time, don't we?"

"In *my* treehouse?"

His chin lifts, and his eyes land on a shelf beside me. I turn to look and see some belongings I didn't notice before. "You see that stuff? It's mine. What in here is yours?"

I look around, though it's hard to see much, due to the moon being our only source of light. Regardless, I don't think I have anything in here at all. Over the years, it slowly got cleared out. "Nothing, I guess. Aside from the whole entire treehouse."

"Doesn't count."

"Yes, it does," I spit out. "It's my place, on my property."

"Eh. Your parents' property. Doesn't count. In fact, I'm almost certain your dad would say I'm welcome anytime I wanna come here."

He's probably right. My dad is pretty tight with Jagger's dad—and Crew's as well as Neo and Maddie's. It's how I imagine Crew, Jagger, and Neo will be one day.

"Whatever. It doesn't matter. Just because I haven't been here in a couple years, doesn't mean you can just take it from me."

"I'll tell ya what," he slides closer, until his knee is bumping mine, "we'll share it."

"Share?" I laugh. "Yeah, right."

His shoulders waggle. "Sure. Why not?"

"How about because you hate me and the feeling is mutual?"

He quirks a brow. "You hate me?"

The expression on his face almost makes me feel guilty for saying so. "Well, yeah. Don't you hate me?"

*Why did I ask that?* Of course he does.

"No," he deadpans.

I wasn't expecting that response. Maybe I don't hate him so much either. But it doesn't change anything. We still can't share this treehouse.

"What would Crew and Neo think if they knew you were sharing anything at all with me?"

"Well, since it's yours, it'd be you sharing with me. Besides, they'd never have to know."

My eyebrows rise. "A secret?"

"Yeah, I guess."

I roll my lips, searching for any sign he's joking. I mean, he has to be. Jagger is Neo's little follower, meaning he does whatever Neo wants, and what he would never approve of is Jagger being anything but malicious toward me.

"Whatever." I wave my hand in the air, blowing out a heavy breath. "It's not like I come here often anyways. Probably won't ever come back now that I know you might be here."

I go to push myself up off the floor, but Jagger's hand lands on my knee, keeping me down. "You really hate me, Scar?"

My mouth opens to speak, but the words don't come out. I'm not sure how to respond to that question. "I...I don't know. I guess I have no feelings whatsoever toward you. You just...sort of exist in my world."

His hand is still on my knee, and the warmth of his touch spreads like wildfire through my body. "Just so you know, I do have a mind of my own."

"Okaaay." I drag out the word, unsure why he's telling me this.

"What I mean is, Neo and Crew don't make decisions for me. If I wanna share a treehouse with you, then I'll share a treehouse with you."

*Is he looking at my lips? Why is he looking at my lips?* My heart is back to galloping in my chest. "That's good to know," I whisper. *Oh no!* I just looked at his lips, too.

His mouth curls up, and when I look him in the eyes, I see him staring back at me. "I like you, Scar. You fight back, and that's not something most girls do when it comes to us."

*I do?*

I'm glad he sees it that way, but I've always assumed I appear weak in their eyes. I suppose I'll have to just keep up the front of being tough because they only see what I show them. "I guess you should keep that in mind when you're pushing me around out there."

He bites his lip and the gesture does something strange to my stomach. "Maybe I will."

Did he move closer to me? He definitely did. Oh my god, is he going to kiss me?

My body freezes when he leans into my space. His lips softly brush against mine.

"Ya know. You said you probably wouldn't come back here again, but I think you should reconsider. Say, tomorrow night?"

I nod because I can't process anything he's saying right now. Do I push him away or slap him?

No. I want this. I want him to kiss me, because as much as I thought I hated him, I know his bullying is the work of Neo Saint. Deep down, Jagger is nothing like that jerk.

His lips part slightly, so I do the same with mine. When his tongue slides into my mouth, I welcome it.

I've never kissed a boy before, but this is exactly how I'd imagined it would be. It's perfect.

Jagger is the first to break the kiss, but his hand stays on my cheek. "First time?" he asks, a softness to his tone.

I nod, feeling the heat rush to my cheeks. "That obvious?"

He shakes his head in slow movements. "Not at all."

"Whoa. What's going on here?"

Jagger jumps back, and I do the same.

I eye the newcomer. "What are you doing here?"

Neo smirks from the ladder. "Just checking in on my friend, but it seems you've got him occupied." His attention shifts to Jagger. "What? Are you two hanging out or something?"

Jagger looks from me to Neo, then back to me. "No. Came here for some privacy and Scar was already here." He climbs to his feet, slouching beneath the low roof. "I was just leaving, though."

Neo laughs as he goes back down the ladder, but as he descends, his phone begins ringing. He drops to the ground and takes the call, while Jagger joins him on solid ground.

"Wait. What?" Neo says, his tone frantic. "No! Tell me what happened? Okay. I'm on my way."

He ends the call, and I crawl over to the opening. "Is everything okay?" I peer down at them on my hands and knees.

Neo looks at me, then Jagger. "It's my mom. Something happened. I have to go."

I gasp. "Is she okay?"

I've never seen Neo this worked up. The worry in his

eyes is apparent and my heart aches for him, and Maddie, too.

"I'll go with you," Jagger tells him. He gives me one last look, swallowing hard while his throat bobs. Then, without a word, they both disappear down the trail.

Right now I need to find Maddie because if something happened to her mom, she'll need me. But I'll be back here tomorrow. And every day Jagger asks me to come, because now that I've had my first kiss, I want more of them —with him.

# CHAPTER

# ONE

## SCAR

Present Day

*This can't be happening again.*

I'm running as fast as I can, dodging sticks on the ground and skirting beneath branches hanging in my way.

*Is he still there?*

I don't stop. My feet keep moving, carrying me quickly to the Square, or anywhere with witnesses.

I can see the roof of the sports complex. I'm almost there.

It's been almost two weeks since my stalker left the note in my bag, and I haven't seen or heard from him since. I thought this was over. That his sick games had ended. There's finally been a bit of tranquility in my life and I got comfortable in it. Far too comfortable, because it's not over. I'm not sure what the endgame is with this psycho prowler, but I'm really fucking scared. Has this person been watching me all this time when I thought he had actually left?

The sound of his steps come closer and closer as my stalker picks up his pace. "Scar," I hear him say.

*Wait. Did he just call me Scar?*

I slow to a brisk walk, still heading for the library.

"Wait up."

The words hit my ear like a song. I'd know that voice anywhere. I stop, but I'm still hesitant. It wasn't long ago a voice recording was played in these same woods, of Maddie and me having a conversation. This could be a recording, too. Dipping around the tree in front of me, I hide behind it and slowly peek around it to make sure it's safe.

When I see him, I gasp. "Oh my god, Jagger!" I remove myself from the tree that I was hugging far too tightly. As Jagger comes closer, I meet him halfway. Once I reach him, I pound my fists to his chest, growling and cursing. "You asshole!"

He laughs. He actually fucking laughs.

"This isn't funny!"

With my wrists now restrained in his hands, he calms down his hysterics while I steady my breathing. "Easy, killer. I was just trying to catch up to you. You know the rules. You can't be out alone."

"And you couldn't have been a little more obvious?" Sarcasm drips from my tone. "Next time...don't bother! I can take care of myself."

"I can see that. You were one trip and fall away from practically throwing yourself into that asshole's hands."

By asshole, he means my stalker, but that's beside the point. "I was fine. Besides, it wasn't him chasing me. It was you."

"Seriously, though. Why didn't you just ask one of us to go with you, or, at the very least, get a Rook to walk with you?"

I jerk my hands away, feeling his nails graze my skin.

Rolling my wrists, I seethe. "Because Crew is at practice still and you were sleeping."

"I wasn't sleeping."

"Yes, you were. I knocked on your door like a hundred times, and when I finally opened it, I saw you sleeping."

"I was just resting my eyes."

"You were snoring. You sounded like a grizzly bear."

"I don't snore."

A sarcastic laugh climbs up my throat. "You're louder than a freight train when you're sleeping."

Jagger tilts his head toward his shoulder with a condescending look. "You watch me sleep often?"

"Oh my god." I punch his shoulder and turn around to finish my trek to the library. "Get over yourself."

He keeps walking behind me and the sound of his heavy steps through the snow only raises my level of annoyance. I should be grateful that he's so concerned, same with Crew, but I'm over this babysitting shit. It's been over a week since I've been followed, had any threats, or seen any evidence that someone is out to get me—aside from Melody and her clique, and Neo, of course. That doesn't count, though. None of them scare me. It's the unknown that sends chills down my spine, but the unknown has seemingly disappeared, and I can finally live normally. Whatever normal is at this place.

"There's a group of students gathered up ahead." I don't turn around or stop walking as I speak. "I've got it from here. You can go home if you want."

The next thing I know, he's at my side. My heart has finally resumed its normal pace, only to quicken again when he throws an arm around my neck, pulling me close. "Come on, Scar. We're friends. Let a friend help you out."

"I don't need help. What I need is a little room to breathe."

Ever since I moved into the Lawless house, I've had Crew and Jagger breathing down my neck. I know they mean well, but it doesn't change the fact that I need my personal space sometimes.

"You can have all the space you want when you're at home. Out here, you need protection."

*Home.* Such a strange word for that house. It doesn't feel like home, at least, not yet. All of my belongings are still in bags. I've been sleeping in Crew's bed because I refuse to sleep on the dirty mattress in my new room. Who knows how many people have fucked on that thing. Fortunately, my new bedroom furniture should be arriving at the house tomorrow.

"Fine," I finally say, "but once we reach the library, you can turn around and go home. Elias is meeting me there and he can walk me home when we're done studying."

He drops his arm from around my shoulders. "Deal." As we keep walking, the only sound is our boots moving through the snow and the distant chatter of students ahead, until Jagger asks, "Does Crew know you're meeting this guy?"

"No, he doesn't. Crew doesn't need to know everything I do." It's not that I'm trying to purposely keep secrets from Crew, but apparently, he threatened Elias and told him to stay away from me. Crew and I had a big argument over it and he said he didn't trust the guy. I told him Elias is my friend, who is also dating Riley, and I can hang out with whoever I want. In the end, we had a screaming match that ended in makeup sex, and we both forgot why we were even fighting in the first place. Doesn't matter, though. I stand true to my words: I can and will choose my own friends.

"Come on now, Scar. You know I can't keep shit from him."

"Never asked you to do that. You can tell him if you want, but all it'll do is piss him off."

"Did you ever stop to think about why it might piss him off?"

I laugh. "Umm. How about because Elias has a dick and Crew's a very jealous guy."

"I have a dick."

My lips roll together, pinching back a smile as I look at Jagger. "Yes, I'm well aware."

"Well. Crew lets you hang out with me."

We reach the library, and I stop at the bottom of the wide cement staircase in front of the building. "Because you're his best friend. Crew trusts you and Neo—well, you, anyways. He doesn't trust many other people."

When I look at Jagger, I see the softness in his eyes when he asks, "Do *you* trust me, Scar?"

That's a tough question to answer because I, too, don't trust many people. It wasn't until very recently that I realized I could even trust Crew, and sometimes, I still have to pinch myself to know it's real. Jagger, on the other hand, has been the least cruel to me and has tried the hardest to get back in my good graces; yet, I still don't know where my trust lies with him. "Should I?"

His fingers brush my cheek, his eyes boring into mine. Goosebumps cascade down my arms and I find myself shivering at his touch. "Probably not in the ways you should."

I choke out the words, "How come?"

"Because I don't trust myself with you."

There's no need to press on that because I know what he means, without even hearing the words. He doesn't trust himself with me, in the same way I don't trust myself with him. Temptation is getting stronger and I'm not sure how long either of us will be able to resist.

The physical attraction is real, and lately, my feelings have been brewing for Jagger. I try to ignore them and maintain whatever friendship we have, but it's getting harder and harder.

My mouth opens to speak, but before I can say the words, his hand drops from my face, and he walks around me.

One glance over my shoulder shows a group of cheerleaders heading toward him, one being Riley. When she spots me, she throws her arm in the air waving. "Scarlett!"

With a subtle wave, I begin toward her. "Hey, Ry. Is Elias inside already?"

"I haven't seen him. We're heading inside the athletic center for practice, but tell him I'll meet him at the dining hall for dinner tonight. Are you joining us?"

"Wish I could, but I told Crew I'd eat at the house tonight. Tomorrow?"

"Tomorrow, it is. And you can also give me all the deets about you two. I know there's a story to tell."

I bite my lip, grinning. "No story."

"Liar," she accuses, and rightfully so. Crew and I haven't made our relationship public knowledge yet, especially since Neo is still up his ass about even socializing with me. It's so strange. Neo lets me live in their house, but he expects Crew and Jagger to still treat me as if I'm their menial, little toy.

"I'll see you at school tomorrow, Ry," I tell her before she waves goodbye and jogs back over to her team.

I give Jagger one last look, and I wish I hadn't because I'm forced to watch some slut put her hand on his chest while giggling. Before I can turn away, though, he peels her hand off him. Something snaps in his eyes and he lifts her arm, twisting her wrist while she tries to pull away. But he doesn't let go. I listen intently as he raises his voice and shouts, "Unless your hand is around my cock, don't touch me again or I'll break your goddamn hand."

I can't help the smile that creeps on my face. Jagger is an asshole, through and through, but lately, for some reason, I get the sweet stuff.

I pull open the large wooden door and step inside the library, inhaling the stale scent of old books and coffee. Best smells in the world.

My eyes immediately land on *my* table, the one I sit at every time I come here, but it's empty. Elias said he'd be here at four. I glance at my wristwatch and see that it's ten after.

A shiny object under the table catches my eye. I walk quietly through the other tables, gripping the strap of my messenger bag. Crouching down, I pick up the old, rusted half-heart. It's like one of those best friend charms you can buy, where one person gets one half, and someone else gets the other. It's not connected to a chain or anything, though there is a hole for one. When I hold it up in the light, I'm able to read the engraving on it. *I'm everywhere you go –Kenna.*

*Kenna.* Where have I heard that name before?

I stuff the charm into the pocket of my coat and stand back up. Searching the room for Elias, I still don't see him, so I drop my bag on the table and get to work without him.

Elias and I come here often to study together. There is something about the library that feels more like home than any other place here at the Academy. Riley has cheer practice four days a week, while Crew has practice those same nights, so Elias and I enjoy each other's company. It's been hell having to keep it from Crew, but I know he'd flip if he knew I was still hanging out with him.

Crew has always been paranoid, thinking everyone is out to get me—even when it was him who was out for me for a while—but lately, he's been extra protective. Even after I moved into the house. I swear something happened, but he keeps telling me just to trust him. For a while, I thought maybe he and the guys caught my stalker and murdered him. Crazy, right? But it was the only explanation why this guy suddenly stopped taunting me. I also wouldn't put it past any of them if they thought the Society was being threatened. But then I realized, if that were the case, Crew would let his guard down versus raising it higher.

Minutes pass of me reading up on common idioms and literary allusions, when I realize it's been more than a few minutes. It's been thirty since I've arrived. *Where the heck is Elias?*

I slide my chair back and slowly get up. Turning and looking, as if I'm expecting him to suddenly arrive. A strange feeling washes over me. It's a feeling I've had countless times since arriving at BCA. The sense that someone is watching me. Almost as if I can feel their eyes burning into my skin. Out of the corner of my eye, I see a shadow, but as soon as my eyes find it, it quickly disappears. Stepping around the chair, I walk slowly toward where it was. Everyone continues on with their quiet work, while I weave through the tables gracefully, heading for the double-faced stacks.

It appears again, this time at the back of the library. Only, it's no shadow—it's the black robe. His back is facing me and the hood is pulled over his head. My heart rate excels, but I don't stop walking. "Stop!" I whisper-yell. "Don't go."

I'm so close. Just a few more steps and I can reach out and grab him and find out who it is, once and for all. But before I'm close enough, a paper drops from his hand and he takes off running. "Wait!" I go to run after him, but I'm stopped when someone grabs me from behind.

My instincts have me pounding my fists into the chest of the perpetrator, but when I realize it's Crew, I quickly stop.

"He was here." I bend down and swipe up the piece of paper, handing it to Crew. "It was him. I know it was."

Crew takes the paper from my hand and slowly opens it, while watching me like I've lost my damn mind. "Who was here?"

"My stalker. The person who's been watching me and leaving these notes." The words fly out of my mouth without me even taking a breath. "He didn't disappear. He's still very much here." I tap the paper in his hand. "Read it."

Crew pinches his eyebrows together and hands it back to me. "It's just a school schedule, Scar."

"What?" I snatch it from his hand, and, sure enough, it's a schedule. "No. It was him. He was wearing the robe." I turn the corner of the shelf and look down the row, but it's empty.

Crew is at my side immediately. "Baby, it's freezing outside. Everyone is wearing winter coats, and I'm sure your mind is just playing tricks on you."

I shake my head, looking at him with desperation in my eyes, practically begging him to believe me. "It had to be him."

I fold the schedule up into a tiny square, gripping it in my palm.

"Come on." He puts an arm around my waist, leading me past the rows of books. "Let's go home and we can talk about this later."

"How'd you even know I was here?"

"Practice ended early. Saw Jagger sitting on the steps out front. He said he was waiting to walk you home, but I told him I'd give you a ride. When I noticed you weren't at your table, but your stuff was, I started looking for you."

*Jagger's been waiting for me this entire time?* As much as I scream, *space*, my heart swells at the thought.

"Was Elias out there?"

He looks at me, brows raised. "No. Why?"

"No reason."

*What in the world happened to Elias?*

I follow Crew's lead to the table, where my books are still out. My eyes continuously glance over my shoulder to see if the person has reappeared. When I unfold the paper in my hands, I catch the name of the student whose schedule I'm holding: *Melody Higgins.*

That's odd. Melody's at cheer practice.

# CHAPTER
# TWO

## SCAR

I HAVEN'T HEARD from Elias since he stood me up yesterday, but Riley is supposed to stop over at some point, so I'm hopeful she can tell me why he never showed.

My eyes lift from the textbook in my hand when Crew walks in my room.

"Last one?" I ask him as he drops a box onto the floor beside me. Sweat drips down his forehead, and if looks could kill, I'd be dead.

"No, Scar. It's not the last one."

He turns and leaves the room—my room—and I crack a smile. He's the one who told me to order whatever I needed for my new room. I only got the necessities—a new mattress, a dresser, a desk, and maybe a couple new outfits. I lean over the box he just brought in. It looks like this might be my clothes. I should probably hide this one before he opens it and realizes I used Blue Blood money to fund a new wardrobe.

I argued hard on my stay here until I had no fight left in me. In the end, I gave in. They're convinced an outsider is after me. They think this person wants to harm the entire Society, with the intention of using me as their weapon. Up until yesterday, I would have argued that I wasn't in danger anymore. Now, I know I'm still being watched.

Regardless, it wasn't my choice to move in here, so I used whatever I could as a bargaining chip. I told them there was no way in hell I was sleeping on the used mattress of a former Lawless member, and Crew handed me a credit card and told me to get what I needed. So I did. I also told them that I want my privacy and a phone. I lost on the phone, but they ensured my privacy—not that they give it to me, anyway. Living with three guys is going to be hell enough. One of them being Neo is straight-up torture. Sometimes I wonder what would be easier on my sanity: giving up and letting my stalker destroy me or allowing Neo to break me down piece by piece, day after day.

"Hey, girl," Riley says, entering with a broad smile on her face.

I close my biology book and push it into my school bag. "And why are you so happy?"

"I shouldn't be, right?" She looks around the room, cringing. "This place is creepy as hell. It's like a gazillion years old. You think anyone's died in this house?"

"There's a very good possibility, Ry. But it's the living we need to fear, not the dead." I push my bag to the side of me. "So, if it's not my phantom room that has you all giddy, what is it?"

She folds her hands together, pressing them to her chest, and beams. "Elias asked me to be his date for the Halloween dance." Her eyes light up with excitement, and it's impossible not to be happy for her. And at least I know Elias is alive after standing me up.

"That's so awesome, Ry. I'm really happy you got a date to a stupid dance, where we're supposed to dress up in ridiculous costumes. Though, I'll pass. Not really my thing. But congrats to you." I'm hoping I didn't sound too pessimistic, but Riley is used to my bitterness, and she does a pretty good job at ignoring it.

"Oh, you're going."

She's also good at talking me into doing things I really don't want to do. Such as this dance. Chances are, she'll dress me up like her little dead doll and put an arm around me while smirking devilishly over her win the entire night.

Doesn't mean I won't argue it. "Nope. Not this time, Ry. I'll do your stupid parties, but dances are a big no."

"You don't have to actually dance—"

"The answer is no."

She falls back on the bare mattress, her feet practically touching my face. "We'll see about that."

I push her feet away and say, "You know how many people have fucked on that bed?" When she jumps off it like it's contaminated—which it is—I laugh.

"Ugh. That's gross." She wipes herself down, snarling grotesquely.

Pushing myself up, I kick the box Crew just brought in until it's against the far wall beneath the window. The blinds are still open, and I look out at the accumulated snow. It's still fall, but winter is well on its way here. It's unfortunate that our autumn season doesn't last long, but it's the price you pay for this gorgeous mountain view.

"Well," Riley begins, "if I can't convince you to attend the dance, how much coaxing will it take for you to come with me to a party at the Ruins tomorrow? There's no school

Thursday, so we can get drunk tomorrow night and sleep in."

I scoff. "It's like thirty degrees outside."

"There'll be a big-ass fire. Besides, we were sort of hoping..." Riley puts on her pouty face, which means she's about to ask for a favor, "...maybe you could convince the almighty Neo Saint to move tonight's festivities underground. Say, the Gathering room?"

That warrants a hefty laugh. "You're kidding, right?" Her stoic expression says she is most definitely not kidding. "You do realize me living in this house doesn't change the fact that Neo hates me, right?"

"You have to have some sort of pull. After all, they've taken you under their wing."

I tug my ear lobe, shaking my head. "No. I've got absolutely no pull when it comes to Neo. If anything, being around him so much is the equivalent of digging my own grave."

Riley doesn't know about my stalker. As far as she's concerned, everything that happened to me was part of the Ladder Games. I never gave her details or told her any different. It's best she doesn't get involved.

"There's some sick truth to that statement, so I'll stop you there."

"Hey," I say, shifting my tone and the subject, "any idea why Elias stood me up at the library yesterday? We were supposed to study and he never showed."

Her mouth curls downward and she shakes her head. "No clue. I saw him this morning and he never mentioned it."

"It's so weird. He always shows."

Crew comes back in the room, pushing a dolly. His

annoyance is apparent as he drops the dolly down and rests his arm on the box. He wipes the sweat from his forehead with his bare arm. "The mattress is the last one."

I smile sheepishly. "Thanks, Crew." I go in for a hug but stop myself, turning up my nose.

"What?" He huffs, before sniffing his own pits. "Do I smell that bad?"

Riley waves her hand over her nose. "I can smell you from here."

Crew smirks. "Get your cute little ass over here." He walks toward me, but I take a step back for each one he takes.

"Stop. Go take a shower. You smell worse than that fifty-year-old mattress."

My back hits the far wall and he reaches out to grab me. "Oh yeah? That bad, huh?"

He pulls my body to his, while I laugh and shriek at the same time. Then, in one swift motion, he spins me around and tackles me onto the old mattress.

I squirm and fight, trying to crawl out from underneath him, but when his lips land on mine, I surrender.

With two hands pinned over my head, Crew grinds himself against my core, not giving a damn that we have an audience. "I'm gonna take a shower then we need to break in that new mattress."

I purse my lips and nod. "Can't wait."

Crew climbs off me, tips his chin to Riley, finally acknowledging her, before he leaves the room.

Once the door closes behind him, I jump off the nasty bed, and Riley is in my face, demanding answers. "What the actual fuck was that?"

Riley doesn't know the details of my relationship with

Crew right now. In fact, Riley doesn't know much of anything pertaining to my life. It actually makes me feel like a shitty friend, but being raised in a society like this one, you learn that the less people know, the better. I'm sure she understands why I don't divulge much information about my past, and it's also why I haven't pried into hers.

My cheeks flush as I turn away to avoid eye contact. "Things have been...developing." I leave it at that, knowing she will dig for more on her own.

The next thing I know, she's back in my face, hands on my shoulders, forcing me to look at her. "Developing?" She drags out the word, her eyes quizzically reading mine.

I shrug my shoulders, letting them dance for a minute before saying, "Yeah. Developing."

"Uh-uh." Her head shakes. "We aren't leaving it at that. I knew you had history with Crew. Knew you were moving in here as an end to the games..." (Yeah, I told her that. See—shitty friend.) "But I had no idea you and Crew were on tickling terms."

"Tickling terms." I laugh at the phrase she's termed for whatever Crew and I have going on. "We're just starting over. That's all. As you know, we once had a thing and we've decided to put the past where it belongs, and this is where it's leading us." I say it all so casually, but there is nothing casual about Crew and me. Not just the relationship that's budding, but also the past that's still greeting us at every turn.

Her hands drop from my shoulders, and her expression becomes more serious, which is exactly what I wanted to avoid. "So, you like him?"

I nod subtly, while searching for the right response, but the only one that comes to mind is the truth. "Yeah, I do like him." A lot actually, but I don't tell her that. Feelings are not something I like to discuss, not even with my therapist back home. It took a solid three months before I even opened my mouth to speak in that office. Once I did, though, it all came out. Riley reminds me a lot of Dr. Barnes, always forcing me to open up and let the truth out.

All the air expels from my lungs when Riley squeezes my chest to hers in a tight hug. "I'm sure outside of this place, that asshole is a wonderful person." The seriousness in her tone has me busting out laughing.

"Nah. He's pretty much still an asshole, but he's my asshole."

I purse my lips tightly. *Did I really just say that?* Is Crew really mine? A short time ago, he belonged to Maddie. If it weren't for the accident, he'd probably still belong to her. Guilt gnaws at my stomach, much like it does every time Crew and I are together as a couple.

A knock at the door has Riley releasing her hold on me. "Come in," I say loud enough for the person on the other side to hear.

"You're pretty brave," Riley says, "not knowing who it is and all."

"Eh. It's gotta be Crew or Jagger. Neo would never knock."

Riley laughs, but I don't find it at all funny. In fact, it's pretty intimidating living in this house with Neo. I walk on eggshells and try to avoid him at all costs. There is no such thing as a pleasant encounter when it comes to that boy.

The door comes open and Jagger is standing there. He doesn't enter, just braces his hands on either side of him against the frame. He's wearing only a pair of gym shorts, sweat sliding down every cut of his abs. I'm speechless, but I'm not the only one.

"Riley," I nudge her and whisper, "pick up your jaw before you trip on it."

She snaps out of her trance and licks her lips. "Right. I should go. I'll see you later." She glances at me with blushed cheeks and a bitten smile.

I nod, giggling at her awkwardness. "Yeah. Later."

Riley turns sideways, sliding past Jagger, who doesn't even bother moving.

Once Riley's gone, Jagger drops his hands and walks toward me with a slow swagger. "What was that all about?"

I find myself licking my lips, too, because, damn, he looks delicious. "Oh, I dunno. Could be you coming in here, looking like that." My eyes skim up and down his body.

Jagger wipes his forearm over his head, wiping up some of the sweat. "Oh yeah?" He smirks. "I don't see you running away all googly-eyed. Does that mean you don't like what you see?"

I blow out a heavy breath of laughter, crouching down and pretending to look for something in my school bag. "I see your ego hasn't deflated at all since I've moved in."

"In my defense, you've only been here a week. Give it some time, and I'm sure you'll be leaving me with little to no self-esteem."

"Wouldn't hurt for any of you guys to be knocked down a few pegs."

He slouches down on the opposite side of the large luggage bag full of the clothes I haven't unpacked. Still unable to look at him, out of fear I'll lose all train of thought and only feed his ego more, I continue to shuffle through some tee shirts.

"Why won't you look at me, Scar?"

My stomach flip-flops, and when I don't respond, he tips my chin up so that I'm looking right at him. "What's there to look at?"

I cast my eyes down, even though he doesn't drop my chin.

God, he's gorgeous. Tall, toned, and tanned. His sultry honey eyes match the dampened tips of hair that shimmer like gold. Every inch of his body is perfectly sculpted.

My heart pitter-patters when his thumb grazes my lower lip.

"Me." He tips my chin again. "Look at me, Scar."

I hate the effect he has on me. I'm still trying to figure Jagger out, but in doing so, I'm finding him more and more attractive. The urge to kiss him is powerful, and I fear if I don't remove myself from this situation right now, I won't be able to fight off my attraction to him any longer. In a perfect world, he'd do something atrocious, like he's done in the past, and I could easily hate him. Only, he's not doing any of those things. Jagger has been warm and kind and helpful. He's walked me home from school every day since I've moved in, while Crew is at practice. And even though I pretend it's annoying, I actually like it. We've had the best conversations, and he can always make me laugh. So while I wish I could hate him, I'm not sure I can.

Jagger is the first person to ever make me hold my breath and stumble over my words. He makes me nervous, and I have no idea why.

"Quit making this weird," I finally say, pushing my bag of clothes toward him and causing him to shift back a few inches.

His hand drops, and he chuckles. "You're so much fun, Scar."

Why does he keep saying my name like that? So sexy and seductive-like? And fun? How am I fun?

The defensive side of me kicks into gear. "What's that supposed to mean?"

He drops back on his ass against the bed, knees bent and his legs spread apart. I give him one glance. One stupid glance and it's not at his face; instead, I'm offered a full view between the legs of his shorts to nothing but his sack resting peacefully against his groin.

I blink my eyes away, feeling my cheeks heat up. When I look back at him—his face this time—he's grinning.

*Oh my god, he knows.*

He knows I just stole a glance at his junk.

I roll my lips together, playing it cool while I pull clothes out of my packed bag. Shirt after shirt falls onto the floor beside me, and before long, the bag is empty.

"What's gotten into you?" he asks with an unwavering tone, as if he doesn't know.

But I don't even know. What has gotten into me? Since when does Jagger, or any guy for that matter, make me feel this flustered? No one ruffles Scarlett Sunder.

"Nothing. I'm just trying to..." My words trail off when Crew walks into the room, holding a shopping bag.

"What's going on in here?" Crew asks, suspicion in his tone.

Jagger pushes himself off the floor and rubs his hands together. "Not much," he steps past Crew, heading for the door and speaking as he walks, "Scar was just looking at my dick."

My jaw drops, and I shout to Jagger as he leaves the room, "I was not!" I look at Crew. "He's lying."

He sets the bag down on the bed, observing me. "What was really going on then?"

"Nothing!" I blurt out defensively. "We were just...talking."

He side-eyes me, knowing there's more to the story. "You sure?"

"Yes, I'm sure! He was only here for a couple minutes, and I'm not even sure what he wanted."

"Oh, I know," he drawls. "I know exactly what Jagger wants." I raise my questioning brows. "He wants you. The question is, do you want him, too?"

"Why are you even asking that? I'm with you." I stand up, chewing on the inside of my cheek.

"You admitted you're drawn to him and that you like his company, so answer the question. Are you falling for my best friend?"

"For the last time, I'm with you, remember? Starting over. Building something fresh and new."

"Okay." He nods, reaching out and grabbing me by the arm. He pulls me close and his spice-scented body wash floods my senses. It's a nice escape from his musty, sweat stench of a few minutes ago. I draw in a deep breath as I fall into his arms. My head rests on his chest as he says, "You'll tell me if anything changes, right?"

I nod against his thumping heart. "Of course."

I'll get over this infatuation I have with Jagger. My future is with Crew. It's always been him and it always will be him.

"What's in the bag?" I ask, changing the subject.

Crew steps back and reaches over to grab the bag. With a

broad smile, he hands it to me. "Got you a little moving-in present to hang on the wall."

I bite back a smile, feeling a swarm of giddiness in my belly. "You did?"

He nods toward the bag in my hand. "Open it up."

I pull apart the twine straps of the paper bag and look inside. My heart doubles in size when I see the *Nightmare Before Christmas* gift inside. "Oh my god, Crew. I love this."

Pulling it out, I hold up the Jack and Sally wall art. It's a metal display with tiny little lights on the back. Crew knows how much I love *Nightmare Before Christmas*. "It's perfect. Thank you, baby." I press my lips to his, knowing that this right here—me and Crew—is exactly what I want.

CHAPTER

# THREE

JAGGER

"PUT SOME DAMN CLOTHES ON." Neo chucks a pillow at me from where he's sitting on the couch. "My date will be here any minute, and I don't need her staring at your half-naked ass before I've had my way with her."

I catch the pillow in midair and use it to wipe the rest of the sweat from my face before throwing it back at him. With a clenched fist, he punches it away and it falls to the ground.

"Throw that thing in the laundry for one of the three Rooks to wash."

Since we had the Gathering to promote the ranks, Rooks are limited. Only three didn't advance, and it sucks ass to be them. They've been our bitches daily, and while I'm not complaining, the remorseful side of me does feel a tinge of guilt. Neo, on the other hand, doesn't have a sympathetic bone in his body.

I drop down on the couch beside him, kicking my feet up on the coffee table in front of us. "So, who's the date?"

33

"Date?" he asks, questioning me. "Did I say date? I meant quick fuck."

"Now that's more like it. I thought something was off about that statement."

"How about you? Got anyone lined up for tonight?"

"Nope," I say with honesty. Right now, the last thing on my mind is girls. Aside from one in particular. One that sleeps in the room next door to mine. That makes even the worst days feel like the best. And one that is completely off-limits because she's with my best friend.

Neo slaps my leg, really fucking hard, and I shriek. "What the fuck?"

"Sucks to be you, man. There's still a lot of untapped pussy on campus. Don't worry, though. I'll break 'em all in for ya."

"I have no doubt you will." I'm staring blankly at my feet on the table when Neo slaps my leg again. "Dude!"

"What the fuck is with you?" he asks, an openness to his tone.

The agitation inside me builds, and if I don't get it out soon, I'll explode. "Nothing! I've just got a lot on my mind."

"Jesus Christ. You, too?"

My brow furrows as I turn to look at him. "What?"

"You're acting just like Crew when he started falling for that bitch—"

"Don't call her that!" I shoot him a glare, fists clenched at my sides.

"And now you're defending her." The doorbell rings, and I breathe out a sigh of relief. Really don't feel like having this conversation with Neo right now. He slaps his own legs, then stands up. Unfortunately, he doesn't stop talking as he approaches the door. "I'll tell you the same thing I've told him countless times. She's not worth it. Get yourself a little hottie for the night, or I'll pass you mine when I'm done. Do whatever the fuck you gotta do, but don't get tangled in that girl's web of lies. You'll live to regret it."

A tall redhead walks in wearing a pair of furry snow boots and a plaid coat that's so big, it makes it look like she has nothing else on.

"Mmm," Neo hums as he grabs her ass. When he does, she giggles and turns around, and I see that she, in fact, doesn't have anything else on. Unless her G-string counts as shorts. "Get that cute little ass bent over my bed and I'll be there in a second."

The girl nibbles at her bottom lip, flips her sleek, red hair over her shoulder, and prances up the stairs like an obedient puppy.

"You see that?" Neo says, "that's what you're missing out on if you don't get over that chick."

I shake my head in annoyance and stretch my legs to pull my phone out of my pocket. Neo ascends the stairs, and when I hear his bedroom door close, I make a call.

"Hey, Dad," I say in a hushed tone. "Did you find anything out yet?"

"Still working on it, son. I'll let you know as soon as I hear anything. And I assume you're still keeping a tight lid on what you know?"

"Told ya I would."

"Good. Let's keep it that way. Your only concern right now is the Academy and the students. Anything on the outside is not your problem—not yet. This goes for Crew and Neo, too. The last thing we need is for that family to find out we're digging."

"All right, Dad. Once again, I'm not saying anything. But

I hate keeping this shit from them, so tell this guy to hurry up."

"How's your grades?"

It's just like him to change the subject. He said what he needed to say and that's that. Screw what I want.

"All *A*'s, like always. Look, I gotta go. Keep me updated, okay?"

"I'll be in touch." Just as I open my mouth to say good-bye, he cuts in, "Oh, and, Jagger, you better not be giving Scarlett a hard time. I told Kol you'd keep an eye on her until this shit is settled."

"You told Kol?" I huff. "So you can tell your friends, but I can't tell mine?"

"Let the Guardians and the Elders handle this, Jagger. You just do what you're supposed to do there and we'll handle everything on the outside."

"But this shit isn't on the outside and the Guardian on the inside isn't doing jack shit."

"You heard what I said. I've got a meeting to get to. I'll be in touch."

The line goes dead, and I aggressively toss my phone into the middle of the room. *Let the Guardians and the Elders handle it.* What a bunch of bullshit. They expect us to endure hell to prepare ourselves for the future, but when we're tossed into the flames, we're expected to drag our own asses out, just because we're in here and they're out there.

"You can't tell your friends what?" Scar asks from behind me.

*Shit.* I spin around quickly. "How long were you standing there?"

She crosses the room to my phone and bends down to pick it up. "Long enough to hear you express your anger about not being able to tell your friends something. So what is it?"

There isn't much I can say to Scar about my conversation with my dad. He's adamant that this stays between us until we know what we're dealing with. The day after we found the Blue Blood shrine in the tunnels, I went back. The guys and I made a pact not to go alone because it could be dangerous, but curiosity got the best of me.

While we were down there, I found a diary. I hid it underneath a pile of papers and went back for it the next day. Turns out, it was the diary of Betty Beckett. The Becketts are a family that has hated every Blue Blood member for decades. Betty was married to the original founder of the BCA property. I only made it through the first couple pages when I put two and two together. That room has been passed down from members of the Beckett family for centuries. It also means, whoever is currently doing the upkeep, is also the person who's been stalking Scar—an outsider, and also a Beckett, or at least someone with a connection to their family. But how and why are the answers I can't seem to find. I called my dad that night and had him look into the Beckett lineage. He contacted one of the Society's Guardians, who is investigating, but so far, nothing.

I get off the couch and eat up the space between us. "It was nothing. Just my dad being my dad."

"Well, if it involves your dad's friends, that means it must involve *my* dad."

She hands me my phone and I take it—fortunately, it's not cracked. "It does. Apparently, my dad told yours that I'd keep an eye on you. Make sure you're safe and all." That part isn't a lie.

"I'm not surprised. They've done that our whole lives. Little good it's done." There's a bite of sarcasm to her tone, and I can understand why after the hostile things we've done to her.

"Hey," I say, grabbing her arm as she stares down at her bare feet, "I told him I would. You know that, right?"

With raised shoulders, she lifts her head. "But did you mean it?"

"Yeah. Of course, I did. Haven't I proved that every day since you moved in? You're here, aren't you?" I'm referencing the house as I look around at the space surrounding us.

"I'm here because of Crew."

I blow out a heavy breath. "Are you serious, Scar? I agreed to let you stay here, too."

She laughs maliciously. "Agreed?"

"Yeah. When Crew mentioned it, I said it was cool. And, somehow, he convinced Neo, too."

"My God. Why are you both so loyal to that jerk?" I'm not sure if it's something I said, or her own thoughts clogging her logic, but she's set off. Her demeanor shifts rapidly from calm to tense. "You know what? Forget it. I don't even need protection. Not from you, and especially not from Neo."

There's a beat of silence before I finally say, "And Crew?"

Her lips purse, and she tucks the stray strand of hair in her face behind her ear. "Crew stood up for me. He stood up for our relationship, and he's not letting Neo dictate his life anymore."

If only that last part were true. Neo dictates everything, even if Scar doesn't see it all. The only reason Neo agreed to let her stay is because Crew convinced him it would be easier to keep an eye on her. Neo still thinks she's the snake

—that there isn't even someone out there fucking with her. Even after finding that room in the tunnels, he somehow convinced himself she orchestrated it and is fooling all of us.

"As he should, if his feelings for you are genuine."

"If?" She pegs me with a sour look. "His feelings are genuine. I know you and Neo don't see it, but Crew and I have something special. We have for a while. It just took us both saying, 'fuck what everyone else thinks,' so we could be together."

"I'm glad for you, Scar. Really, I am." The emptiness in my words is apparent, and I can tell by the look on her face that my words didn't appease her in the slightest.

Her arms cross over her chest and she pops her hip. "Really? Then why do you act so pissed about it?"

I'm not sure how to respond without sounding jealous, because I'm *not* jealous. Sure, Scar has been taking up a lot of Crew's time. And the way Scar speaks like he's some saint all of a sudden is annoying as hell. But I'm not jealous of their relationship. Maybe there's a small part of me that wishes it was me instead. That I would have been the one to comfort her after Maddie's accident, or the one to stand up to Neo in her defense. But I didn't do any of that. He did.

"I'm not pissed at all," I finally say, "I just think it's a little premature for you and Crew to start living out your fairy-tale relationship after everything he's done to you."

She's on the defensive and the last thing I want is to piss her off right now, but the scowl on her face says it's too late for that. "You mean everything you've all done to me?"

I could tell her that, in all honesty, everything that happened was Neo's doing and we followed along because of the pact we made before taking on the Lawless role. "I'll admit, we haven't made things easy for you."

"Haven't made things easy?" She barks out a laugh. "How about, you've made my life hell?"

*And still are.*

"Look, Scar. We fucked up. All I'm saying is, take things slow with Crew. There's no need to rush into things. Not to mention, Maddie is still lying in a coma with no idea Crew won't be waiting for her when she wakes up." Immediately, I eat my words. I went too far. I run my hand over my forehead, eyes wide on hers. "Shit. I'm sorry, Scar. I didn't mean—"

"Don't." She holds up a hand, shutting me up. When she turns to walk away, her pain obvious, I grab her by the arm, but she quickly jerks back. "Don't touch me."

"Just let her go, man." Neo walks in the room, sweeping his hand in the air. "She's a waste of time."

Scar stops walking, pins Neo with a hard glare, like she wants to say something vulgar. As abrupt as she stopped, she begins walking again, stomping with heavy steps up the stairs.

I shake my head in disappointment as Neo snatches a half-empty bottle of whiskey off the table beside the couch.

"Was that really necessary?"

"More than necessary. We can't let that girl get too comfortable in our lives."

He unscrews the top and tips the bottle back, taking a long, slow swig.

"Slow down, man. It's only 4 o'clock."

He pulls the bottle away from his lips, smacking them together and sliding his tongue across his bottom lip. His mouth tugs up in a grin. "It's five o'clock somewhere. Besides, need to build my tolerance before the party tomorrow night."

"You have the tolerance of an alcoholic. And what's this party you speak of?"

"It seems the cheerleaders have thrown together a little shindig at the Ruins tomorrow night, so I put together a little something of my own." The mischievous look on his face tells me he's definitely up to something.

"Care to elaborate?"

His shoulders rise and fall as holds tight to the still open bottle of liquor. "Party at our house. We'll call it *a house-warming party for our new housemate.*"

"Aren't you the one who just said we didn't want her getting too comfortable here?"

"Oh, she won't be comfortable. That, I can promise you."

"Pretty sure if Scar goes to any party, it'll be with Riley."

"Like hell she will." He scoffs. "Part of the deal of her moving in was that she only goes out if one of us is with her. Which we won't be. Not you. Not me. And sure as hell not Crew."

My fingertips press to my eye sockets, and I rub vigorously. "Whatever, I'll let you be the one to tell her that."

His head shakes and his lips twitch. "Nah. Think we'll let Crew do the honor."

When I have no response to this never-ending bullshit, Neo continues, "Come upstairs with me." He angles his head to the right, motioning me to follow him. "Got something for ya."

Dropping my shoulders, I scratch the top of my head and humor him by following. "I'm not sure I wanna know what that means. You're not exactly the giving type."

He huffs out a breath. "After this, you'll be thanking me. Guaranteed."

"Doubtful," I mutter under my breath as we reach the top of the stairs. Neo turns left, instead of right, which is where his bedroom is. "Where's this *surprise?*"

When we pass by Scar's room, I look inside her open door. There are opened boxes scattered around and clothes flung everywhere. Then I see her and Crew lying on the bed. His hand is pinching the skin of her ass that hangs out of her shorts. Her head rests on his bare chest and they're both smiling, which feels like a punch in the gut.

"I've gotta go deal with some bullshit," I hear him say to her. "It shouldn't take long."

Is that what our duties are now? Bullshit? A couple weeks ago, I wouldn't care less what he refers to our duties as, but lately, I'm really fucking annoyed with anything Crew says or does.

I'm not even paying attention to Neo as he walks into my room. "What are you doing?" I ask, still in his shadow.

My questions are answered when I see the naked chick on my bed. Neo peels off his shirt and pounces on her while I drop my head back. *Fuck my life.*

"This is my surprise?" I ask him, and he looks at me with a grin that says, *You're welcome.*

"I've got shit to do." I point a thumb over my shoulder, looking into the eyes of the girl. "Out. Now."

Completely ignoring me, she leans back on her elbows and spreads her legs, giving me a full show of what's between them. It's a beautiful sight, but not one I'm interested in right now.

Neo, who's on his side next to her, slips a single finger inside her pussy, and it's hard not to watch. "Come on, dude, I got her all wet and ready for ya."

It's not the first time we've shared a girl. Hell, Crew, Neo, and I have shared multiple girls. Some, at the same time. Other times, passing over seconds or thirds. My hesitation has nothing to do with the situation and more to do with the fact that I'm not interested in this one.

"Fine," Neo says, sliding his finger out and running it down his tongue. "I'll leave you two alone then." His mouth ghosts hers, but when she goes to kiss him, he pulls back. "Come see me when you're done." He bops her nose like she's a child, then climbs off the bed.

He quickly closes the space between us, snatching his shirt off the floor on the way. "Her name is Amanda. She's got big tits and she likes it rough." He slaps my shoulder before walking out, leaving the door open behind him.

"Get up," I bark the order, and Amanda does as she's told, the sultry expression on her face never fading. She parades toward me, accentuating the rise and fall of each hip with her slow steps. "Put some damn clothes on and leave this house. Now."

Closing in on me, she rubs her shoulder against my chest then slides around me. With her chin resting on my shoulder, she says, in a breathy-whisper, "I promised your friend I'd show you a good time."

"I'm relieving you of that promise. Now, get dressed and leave before I throw your naked ass out in the snow."

Still not obeying, she caresses my body with her bare one and comes around from behind me, standing directly in front of me. She takes one of my hands and raises it to her breasts.

Look. I'm a man who enjoys women very much. I'm only human, so naturally, I give her luscious breast a squeeze. Running a finger along the hem of my shorts, she arches her back and her nipples pucker against my chest. In one swift motion, her hand goes down my gym shorts, heading straight for my semi-erect cock.

When her fingers wrap around my girth, I growl.

She's seductive, I'll give her that. Pretty sexy, too. If this were another time in my life, I'd already be quenching her thirst with my cum.

With her hand still wrapped around me, she drops to her knees, sliding my shorts down with her. They pool around my ankles, and I'm fucking screwed when she begins stroking me with a tight grip.

Her tongue darts out, wetting her bottom lip as she peers up at me with lust-filled eyes. "I swear it'll be worth it if you let me keep my promise."

*Fuck me.* Every voice in my head tells me to stop her, but I'm weak to those juicy lips and my cock, that's now rock hard, is twitching for her.

A brush of air hits my backside as my door flies farther open. One glance over my shoulder has me shoving Amanda back, and she falls on the floor. I reach down quickly, pulling up my shorts, my eyes never leaving Scar's.

"Shit. The door was open. I'm sorry." She turns hastily and leaves the room, keeping the door open.

"Scar," I call out, "Wait." I'm not sure why I'm chasing after her, like I just did something wrong, but I am. "Hey," I say, loud enough for her to hear, but she continues to walk briskly down the hall toward Crew's room.

"Scar! Would you fucking wait a second?" Her feet stop moving, but she doesn't turn around. I jog to catch up to her, and when I do, I stop directly behind her. "Where are you going?"

"Away from you."

I put a hand on her shoulder, softly pulling to get her to

turn around, but she tenses up and holds her stance. "Are you mad at me?"

Finally, she turns to look at me. Taking a step back, she crosses her arms over her chest, which is something I notice she does often when she's upset. If that isn't insight into her mood, the scowl on her face sure as hell is. "Why would I be mad?"

I chuckle, though the sound is empty of any humor. "If you're not mad, why are you trying to get away from me?"

There's disappointment, mixed with anger, in her eyes, and they're fixed right on mine. "Because," she blows out a heavy breath, "I just walked in on you with your," her hands wave up and down my crotch, "thing out." Her cheeks tinge pink, and it's cute as hell.

I fight the smile growing on my face. "My thing?"

"Shut up. You know what I mean."

"No, I don't. What thing, Scar?"

If I thought I'd seen every emotion on Scar's face, I was wrong because her cheeks are the brightest shade of embarrassment I've ever seen.

I laugh when her response is an eye roll. "You have the mouth of a sailor, but you can't say dick when it's referencing mine? Besides, it's not the first time you stole a glance today."

Her hands plant to her face, hiding it. "Oh my god, Jagger. Stop it. You're making this shit awkward again."

Reaching out, I grab her hands, peeling them away from her face. "Nothing ever has to be awkward with us."

She blinks her eyes at me, and they soften on impact. "The door was open and I—"

"It's fine," I laugh, "I was, like, two seconds away from stopping her anyways."

"Liar."

"Dead serious." At least, I think I am. Pretty sure I was gonna stop her. Maybe not, but I definitely would now. "What were you coming into my room for anyways?"

Scar purses her lips, head angled toward her shoulder. "I came to apologize."

My neck cranes back. "For what?"

"For being a bitch earlier."

I'm taken aback because, for one, Scar doesn't apologize often. And two, I'm the one who should be throwing out apologies. "You don't have to apologize. If anyone should say sorry, it's me. That whole Maddie thing...I didn't mean it. You and Crew aren't doing anything wrong."

"Aren't we, though? I mean, Maddie's my best friend, and when she wakes up, she's still going to love Crew."

"Scar," I say with sympathy in my tone, "if Maddie was going to wake up—"

She stops me by shaking her head rapidly. "Don't go there."

"Babe," Crew says from behind me, and Scar's eyes shoot over my shoulder, immediately dropping my hands.

My shoulders slouch as I turn around, blowing out a wisp of air through my flared nostrils. *Every fucking time I try to talk to her.*

"I thought you had to go deal with something?" Scar asks him. They meet each other halfway in the hall and I watch the interaction because I'm nosey and I wanna know how much it pisses him off when I'm around Scar now.

"Sled won't start. What are you two doing?" He looks at me, then back to Scar.

I shrug. "Just talking. That okay with you?"

Neo bursts into the hall. "Cole!" He raises his voice, stalking toward me. "What the hell, man? You just left her?"

"What's he talking about?" Crew asks.

Neo, being the jackass he is, takes it upon himself to explain. "Apparently, Scar walked in on our boy, who was about to get laid, and he dropped the girl like a dead fly to take off after your girlfriend."

Crew cranes his neck, his posture stiffening. "Why?" he asks, his searing eyes bolted to mine. "Why'd you run after Scar?"

"Would you guys quit this shit!" Scar shouts. "Who fucking cares? Neo probably orchestrated this whole thing because he's a master manipulator. Don't you guys see what he's trying to do? He wants you to turn against each other."

"Shut your fucking mouth," Neo barks at her, and my blood reaches a boiling point.

I start toward him, each step becoming more and more thunderous. He disrespected her for the last time.

Before I can do anything about it, Crew shoves Neo and his back hits the wall. Gripping him by the collar of his black tee shirt, Crew lifts him up. "You ever talk to her like that again and you'll be the next missing case at this Academy."

*Damn.* Boy really did grow some balls. I'm impressed.

Scar takes a step back and I put an arm around her waist, guiding her a few feet away, in case they start throwing down.

Neo, being much stronger than Crew, pushes him, which gives them both some much-needed space. I remove my arm from Scar's waist and use the opportunity to step between the guys. With my hands spread, I shout, "Both of you, quit this shit! You're friends, remember?"

"Fuck that nonsense," Neo scoffs, stepping around us, "he's not my fucking friend. Not lately anyway."

Crew doesn't even look at me as he takes Scar's hand and leads her down the hall. As they go, she glances at me over her shoulder, giving me a sorrowful look, then turns into Crew's room, leaving so many unanswered questions in my head.

CHAPTER

# FOUR

SCAR

CREW CLOSES his door and begins pacing the room. My heart beats rapidly in my chest because I'm not sure what's going through his head. Is he upset with me because of the Jagger situation, or is he upset with Neo because...well, he's Neo?

He's on his fourth lap across the room when I reach out and grab his arm. "What's wrong, Crew?"

Fuming, he jerks away and keeps on his path. "Everything is fucking wrong."

I'm not sure what I can do to help the situation. Honestly, I'm not sure there is anything I can do. The last thing I want is to put myself in the middle of their quarrels, even though they usually do center around me. If it weren't for me, these guys would be having the senior year of their lives.

*No.* They brought me here. I didn't ask for this; they did.

"Would you fucking stop?" My voice rises, much higher than I intended it to. It grabs his attention, so I'm not that regretful.

Crew stops in front of his unmade bed, his posture lax. When he doesn't say anything, I do all the talking.

"If this is about Jagger, you need to quit being so jealous. I've told you time and time again—"

He rapidly fires a response. "It's not about him."

"Okay, well, if it's Neo, then I don't know what to say because there probably isn't anything that will fix this, unless you start treating me as shitty as he does."

He sits down on the end of the bed, legs dangling over the cherry oak footboard. "He's such a fucking asshole."

"You guys are like brothers. He'll get over it eventually."

Turning his head, he looks at me. "I'm not so sure about that."

"Why, though? I don't get it. It's been so long and I still don't understand." I walk over to where he's sitting and position myself between his legs. "Make me understand, Crew."

His eyes lift to mine. "I wish I could."

My head bobs slowly. "The rules? The Lawless? The secrets?"

He nods.

"Look. There's a lot that happens that we are sworn to secrecy on. Pacts and oaths were made and it doesn't excuse the shit I've done, but they've stolen my voice."

"What kind of pacts and oaths?"

"A brotherhood pact with the guys and an oath to the Blue Bloods."

I'm not surprised by any of this. I've always known the guys have oaths to the Society that the girls don't. I'm just wondering why it's an issue all of a sudden. "Does every Lawless group have this pact?"

He nods again.

That explains why my dad is so faithful to Neo's asshole dad. His other Lawless brothers are not terrible human beings; in fact, Jagger's and Crew's dads are pretty decent, but Sebastian Saint is the worst, and I've always wondered why my dad puts up with his shit. Now I know—he has to.

"This is why I never wanted to be part of this shit. The Blue Bloods have stolen our lives, Crew."

"It's not forever." His words are meant to be endearing, but they're the exact opposite, because they're empty of the truth.

"It is forever, though. Unless we want to be condemned to a life as a deserter and a target for the members, *it is forever*."

Crew sighs heavily, reaching for my hands. "Then I guess we have no choice, do we?"

"No. We don't."

He pulls me down on top of him, my body blanketing his. "You know what's more important to me than a pact or an oath?" I raise my brows at his question. "You. I won't let them come between us again, Scar."

My lips twitch with a smile. "Promise?"

Fingers weave into my hair, pulling my head down to his. Our foreheads rest against one another's. "I promise."

A wide grin grows on Crew's face as his fingers dance up my leg. Our mouths magnetically connect and goosebumps cascade down my body. No one has ever made me feel the way Crew does from just a single touch. When I'm with him, I feel like the most beautiful girl in the world. Everything about the past year escapes my mind and I'm back to the place we were before it all went to hell. Back to a time when our secret was safe and no obstacles stood in our way.

"I love you," he whispers against my lips, and I inhale his single breath.

My heart swells, and I want to stay in this moment for an eternity. "I love you, too."

No matter what happens going forward, I trust that Crew will be there. On my side. In my corner.

Bypassing my tee shirt, Crew slips his hand beneath a cup of my bra. My stomach tightens and I arch my back, seeking any friction he will give me. When his cock grinds against my leg, I moan into his mouth. "I need you."

His response is a smirk and a nibble on my bottom lip. "Tell me what you want and I'll give it to you." He climbs on top of me, blanketing my body with his, while sliding up and down, his erection a tease against my core.

My hands cradle his head. Fingers combing through his thick, messy hair. "You. Inside me." Our mouths part and I slide my tongue inside, wrapping it around his, wanting to hold it hostage until he gives me exactly what I need.

With my legs straight beneath him, I bring one up, then the other, until he's settled between my thighs.

I deepen this kiss, my heart in a race against his. I can feel it pounding into my chest, overpowering the butterflies that are swarming through my stomach.

I want it to always be like this. Those feelings that I can't ignore. The dire need to have him closer when he's literally lying on top of me.

Crew gets on his knees that are pressed between my legs. He moves his hands behind me, levitating my back off the bed.

His soft sage eyes stare back into mine. *Take me, Crew. Own me.*

My shirt is the first to go, then my bra. Crew leans

forward, taking the bud of my nipple in his mouth. His teeth graze my sensitive flesh and I whimper. He moves to the next one before his mouth presses to mine again. Gently, I'm laid back down, and he disappears down my body, ridding me of my shorts and quickly finding that I'm not wearing any panties.

"Mmm," he hums into the crease between my legs, "I've missed this view."

I close my eyes, licking my lips when his mouth forms an O and he kisses my pussy. His tongue darts out, flicking my clit, and I grab a fistful of his hair, guiding him where I want him while riding his face.

He sticks a finger inside me, then another. "You taste so fucking good." The stubble of his face scratches against my inner thighs, but I fucking love it. My man feasting on me like I'm his favorite dessert.

Two fingers curl, pumping inside me. My hips rise and fall as electricity courses through my body. "Crew," I cry out, knowing how much he likes it when I say his name.

"That's right, baby. Come for me."

His head lifts and he watches as he fingers me. Moving faster, digging deeper, and I lose all control. "Oh god." I lift my ass off the bed. My stomach clenches, walls tightening as I squeeze his fingers.

I'm in a state of euphoria as I come down from my high. Crew pulls his fingers out and removes his clothes. My legs part for him, wrapping around his hips, and the next thing I know, he's filling me back up with his cock. His sticky fingers squeeze my waist, his chest elevated over mine.

"You're so fucking beautiful," he says, before kissing my mouth and giving me a taste of myself.

His cock swells inside me while I inch farther up on the

bed until my head is banging into the headboard. Over and over again.

Shrills of ecstasy tear through my vocal cords.

His thrusts become deeper and faster, breaths ragged and unfulfilled. "Fuck, baby." He growls before diving inside me once more. His movements slow, and he drops down on top of me. I run my fingers over his forehead, wiping away the beads of sweat that accumulated there.

After a few minutes of lying here in a breathless state, Crew rolls off me so I can go to the bathroom and get cleaned up.

When I return, he's lying on his side, his head propped with his hand. He pats the open space on the mattress beside him.

"I got some bad news." A stoic expression washes over him and my fingers twitch with nervousness.

"What?" I drawl, plopping down on the bed next to him. I'm on my side, too, staring into his worried eyes.

"I can't go to the party tomorrow."

"Crew, no! I don't wanna go without you."

"That's good. Because you're not. You're staying here with me." He bites his lip, and it's a failed attempt at trying to sway me. It's not working. Not even a little. Okay. Maybe a little.

"I promised Ry I'd go. I can't ditch her like that."

He lifts his shoulder. "Invite her here."

"She has to go. The cheerleaders are throwing the party. In fact, she wanted me to see if you guys would let them move it out of the snow and into the Gathering room."

Crew chews on his lip, deep in thought, before he finally says, "I've got an idea. We let them have the party underground and give you the credit, so Riley isn't mad, and you stay here with me, so we can attend Neo's mandatory party."

I scoff. "Mandatory?"

"Pacts and oaths, remember?"

My cheeks puff and I blow out the pent-up air in one breath. "So damn stupid, but fine."

Crew squeezes my waist, a smile playing at his lips. "You're not mad?"

"I know you don't have a choice. I mean, I could still go, but I don't want to if you're not there."

"Good. Because I wouldn't let you go without one of us guys."

I scowl at him playfully. "Elias will be there, among many other guys."

"Exactly my point."

# CHAPTER
# FIVE

CREW

After yesterday's chaos, Scar and I had a nice, quiet dinner alone. Unless we're in one of our rooms, alone time together has been scarce. I'm always either at practice or school, and she's been spending a lot of her free time with Jagger.

Practice has ended for the day and the party is about to start, and I'm hoping like hell we can have a peaceful night, but something tells me that's asking too much in this damn house. On a positive note, Scar's here and she's safe.

I have to keep reminding myself of that. It doesn't matter that Jagger has had his eyes on her since the second she arrived or that I catch him watching her from afar, likely daydreaming about how life would be if he were in my place. The thought of any guy worming their way into Scar's life irks me to the core. It makes me fucking crazy. That Elias guy—hell no. I don't want her anywhere near that douchebag. But Jagger—he's my best friend, and if I had to trust anyone with her, it would be him. Yet, it still bothers me. I think it's mostly because I know Scar has some sort of connection with him, too. I've seen it. It's too obvious to ignore.

Now she's living here under our protection and it's the best choice I've made. Even if it comes with the cost of potentially losing her, her safety is all I'm concerned with. Neo thinks she's here so we can keep an eye on her because he believes she's playing us in her own little game, but I'm hopeful her stay will shine light on the situation and he'll see that Scar is a victim and not an enemy. She's a tough girl, but she's not the vicious person he wants everyone to believe she is.

The last thing I want to do is cause any more emotional turmoil for Scar. So for now, I'll let Jagger watch her, waiting and hoping that one day she'll look at him the way she looks at me. Too bad for him, that'll never happen.

As for Neo...no one can predict what's going on in that twisted mind.

Scar's bedroom door opens, and I drop my foot from the wall in the hallway and stick my phone in my back pocket. When I get a good look at her, I bite my balled fist. Looking that good should be illegal. Or, at the very least, not allowed in public. "Damn, baby." I tug at her top that sits just above her belly button. When I stretch it down, it springs right back up. "You do know it's freezing outside, right? Why don't you go grab a sweatshirt?"

She chuckles, looking at me like I'm joking, which I'm sure as shit not. "I'll be fine." Grabbing my hand, she tugs me down the hallway. Sensing my reluctance, she stops. "What's wrong?"

I take her by the waist, pinning her against the wall beside the staircase. My fingers sink into the flesh of skin that should be covered. "You're too fucking sexy for your own good." I kiss her lips, feeling thankful there won't be a bunch of horny-ass guys gawking at her tonight.

"I'm glad you think so." She smirks against my mouth. "Which is exactly why I'm not covering myself up. It's all for you."

"Better be just for me." I grind my aching cock against her, and if we don't get down those stairs right now, we might never make it. I'm two seconds away from taking her through Jagger's open door and fucking her on his bed.

"Always is," she mutters, and it's a seductive whisper that plays on my hormones. One that tells me she wants to be fucked right now.

Jagger comes out of his room, and I didn't even realize he was in there. Scar slips out of her place between me and the wall. "Hey, Jagger," she croaks, and it has me pinching my eyebrows together. Does it bother her that he sees us close like this?

*Fuck.*

*I need to get out of my own head.*

His eyes skate from hers to mine. "Heading down to the party?"

I tip my chin. "Yeah. If that's what you call it."

"Why do you say that?" Scar asks, completely oblivious to what we're about to embark on. Neo, being the fucking idiot he is, decided to make this an all-girls' party, while forcing our attendance—meaning mine and Jagger's. With us three here, that leaves no opportunity for Scar to attend the party at the Ruins. It's a control scheme on Neo's part.

"Neo put it together," I tell her. "Enough said."

Scar clicks her tongue on the roof of her mouth. "True."

"Guess I'll see you down there, then," Jagger says, giving Scar a crescent smile before jogging down the staircase.

I watch her watch him, feeling a splinter of jealousy in my gut.

Her gaze snaps to mine, and she catches my scowl. "What's wrong?"

"Nothing," I tell her, tone flat.

A smile parts her lips and she takes my hand. "Let's go, grumpass."

"Grumpass?" I chuckle. "What's with the name-calling?"

We walk downstairs, holding hands, as she elaborates, "What's with the sour attitude lately?"

"Just observing the situation. Taking it all in."

"Situation?" she drawls. "As in, us?"

My shoulders rise and fall. "Us. You. Him."

Scar side-eyes me, and I can tell she wants to push more, but when we reach the bottom, her train of thought is rail-roaded. She takes a look around, cringing at our guests. "Now I see what you meant. Leave it to Neo to host a party full of half-naked girls."

"We don't have to stay long. We're in the house. That's all that matters."

Scar slides up to me, her face an inch from mine, and she grins. "What did you have in mind?"

"Oh, I dunno. You, me, and a hot shower."

"Maybe tomorrow," Neo says, killing our vibe. "Until then, Lucy needs help tapping the keg."

Scar sulks into my shoulder, mumbling, "Does he ever go away?"

"Unfortunately not. Guess I've got work to do." I take her hand, ready to head for the kitchen, where the keg is usually placed when a party's here.

Neo grabs me by the shoulder. "Not so fast." I growl,

eyes rolling as he continues, "I need to talk to Scar about something."

I don't like this. Not one bit.

"It's fine," she says, peering up at me. "I can take care of myself."

I know that to be true, but I don't like the idea of Neo getting in her head again. He'd love nothing more than to turn Scar and me against each other for his own personal gain.

"All right. I'll be right back." I kiss her lips then let her slip out of my reach. I don't go far, though. Lucy and the keg can wait.

Instead, I press my back to the wall in the kitchen, and I listen.

"Glad you could make it to my party," Neo says, using a condescending tone.

"As if I had a choice." I can picture it now. She's standing there, arms crossed over her chest and a Cheshire grin on her face.

"That's true, but you're here nonetheless."

"What'd you want, Neo? I have much better things to do."

"I'm sure you do. There's a lot of girls here. Maybe a little three-way is in your near future? Ya know, Crew's always enjoyed the company of many women at the same time."

*Fucking asshole!*

It's taking everything in me not to turn this corner and shove his face into the wall.

"Maybe so. But with me, he doesn't need more than one. Can you say the same for yourself when it comes to the ladies? Or is that why you have to pass them on to your friends when you're finished? So they aren't left unsatisfied?"

Laughter climbs up my throat. Fortunately, "I Ain't Worried" by OneRepublic is playing loud enough to drown out the sound.

"You're a real bitch, you know that?"

"Sure do. What about it?"

I'm not sure why I was ever worried. Scar can most definitely handle her own when it comes to Neo. Which says a lot, considering he's a tough one to handle.

"Keep in mind, Scar...you're only here because I allow it. Piss me off and I'll throw you to the fucking dogs."

"Weird," she huffs out on a breath of laughter, "I thought you were a dog?"

"That's where you're wrong, baby. I'm no dog. I'm the big bad wolf your mama warned you about and you better watch your fucking back because I'll eat you alive the second you screw up. I'm watching and I'm waiting. I'm fucking hungry as hell, Scar."

I can tell she's getting bored with this back and forth by the sound of her sigh. "I'm not scared of you, Neo. You can throw out threats, but they're not sticking. Now say what you need to say, so I can get as far away from you as possible."

"You should be scared because I have knowledge that can shatter your entire world. Now you have to decide if you really want to drag Crew into your mess."

I turn the corner, blood boiling. "That's enough," I lash out at Neo, as I scoop one arm around Scar's waist, lugging her toward me. "Leave her the hell alone."

"It's fine, Crew." Scar pats a hand to my heaving chest,

glaring at Neo. "He doesn't intimidate me. Neo just needs to use big, angry words to pacify his sad, little penis."

Neo smirks, shaking his finger at Scar. "You're gonna pay for that."

"Dude, just get lost. There's a dozen chicks here. Why fuck with mine?" I'm seconds away from tearing him apart, limb by limb, so it's in his best interests to walk away while he has the chance.

Neo sweeps the air with his hand. "Fucking traitor," he grumbles as he walks away.

I look at Scar with apologetic eyes. "I'm sorry. I should've never left you alone with him."

"Don't be," she says, "I told you I'd be fine, and I was. Neo's words don't hurt me. I am curious, though." Her head tilts slightly toward her shoulder. "What did he mean when he said he has knowledge that can 'shatter my world'?"

I'm as dumbfounded as she is on that one. I can only assume he's referring to Maddie's accident again, but we all know he's grasping at straws at that one. "No clue." Scar bites her lip nervously, so I ask, "Why? Are you worried about it?"

"I'm not sure yet. Neo always spits vile words and threats at me, but the confidence in his tone this time was a little unnerving."

I pull her in for a reassuring hug. "Don't worry about him. Neo might think he hates you, but I can guarantee he hates himself more."

Her head rests on my shoulder, and when I glance to the left, I see Jagger on the couch—watching us.

# SIX

## JAGGER

At this point, I think I'd rather be at the party at the Ruins over this shit: sitting here watching Crew, who's holding on to Scar, while a dozen chicks prance around in skimpy clothes, all trying to impress their almighty Lawless members—me included. I probably should have jumped up in Crew's defense during his verbal altercation with Neo, but I wanted to let things play out the way they should.

I knew exactly what Neo was doing when he arranged this little gathering. He wants to make Scar squirm. He's hungry for her discomfort and he thinks this party would do the trick. Obviously, he doesn't know her at all.

Scar doesn't give a flying fuck that Crew is one of only three guys here with all these smoking hot babes. What Neo failed to realize is that Scar's confidence soars right along with her, 'I don't give a fuck' attitude. If anyone is squirming, it's Neo. Melody—who is a cheerleader but ditched her own party—is, once again, trying her damnedest to get Neo's attention. He can't stand that slut and why he invited her into our home is a mystery I don't care to try and solve.

Right now, all I'm waiting for is that one moment where Crew lets his guard down and Scar slips out of his hold. I just wanna talk to her. Make sure things are cool after I put my foot in my mouth earlier today. Unfortunately, Crew has attached himself to her like a leech and I don't see him losing his hold anytime soon.

Neo's voice comes from behind me and snaps me out of my fixation on Scar. "There's a dozen chicks here who would willingly open their mouths for your dick, and you're watching the one you shouldn't want."

I tip back my bottle of dark lager and take a small sip, ignoring the shithead chirping in my ear.

"All right," Neo says with a heavy breath, as he drops down beside me on the couch, "you like her. I can see that. So go get her."

With the rim of the bottle pressed to my lips, I turn my head to look at him. "Come again?"

"I said, go get her. Crew doesn't own Scar. In fact, I'm not even sure they've given themselves a title. She's open for the taking."

Is he being serious right now? Crew is supposed to be one of his best friends. Yet, he's telling me to go after her. Not to mention, he loathes her. "Are you high?"

"No." He chuckles, but his squinted eyes and the film of pink covering the whites of them tell me he's lying. "All right, maybe a little. But, I'm dead fucking serious."

I move forward, setting my half-full bottle on the table, while giving Neo my full attention. "You hate Scar, so how about you tell me what the fuck you're up to."

"Hate's a strong word, but I'll go with it. I'm just saying, maybe there's someone far more devious who I loathe more."

"Whoa. Are you talking about Crew?"

Neo sinks back into the couch, his eyes full of sinister intentions. "He's fucking playing us, Jagger."

This conversation just got interesting. "Playing us, how?"

Neo stares Crew down as he peppers Scar's neck with kisses, making her squirm and giggle in his arms. "He knows what she did to my sister. But look at him. He has no intention of helping me bring her down. He brought her into this house for his own personal gain."

I knew that already. Knew Neo was still hell-bent that Scar is the reason Maddie fell. Neo thinks she's orchestrating this whole stalker thing, too. We haven't told Scar about what we found in the tunnels because Neo thinks we're now two steps ahead of her. The truth is, Neo's stuck in his own revenge game while Crew is living in la-la land with the girl of his dreams. I'm the only one who knows the truth. Scar isn't making anything up. Someone is after her, and while these guys are fucking around with their own shit, I'm the one who is making sure she's safe.

"It's not her. Someone *is* after her. Maybe even all of us," I say with complete seriousness.

"Don't tell me you're believing this bullshit, too?"

I just shake my head because, without facts, Neo won't believe a damn thing I say. "Doesn't matter what I believe."

"Look, man." He springs up to a sitting position, his hands on his knees. "Even if Scar isn't making this shit up and someone really is after her, it doesn't change the fact that Crew's loyalty has shifted. It shifted the day Maddie fell. His sights are set on Scar and that's all he fucking cares about. He forgot all about the girl he supposedly loved when she went to sleep and never woke up."

This is far too personal for Neo. I want to sympathize with the way he's feeling. The guy lost his mom and his twin sister, who was his best friend. His dad is absent and only cares about his political status and the perfect picture his family paints for the world to see. Neo lives in his own head, and he only sees what his mind tells him to see.

I'm gonna fix this, though. I'll get to the truth, one way or another. I'll clear Scar's name, and hopefully, one day, Crew and Neo can repair the damage that was caused from this tragedy.

Neo is right about one thing, though. Crew doesn't own Scar. Her heart is wide open for the taking. Assuming Crew hasn't stolen all of it yet.

I watch as Crew plants a kiss on Scar's cheek, whispers something to her, then walks away.

Scar looks around the room and I can tell she's feeling a bit out of place. A couple girls use the opportunity to ambush Crew, seeing an opening of their own. She locks eyes with him momentarily then turns around unfazed.

Neo slaps a hand on my leg. "Now's your chance."

Using this opportunity, I stand up, snatch my beer off the table, and head straight for her as she walks into the kitchen.

I'm stopped by Amber, a senior, who looks like she's had too much to drink. "Hey, Jagger. Great party." Her body sways as she tries to steady herself on another girl's arm.

I look past her, seeing that Scar has now walked out the sliding glass doors to the porch. "I'm busy."

Amber holds up a shot glass filled to the brim with clear liquid. "Have a drink with me. It's tequila."

"Fucking move!" I attempt to dip around her, but

another girl wearing a bikini joins her side, all three completely blocking my entrance into the kitchen.

The new girl slithers up to me. The warmth of her tits pressed against my arm is enticing, but it's not enough to keep me here.

"I saw Neo checking the three of you out earlier. Why don't you give him some attention? I'm sure it'll make his day."

It's a lie, but it works. Three pairs of eyes shoot over my shoulder, in search of Neo. I manage to slip between them and into the kitchen. A glance over my shoulder shows them parading toward Neo like he's theirs for the taking. That was almost too easy.

When I turn back around, I crash right into Crew. He's holding a can of fruity seltzer, likely for Scar, and a bottle of beer. "Have you seen Scar?" he asks, his gaze dancing over my shoulder.

My lips purse together and I skim the room casually. "No," I lie, "haven't seen her."

He steps past me in search of his girlfriend, while I go straight to where she's at.

# CHAPTER
# SEVEN

SCAR

"Everything okay?" Jagger's voice comes from beside me. He leans on the porch railing, sinking the sleeves of his black hoodie into the snow.

"Yeah," I wheeze, "just needed some fresh air."

My entire body shakes and I'm starting to think coming out here in a short-sleeved tee shirt with thin leggings was a bad idea.

"You're shivering," Jagger says as he peels off his hoodie.

He goes to hand it to me, but I shoot a thumb over my shoulder. "I'm okay. Really. I should probably go back inside."

"What's the rush?" The hoodie comes over my shoulders, the long sleeves hanging down in front of me.

"Thank you." I smile as I hug the hoodie to my body, while absorbing any sliver of warmth it brings me. "Crew went to get me a drink and he's probably wondering where I'm at."

"Actually, I think he's talking to Neo right now. Probably best to avoid that situation if you can."

*Ugh.* He's right. Neo is probably drilling nonsense into Crew's head. Fortunately, I trust Crew, and I know he won't be swayed by Neo's bullshit theories. I'll give them their time; otherwise, I'll walk in there looking like the bad guy Neo already sees me as.

I turn back around, looking out into the dark field that meets the forest. The snow is only lightly falling, which is nice, but the accumulation is quite deep. Making small talk, I say, "I don't remember the snow ever falling this early back home."

Jagger shares my view as he leans into the snow-covered railing again, this time, bare armed. "It's a whole different world in Boulder Cove."

"No kidding. I'm not sure anything could have prepared me for what I walked in on at this place."

He turns to look at me while I stare straight ahead. "Are we still talking about the weather?"

I shrug my shoulders because it's the easiest response, but, deep down, there is so much I want to say.

I straighten my back and turn to face him. "What changed, Jagger?" When he cocks an eyebrow, I elaborate. "I know Neo's seen me as a threat since we were kids, but you and Crew never cared about his dislike for me back then. I've had this conversation with Crew already, but why did you turn on me the way you did?"

His shoulders drop in defeat. "It was the games, Scar. I had to."

"I'm not talking about the games. I'm talking about everything after Maddie's fall, up until I arrived here."

Jagger was never as malicious as Neo was, or even Crew. I could tell he always wanted to stay impartial, but it doesn't change the fact that he still went along with the cruelty toward me.

He blows out a heavy breath then looks back at the open doors into the kitchen. I follow his line of sight and see only one girl in there, which means the others are likely attached to Crew and Neo. When he looks back at me, he takes me by the arm, causing me to hold tighter to his sweatshirt that's wrapped around me. "Come here," he says, leading me to the end of the porch.

Once we're out of sight, he drops his hand from my arm. He must be willing to share something important with me if he moved us out of anyone's prying eyes.

"I never wanted to hurt you, Scar. The thing is, there's so much that happens behind the scenes for the men in the Society, and even more when you're made a Lawless member. The guys and I always knew we'd take this role because of our lineage, but when we accepted it, we...or I... had no idea what it truly entailed."

"I know all that. Crew told me as much, but I want to know what any of it has to do with me."

He licks his lips, biding time because I know, and he knows, he can only say so much. I've learned not to pry when it comes to any member's placement in the Society because it's sticky, but if I'm involved, I have every right to know.

"Loyalty. We made a pact and we stick to it. Neo changed after his mom died. You know that. After Maddie's accident, he became irrational—unreasonable. He convinced us you were involved in Maddie's fall. To what extent, I'm not sure, but he wanted to make you pay, and we followed in line."

"And what about now? Where is Neo's loyalty to you and Crew?"

"Honestly? I'd bet it's nonexistent. Neo only cares about one thing right now and that's revenge against anyone who hurt Maddie. He doesn't even care that there's a threat to the students at the Academy and the Society."

"Wait. What?" I spit out. "Someone is threatening the students *and the Society*?"

*Why am I just now hearing about this?*

Jagger's face drops, and I can tell he said too much by the look on his face. "It's fine. We've got it all under control."

"Jagger," I drawl, "tell me what you meant."

Just as he opens his mouth to speak, the screeching howls of girls from inside ring in my ears.

Jagger and I both look at each other, wide-eyed. "What was that?" we both say in unison.

He heads for the door and I follow behind him quickly. One look inside the open doors shows a pitch-black room. Two girls come barreling out the door, crashing into me and knocking the sweatshirt from around my shoulders.

"What happened to the lights?" I ask them, bending down and picking up Jagger's sweatshirt. I shake it off, then ball it up and hug it to my chest. The lingering snow on it seeps into my skin and I shiver.

"Someone's in there," one of the girls says, and I notice she's wearing a bikini.

I hand her the sweatshirt because she needs it more than I do. "Here, wrap this around you, then tell me what the hell you mean by *someone's in there*."

"Jill and Lucy were looking for a bathroom when the lights went out and they went into the wrong room and saw a man in a black robe with a ski mask over his face. He grabbed Lucy, but when she screamed, he shoved her into some boxes then he took off running."

Jagger takes me by the hand, pulling me inside, while more girls come out onto the porch. There's not much light, but it's a half moon, so it's more than what they're getting inside.

"Scar," I hear Crew shouting, "where the fuck are you?"

"I'm here."

Crew comes running toward me, his arms wrap around my waist and he buries his face in my hair. "Jesus, Scar. Where the hell have you been? I thought something happened to you."

"I was outside…" I look over and see that Jagger is now gone. "I'm fine. What the hell happened?"

"Fuck if I know. The lights went out and the next thing I know, some girls are screaming that there's a creep in the house, which made all the other girls freak out and start running."

Outside, one of the girls mentioned someone falling into boxes. "My room." I pull out of Crew's embrace and head into the living room, where it's eerily quiet all of a sudden. Someone lit a candle, so there's a sliver of light, but I pay no attention to who is in here. I make a beeline for the staircase and go up, Crew following closely behind me.

"What are you doing?" he asks, his hand on my waist.

"I think the creep was in my room."

Crew asks more questions, but they slip through my ears as empty words. I go straight to my room, where the door is wide open. *I know I closed it earlier.*

It doesn't mean much because girls are nosey as hell and

they were likely snooping around, but in this situation, red flags are raised.

"What the fuck happened?" Neo appears out of nowhere, holding out his phone with the flashlight turned on. His voice is stern and serious and it sends chills down my back.

"Scar thinks someone was in her room," Crew tells him.

"I don't *think*. I know. Gimme your phone," I say to Neo, not waiting for him to do me the courtesy of handing it over. I jerk it from his hand and shine it around my room, looking for anything out of the ordinary.

"Quit fucking around, Scar. You know damn well no one is in your room. Where the hell were you when the lights went out?"

I shine the light directly in Neo's beady olive eyes. "You think I did this?" I should feel hurt that he'd accuse me of such a thing, but I'm not hurt, I'm angry. I'm fucking furious.

I eat up the space between us, one heavy step at a time. "Get off your fucking high horse." I shove my hands to his chest, phone still clenched between my fingertips. "Put your hatred for me aside for two fucking minutes and maybe you'll see that this isn't some sick game on my part. Someone is out there and they want to hurt, not only me, but all of us."

I'm not sure how true my words are, considering I have no idea why anyone would want to hurt the Society, but Jagger said there is a threat out there and this proves that it's true.

I shove Neo again, walking him into the wall behind him. All the while, the sinister grin on his face only spreads.

A chuckle escapes him, and it enrages me. I slam his

phone to the ground. Crew comes up from behind, but I pay him no attention.

"What the hell is your fucking problem, Neo? Tell me! Tell me why you hate me so much that you think I'd scheme and try to make myself look like a victim?"

The phone points directly at the ceiling, but it's enough light to see the amused look on his face. It sickens me. It makes my stomach turn, and I want nothing more than to feed him my fist while sending his teeth down his disgusting throat.

"Answer me!" I scream, losing all control.

The laughter that escapes him is insulting. Rage consumes me as I draw my fist back, ready to lay it on his pretty face. Unfortunately, Crew grabs my wrist. "Calm down, baby."

My attention shifts to Crew, who is grating on my nerves right now. He should have just let me punch this fucker. "Calm down?" I huff. "Do you hear what he's accusing me of?"

"There are no accusations if there's proof of the truth." Neo's words hit my ears and something even more villainous snaps inside me.

"Or one could say that your accusations are really a confession. I was outside with Jagger the entire time—"

Crew drums his fingers against my wrist. "You were with Jagger?"

My one-track mind ignores him while I drill Neo, "Tell me, Neo. Where were you when the lights went out?"

He laughs a hollow sound. "Are you accusing me?"

"Maybe I am. This could all be you. Taunting me, trying to break me. You have the motive and the means." I jerk my arm away from Crew, not trying to be rude, but also feeling the dire need to defend myself to Neo from all angles.

Crew puts an arm around my waist from behind, holding me back.

"First of all," Neo begins, picking his phone off the floor, "I've never made it a secret that I don't like you, Scar. If I want to hurt you, I'll do it in the light of day with witnesses surrounding me. Second, I was with Crew and about six other girls who can back my story. Not that I need to explain anything to you."

For a while I considered Neo being the mystery person out there who's been fucking with me. Though, my gut tells me it isn't him since a lot of the weird notes popping up involved Maddie, and I know he wouldn't use her that way, but I still won't completely rule him out.

Crew comes to his defense. "It's true. He was with me."

I find it interesting that Crew is defending Neo in this case, but he hasn't said a damn word about me being innocent.

I glance over my shoulder at Crew. "Do you think I've been lying this whole time?" I need to hear him say it out loud, in front of Neo. Crew knows damn well I'm not lying about what's been going on. He knows I'm not playing the victim. But has he told Neo that?

"Not at all," he says in one breath. His gaze lands on Neo. "She's not doing this. You and I both know that. You've gotta let this go, man."

His words sing to my ears because this moment right here solidifies everything between Crew and me. I don't want him to ever have to choose between me and his friends, but it's comforting to know that when push comes to shove, he's in my corner.

When I look back at Neo, it's like the anger has been washed from his face, and he's left with emotions he doesn't know how to handle. He wants so badly to blame me for everything awful in his life because it's easier than admitting there is no one to blame. He can't seek revenge if there is no one to endure the acts.

"Jagger," Neo shouts through the momentary bout of silence. Everything is quiet. It sounds like the group downstairs just disappeared.

When Jagger doesn't come, Neo pulls out his phone, and I assume it's to text him.

"Where did everyone go?" I whisper to Crew.

"We told all the girls to go to the Ruins. Party here is over."

I'm not sure what this party was even about, but I'm sure it was some fucked-up attempt to stop me from hanging out with my real friends. Maybe Neo was hoping some cute girls being around would take Crew's attention off me. I know he hates that Crew and I are together, and he'll do anything in his power to break us up.

I turn around to look at Crew. My hands wrap around his torso and I speak as if Neo isn't standing directly behind me. Or maybe I want him to hear what I'm about to say. "Thank you for believing in me. I don't know how I'd get through any of this without you."

His lips press softly to mine. "You'll never have to find out."

"Unless someone pushes her off a cliff. Then what? Will you move on to her new bestie? Seems to be your M.O."

"Fuck you," Crew spats, "my feelings for Scar have nothing to do with Maddie."

Jagger finally emerges and his timing couldn't be more perfect. "Everyone okay in here?"

"Where the hell have you been?" Neo barks at him.

"Walked with the girls to meet up with a Rook to take them to the other party." Jagger's eyes dance around from person to person. "What's with all the tension in here?"

"Were you with Scar when the lights went out?" Neo asks, getting straight to the point.

I sigh, utterly annoyed that he refuses to believe a single word I say.

"Yeah. We were outside on the porch. Why?"

Crew tugs me to his side, glaring at Neo. "Neo thinks she did it."

"Seriously?" Jagger looks at me, eyes skating down to Crew's hand that's squeezing my hip, then quickly back up. "Scar was with me the entire time. Some chick said a guy in a robe and mask grabbed Lucy Winters. Definitely wasn't Scar."

"We have to look at things from every angle," Neo tells him, sounding far too confident for such an uncertain guy. "But now we know it wasn't her." The condescending look he flashes me irks me to the core, but I throw it right back at him.

My shoulders tighten, and I stand tall. "Which I already told you and you should have believed."

"What's that over there?" Jagger asks, and we all follow his line of sight. He picks something up off the floor. A paper, maybe? He holds it up, and I see that it's a white business envelope. "Is this yours?"

I shake my head no. "Never seen that before." I slip out of Crew's hold and walk over to Jagger, peering at the envelope as he peels back the flap. My heart gallops in my chest, and as much as I want to know what's inside, another part of me doesn't want to acknowledge that this is happening again.

Neo, being the control freak he is, snags the envelope from Jagger's hand before he can see the contents. His finger slides under the lip, and he reaches inside. When he pulls his hand out, he's holding a picture.

It takes me a second, but I come to realize, it's a picture of me.

"That's me...when I was only a child. It looks like one of my birthday parties. Why would this guy have a picture of me as a child?" Panic ensues, and I take it from Neo. It looks like it was taken through a window. Like someone was standing outside of my family home, watching us. I look at the guys, who are all staring at me like they're waiting for me to lose my shit. No one says anything, so I take it upon myself to ask the question that I'm sure we all have. "Where did this come from?" I flip the picture over and there's something written on the back.

*I was at every birthday. You just didn't know.*

My heart sinks into my stomach, and I cringe at the words. I was being watched all these years?

When no one responds, I raise my voice. "Where the fuck did this come from, dammit!"

Neo points a flashlight right at me and I know he's waiting for the reaction he craves. He wants to see my fear. I glower at him, wishing I could find a way to blame this all on him.

When Crew and Jagger share a cryptic look before focusing their attention on Neo, I lose it. "Would someone fucking say something?"

"Baby," Crew begins, "there's something I need to tell you—" Before he can finish, he's rudely cut off by Neo.

"Don't you dare tell her," Neo snaps, now shining his light on Crew.

"Fuck off, Neo. Can't you see now that Scar isn't behind this? Someone else is doing this, and it's not just about her anymore."

Jagger steps forward, finally having something to say. "Crew's right. If we're going to protect Scar and bring this fucker down, she needs to know everything."

Neo shakes his head in disapproval. His sheer hatred for this situation radiating through the room. Because it's now that Neo finally realizes he's been wrong all along. He's always wanted to blame me for everything bad in his life, and for the first time ever, he knows I'm not to blame, and it fucking kills him.

"Tell me," I say, looking at Crew, then Jagger, and finally Neo. "Someone tell me what the hell is going on."

To my surprise, it's Neo who speaks up. "You want the truth?"

Crew steps in front of me, blocking my view of Neo. "I've got this. You two go figure out the light situation."

There's a few mumbles before the guys backtrack in the direction of the door. "Holler if you need us," Jagger says to Crew, but his eyes are on me.

Once they're gone, so is the light. Crew and I are left standing beside my bed with the glow of the moon shining through my window.

He takes the picture from my hands and drops it down on the bed before wrapping his fingers around mine. "I should've told you a while ago, but I thought I was protecting you."

I scowl back at him, not liking where this is going. "Told me what?"

"Remember when I was locked in the tunnels?" he asks, and I nod. "I found a door we'd never seen before. Or maybe we did and it was different then. It had a combination lock on it, and with some help, me and the guys got through to the other side."

"And?" I press, wanting him to get to the point.

"And we found a room full of Blue Blood paraphernalia." I can see the disdain in his eyes as he continues, "It was fucking insane. There were newspaper clippings, old artifacts, pictures—"

"My pictures?"

"No. Well, yeah. Once we were in there, we found another room." He swallows hard, and it makes me do the same. "It was a room full of...you."

"Of me?" I stretch my neck. "What's that even mean?"

"It was this fucked-up shrine of you, Scar. All it took was one look in that room to know this sicko was obsessed with you."

I gasp, feeling like my chest is caving in. "You're kidding, right?"

He shakes his no and each movement makes me feel more and more dizzy. I step back, bumping into the new mattress, so I sit down. "I knew it," I say, hardly recognizing my own voice. "I knew I wasn't imagining all this."

"You weren't. Neo's a damn idiot. Don't listen to anything he says."

His words elude me as I focus on the fact that Crew knew—they all did. "You knew this whole time and didn't tell me?"

"I wanted to tell you, but Jagger and I both thought it

was better this way. We didn't want you to worry. But I swear, I planned to tell you the second we had a concrete suspect."

"Or Neo didn't want me to know what you guys found because he was convinced it was me and he wanted to stay two steps ahead?"

"No," he huffs, "Neo wanted to *expose you* from the start, but we were able to persuade him to wait. We wanted to find something that could prove it wasn't you. And now we have."

My gut wretches. Since when do I have to prove myself to anyone, especially Neo Saint? First, he thinks I'm the reason Maddie fell, and now, he thinks I'm crying victim from my own game.

I jump up and storm out of the room.

"Scar, wait," Crew says as he jogs up to my side, "I didn't mean to hurt you."

"You never do, Crew." Sarcasm drips from my words and guilt immediately gnaws at my stomach. I stop walking and he does the same. "I'm sorry. I didn't mean it like that. I'm just so fed up with all this bullshit. When does it end, Crew?"

"I know, baby. This whole situation is fucked up. We're all just doing the best we can." His arms wrap around me and I fall into him, basking in this moment of safety.

He holds me for what feels like minutes as more questions invade my mind.

*Who would do this? Why do it to me?*

There's only one way to find out. This person is good, but everyone fucks up occasionally. There has to be some sort of evidence that we can find to try and figure out who is doing this.

I lean back slightly, looking up at Crew. "I'd like to see the room in the tunnels."

His body tenses as soon as my words hit his ears. Peering down at me, he says, "I don't think that's a good idea."

I won't take no for an answer, though, and if no is the only one he gives me, I'll find another way.

"If that room is full of information about me and my personal life, I want to see it."

He doesn't say anything. The only sound is the shuffling of feet on the hardwood floor in Neo's room.

Crew turns his ear toward the door, listening. "Sounds like he's on the phone with the headmaster. Probably giving 'em hell about getting the power back on."

My hands plant on my hips, and I glower at him. "You're deflecting."

"Am not."

"Are so. I want to see the room, Crew."

He sighs heavily, weaving his fingers through his hair. "Lemme talk to the guys."

I shake my head in disappointment, because I know they'll make every excuse for me not to go.

"Fine," I say, knowing that it's not fine.

I guess if I want to see the room in the tunnels, I'll have to find it myself.

Suddenly, Neo's bedroom door flies open. "We have to go," he says, "bring the girl."

*The girl?* Dickhead!

"Go where?" Crew asks.

Neo stalks past us, raising his voice as he heads down the hall. "The Ruins. There's been a situation."

CHAPTER

# EIGHT

JAGGER

"Fuck!" Crew shouts as he tosses his helmet at his sled. "Still won't fucking start."

Scar hugs Crew's spare helmet to her black down-filled jacket, shivering under the lamppost in the driveway.

Neo revs his engine, not giving a damn that Crew's sled isn't running. "Hurry your asses up!" He revs it again, ready to tear up the trails, leaving us in a dust of snow.

"Stop his ass," I tell Crew, "tell him you need a ride. Scar can go with me."

Crew looks at Scar for approval, and she immediately says, "Well, I'm definitely not riding with Neo." She pulls the helmet on her head and steps toward me, before turning around to look at Crew. "I'll see you there?"

He nods in response, but I can tell he doesn't like this situation. "Be safe," he says, his words directed at me. "Anything happens to her and—"

"Calm the fuck down. Nothing's gonna happen to her." Crew's well aware that I'm an adrenaline junkie who lives

83

for speed and a thrill, but with Scar in tow, I'll take it nice and slow.

Scar swings a leg over the sled and settles in behind me. Her arms wrap around my waist, and suddenly, I believe in the saying, *everything happens for a reason.*

I pull down the heated shield on my helmet, my coy smile out of sight. "Ready?"

My fingers teeter over the throttle while Scar's body heat seeps through my heavy ski coat. Her touch alone could thaw fourth-degree frostbite.

We take off, and I'm not sure Scar knows exactly what she's gotten herself into by hopping on the back of my sled. Of course I'll play it safe, but beneath us is one of the fastest and fiercest snowmobiles on the market. Naturally, I have to show off a little.

Giving it some gas, she squeezes my waist, as anticipated.

The beak of her helmet rests on my shoulder, and it's taking everything in me not to turn off this trail and get lost together.

It's tempting.

So fucking tempting.

In a knee-jerk reaction, I swing a left.

Neo and Crew can handle whatever is going down at the Ruins.

Scar knows these trails well enough by now to know we aren't going in the right direction, but she doesn't say a word, at least, not that I can hear.

Instead, she hugs me tighter. My heart pounds beneath the layers of clothing on my chest. This girl is making me reckless. Her face pops into my every thought, my every dream. It always has. I've had feelings for Scar since we were kids. Probably even longer than Crew has. I never told a soul, though. Not even her.

*She's not coming.*

*Should've known. Especially after everything that went down yesterday. I shouldn't be here either. I should be with Neo and Crew and everyone else who stopped by the Saint house to pay their respects to his family. Instead, I'm here. Waiting and wishing on some off chance that Scar will actually show.*

*With my feet on solid ground, I pace in front of the treehouse, tossing my phone back and forth in my hands. I glance at it and see a missed call from Neo. Seconds later, a voice mail chimes in.*

*This was a waste of time. I should be with my friends.*

*The sound of crunching leaves grabs my attention, and suddenly, 'I should be with my friends' and 'I'm staying here' are waging a war in my head.*

*My eyes perk up, and I see her.*

*"You came," I say, biting down on my smile. The giddiness inside me quickly dissipates when I see the sadness in her expression. "You okay?" I ask, immediately regretting the question because, of course, she's not okay. None of us are.*

*Her lips purse together, and she shakes her head. "I just can't believe she's gone. Maddie's mom was one of the sweetest women I've ever known."*

*It's true. Carian Saint was kindness and warmth personified. Yesterday, while we were at this exact location, Neo got the call that something happened. Minutes later, we were told Carian was crossing the street when she was struck by a car. She died on the scene.*

*I wrap my arms around Scar, knowing it won't ease the pain, but hoping it'll give us both some sort of comfort during this tragic time. No words are spoken. I just hold her until she doesn't want me to anymore.*

*When she steps back, wiping the tears from her eyes, I ask, "How's Maddie holding up?"*

*She draws in a bumpy breath, her entire body quivering. "Not good. And Neo?"*

*"Same, but he won't admit it. He's shut down. Likely numb from the pain."*

*"It's probably better that way. At least for now."*

*My phone buzzes again, and Scar looks down at my jeans pocket. "You should get that. It might be him."*

*I pull it out and take the call while Scar turns around and cries into the sleeve of her oversized flannel.*

*"Hey," I say to Crew.*

*"Where are you at? Neo's been trying to reach you."*

*"I'm...around. How's he doing?"*

*"Terrible. Apparently, his dad wants the investigation done on the down-low so they can avoid any public attention. Neo's pissed."*

*"What can we do?" I ask him, but as I do, I notice Neo stalking toward me. "Hey. He's here. I'll call you back."*

*"Hey, man. Doing okay?" I ask him as I end the call. He doesn't say anything, just glares at me while he continues to stomp his feet in my direction. "How'd you know I was out here?"*

*"Why wouldn't you be? She's here." He aggressively slaps my phone from my hand, sending it to the ground. "My mom dies and this is what you do? Come out here with her?"*

*Scar comes forward, her tone tranquil. "We weren't—"*

*"Shut up. I wasn't talking to you." Neo growls, his fiery gaze now on Scar.*

*"I'm gonna go," she says apologetically. "I'm sorry about your mom. Let me know if you or Maddie need anything at all."*

*"We don't need a damn thing from you. Crew is with Maddie, so just go back to your house and stay away from her."*

*Scar nods, tears threatening to fall from the corners of her eyes.*

*If this were any other day, she'd spit cruel words right back at Neo. But she knows this isn't the time for that.*

*When she turns to leave, I jog up to her to say goodbye. "I'm gonna stay with Neo, but call me later if you wanna talk."*

*"Thanks, Jagger."*

*Probably not the time for this either, but I say, "Try again tomorrow?"*

*She forces a smile on her face. "Sure. Tomorrow."*

I bring the sled to a stop in front of the old Ferris wheel, engine still running. Scar unleashes her hold on me and lifts the helmet over her head. "What are we doing here?"

Once I've got my helmet off, too, I turn my head, so she can hear me. Damn, I didn't think I'd be this nervous. My heart is ready to flee from my body. After all these years, I'm finally doing something for myself. I'm telling her the truth about how I feel. I kill the engine, leaving us in silence. "There's something I need to tell you, Scar."

"Can it wait? I'm really worried about what's going down at the Ruins. Riley's there and Crew's gonna wonder where we're at."

And just like that, my heart splinters. "Yeah. Of course. We'll try again tomorrow." Same song, different dance.

*What the fuck was I thinking?*

# NINE

SCAR

JAGGER DRIVES STRAIGHT through a crowd of people in front of the Ruins, everyone clearing a path for us. As soon as we stop, I tear the helmet off my head and let it fall to the ground. "Crew," I holler, knowing he won't hear me because he's nowhere in sight. "Where is he?" I ask Jagger, who grabs my hand and pulls me toward the front of the crowd.

"What the hell happened?" he asks a random guy who's climbing up the ladder from the tunnels.

"There was an attack."

My eyes widen, and I gasp. "Who?"

"Where?" Jagger asks the guy.

"Hannah Merrill. She's pretty far down. Apparently, her friend Melody found her unconscious. When she came to, she said someone in a mask and a robe threw her into the wall and she hit her head."

"Is Crew down there?"

"Yeah. He and Neo both are."

Jagger turns around to look at the crowd, draining the blood from my hand. "Everyone, go back to your dorms. If you're caught in the tunnels going forward, there will be consequences."

My eyes dance around in search of Riley.

Jagger catches my apprehension. "Who are you looking for?"

"Riley and Elias. I don't see them anywhere."

Jagger pulls his phone out of his pocket, talking as he types. "I'm sure they're here somewhere." He lifts the phone to his ear, and I can hear it ringing on the other end.

*I need to go find Riley and Elias.*

I try to pull my hand from Jagger's, but his eyes snap to mine and he shakes his head.

"Shouldn't we, like, call an ambulance or something?"

Once again, he shakes his head no.

"Where the fuck are you?" he says into the phone. "She's with me. She's fine." His eyes stay cemented to mine and I wish he'd hurry up, so I know what the hell's going on.

"Ask them if they've seen Riley or Elias."

"What the hell? All right, I'm coming down." Jagger ends the call.

"You didn't ask!"

"Your friends are fine. Come with me." He leads me to the ladder, gesturing for me to go first. As I descend, I stop and peer up at him. "Will you have someone check on Elias and Riley? Make sure they're okay?"

He nods subtly. "Sure. If it's that important to you."

I continue down, Jagger following. As soon as my feet hit the ground, I'm being swept up in Crew's arms. "What the hell took you guys so long?"

I look over his shoulder at Jagger, who's already watching us. "Got caught up on a branch on the trail," I lie. It's better this way.

Jagger takes in a deep breath and walks around us, leaving Crew and me alone at the entrance.

"How's Hannah?" I ask him.

"A little disorientated. She's got a nice-size gash on her head but the on-call doctor is with her."

"Good. I'm glad someone called him." I don't bother asking about the authorities because everyone here knows that outside law enforcement doesn't get involved. However, the Lawless are required to report incidents like this to the Elders. "Did you call Neo's dad?"

He shakes his head in slow movements as he chews on his bottom lip. "No. We're not involving the Chairman or the Elders. If we pull them into this, they'll hinder our ability to catch this guy. And *we will* catch this guy."

I wrap my arms around his neck, my head resting against his collarbone. "I hope you're right."

Suddenly, something hits me. "Hey," I say, pulling back, "is Melody with Hannah?"

"Yeah. Why?"

"Remember that schedule I found in the library when I was certain someone was watching me?"

"I remember. What about it?"

"It was Melody's. Don't you think it's a little strange that I found her schedule when I saw that guy and now her best friend was attacked?"

"Probably a coincidence."

"It's worth asking about, though. Don't ya think? What if this guy is after Melody, too?"

"I'm not worried about Melody or Hannah. I'm worried about you." He kisses my lips before drawing back to get a better look at me. "So, Jagger got the sled caught up on a branch, huh?"

I nod, feeling a twinge of guilt for not telling him the truth. When I said that, I was still in a state of panic and the words just flew out of my mouth. I thought it would be better if he didn't know, but my conscience doesn't agree.

"That's weird. I took the same trail that leads here, and I didn't see any debris on my way. Must've fallen after I passed through."

"I lied," I blurt out, unable to keep up with my story. "I'm sorry, Crew, but I lied. There was no branch."

He takes a step back, rubbing his chin. "Okay," he drags out the word. "So what really happened?"

I massage my temple, hating the position I'm in. The last thing I want is to start an argument between Jagger and Crew. Crew is already convinced I have feelings for Jagger and this will only add to that assumption.

"I really don't know," I tell him, truthfully. "I noticed we turned off the trail, but I didn't say anything. I thought maybe he had to stop somewhere on the way."

Crew sighs heavily. "Just tell me what the fuck happened, Scar."

"Nothing," I gulp, "it's the honest truth. Nothing happened. We pulled over—"

"Where?"

*Dammit.* I draw in a full breath. I really don't want to give up Jagger's special spot. "Just...somewhere."

"And?"

It feels like I'm being grilled right now and I hate it. "And nothing. He said he wanted to talk to me about something, then I asked him if it could wait because I wanted to get here..." my hands run down his sleeved arms, "...to you."

Crew licks his lips, overthinking this, I'm sure. "You're sure that's all that happened?"

I tilt my head to the side, cracking a smile. It's kinda cute when he's jealous. "I'm sure." I slither up to him, bringing my hands around his neck, and clasp them together. I lift my chin and his eyes peer down on me. He's still scowling, but I think I can change that. My lips meet his and I instantly feel his body relax against mine. "I'm here now. With you."

He smacks my ass with both hands, hard, and my body jolts. His fingers curl into the flesh of my cheeks. "Let's keep it that way."

"Scarlett!" I hear Riley bellow from above ground. "Are you down there?"

"I'm here," I holler back, hurrying over to the ladder. I look up and see her panic-stricken face. "I'm okay."

She clutches her chest. "Thank fuck. I thought you were dead."

I laugh at her hysterics. "Why would you think that?"

"Oh, I dunno. Maybe because of the company you keep. Or because I heard a girl was beaten to a bloody pulp down there."

*That's the rumor mill for ya...*

Riley begins to shimmy down the ladder, her ass on display under her jean miniskirt.

"Hannah is fine, too. She just hit her head on the wall."

The minute her feet touch the ground, she throws herself at me. "Don't you ever scare me like that again."

"Everyone is fine. I promise."

She takes a step back, hands pressed to my shoulders. "This time! What about next time? What about when it's you? I knew you moving in with those guys was a bad idea." She looks over my shoulder, acknowledging Crew. "Sorry, but it's true."

I glance at Crew, who has his hands up in the air. "No

offense taken. But I think we both know Scar is safer with us."

"Doubtful," she hisses at him, and I'm a bit surprised by her confrontational tone. Riley is usually timid and reserved when it comes to the Lawless.

"Where's Elias?" I ask her, needing to change the subject quickly before it escalates into another situation I'm stuck in the middle of.

"Everyone was sent back to their dorms, but there was no way in hell I was going there without making sure you were safe first."

"Ry!" I stammer. "You've been out there alone when there's a madman on the loose? What the hell were you thinking?"

"I was thinking that if someone wanted to hurt me, they could have done it already. I'm out alone all the time. It's you I'm worried about."

My neck stretches back in confusion. "Me? Why?" I think we all have every reason to be worried, but what I don't understand is why Riley is so concerned about my safety all of a sudden. She doesn't even know this crazy guy is targeting me.

"I heard everyone talking about what happened at the Lawless house. Someone broke into your room?"

Crew comes up to my side, putting an arm around my waist. "Scar is safe. As we promised you she would be."

Riley glowers at Crew, and they exchange unspoken words. It's like a battle over who can keep me the safest, and, truthfully, it's really uncomfortable. "Both of you, stop! Contrary to what you might think, I'm perfectly capable of taking care of myself." I simper, looking at Riley. "Crew is right, though. They wouldn't let anything happen to me."

She scratches the back of her head, assessing Crew before looking at me and saying, "Fine. Why don't you walk home with me and stay at my place tonight until they get the power back on at the guys' house."

"No," Crew blurts out, warranting a quizzical look from both Riley and me. "I don't want her in the dorms. Neo called the headmaster and she assured him the power will be back on tonight."

"Scarlett?" Riley says, wanting to know how I feel about this situation.

"Crew is right. It's best if I stay at their house." An idea pops into my head. "But since the parties were both a bust, we could still hang out tonight."

Riley's eyes light up. "I love that idea!" Her arms fly around the upper half of my body. "I've missed you since you moved out."

Crew and I share a look. "She's always like this," I tell him.

"If by *always like this*, you mean super happy to hang out with my bestie, then yes!"

"Okay. It's settled then," Crew says, clearly bored with this conversation. "I have to go check on things with the guys, so your hangout will have to wait." He takes my hand, and Riley grabs the other.

"Wait," Riley says, tugging me in her direction, "why don't we go back to my room until Crew is done and he can stop and pick you up after?"

It's a good thing we don't have school tomorrow, even though it's a Thursday. I have a feeling it's going to be a very long night.

"All right," Crew says, eyes on me, "I'll get someone I

trust to walk you both to the dorm and I'll swing by when we're done here."

I squeeze his hand, seeking reassurance. "You sure you don't mind?"

"Nah. This shouldn't take long." He leans close, lips brushing my ear. "But I expect you to pay me a visit in my room when we get home tonight."

A smile plays on my lips and I whisper back, "I'll do my very best."

"Ya know. I could get used to this," Riley says as she kicks out her leg, shaking off the snow that's seeping into her ankle boot.

"What's that? Freezing your ass off in a miniskirt in frigid temperatures?"

"No," she chuckles, "having a bodyguard."

I look over my shoulder at Victor, who's following quietly behind us. Unfortunately, ol' boy Vic fucked up again and he was never promoted from Rook rank. Now, he really is the Lawless's bitch. He was given strict orders to follow us to the Foxes' Den.

As we near the end of the trail, I spot Elias. He's walking toward us, bundled up in a trench coat with a trapper hat on his head. "There you are," he says to Riley, "I've been looking everywhere."

"Aren't you supposed to be at your dorm?"

"Technically, yes. But the Lawless are still in the tunnels. What they don't know won't..."

His words trail off when he looks at me. I get the impression he thinks I've left his side and joined the

Lawless. "Don't worry, Elias." I pat his shoulder. "Your secrets are safe with me. Under one condition."

His eyes perk up. "A condition?"

"Mhmm. You tell me why you stood me up yesterday. I waited for you at the library and you never showed up."

Elias breaks eye contact, gazing past my shoulder. "Actually, I did show." He looks back at me, an expression of indignation on his face. "Your boy, Jagger, sent me away."

"He what?" I gasp. *Jagger sent him away?*

"Yup. Made me go fetch a keg for their party and bring it to their house."

"Why would he do that?"

"Because he's Jagger—a member of the Lawless—and they're grade-A dickheads."

Jagger isn't usually a bully to the other students. He doesn't order them around in the way that Crew and Neo do. It can only mean one thing...he was keeping Elias away from me.

He was either concerned for my safety, or he was jealous. And I don't know what to do with either concept.

"I guess I have no choice but to forgive you and keep your secret then."

"Good." He beams. "Then what'd ya say we hit up the snack store and stuff our faces on the library steps like old times."

"Oooh," Riley beams, "that's a great idea."

I wince. "I don't think that's a great idea. Crew will be at the dorms to pick me up soon and I promised we'd be there. I don't want him to worry. Not to mention, someone was attacked tonight. Shouldn't we play it safe for a while?"

"Oh, come on, Scar," Riley says, and it's odd because she

never calls me Scar. "Live a little. We're only seniors once and these guys already have you on a tight leash."

She makes a good point. They have been keeping close tabs on me. I get it, but living a little sounds pretty damn nice.

Victor steps in front of us. "Let's go, ladies. I've got orders to fulfill."

"No worries," Elias tells him. "I've got them from here."

Victor laughs in a mocking tone. "Fuck that. I'm not pissing those guys off any more than I already have."

"Vic," I say, throwing an arm around his shoulders, "can I call you, Vic? We're old friends, right?" He shakes his head, not liking where this is going. "You already broke one rule. You weren't supposed to talk to us. Besides, Elias will make sure we get where we need to be."

His shoulders slump, and he pulls away from me. "You're gonna get me in a lot of fucking trouble. Ya know that?"

"I'll make sure there is no trouble for you. Promise." I'm not sure if he believes me, but he has to know I do have some pull with Crew and Jagger now. I do live in their house, after all.

"Fine," Victor grumbles. "But if they find out and—"

"They won't," I assure him. My hands land on his shoulders and I spin him in the opposite direction, toward the boys' dorms. "Go back to your room and everything will be fine."

Against his better judgment, he leaves with a heavy sigh. Once he's out of sight, Riley snickers. "Damn, girl. You really have a way with the guys here. I'm impressed."

I laugh it off because while it may be true, Riley also has

no idea why I have a way with the guys. It all comes down to the secrets we keep.

We're walking slowly, side by side, while Elias and Riley hold hands and discuss Hannah and the attack. The sidewalks are eerily quiet since the students were sent back to their dorms. A lamppost flickers in the distance and a hair-raising sensation washes over me.

Maybe it was a bad idea to send Victor away. I'm really doubting Elias's ability to protect us, should this crazy guy come after one of us. Elias is a smart guy, but he lacks any brawn, and there's no doubt in my mind he'd be overpowered by just about any guy at the Academy.

"We should just go to the dorm," I spit out, interrupting their conversation. They both look at me, surprised by my outburst. "What if the person who broke into my room and attacked Hannah and Lucy is still out there?" I look around, getting the sense we're being watched.

"Chill out, babe. We're fine," Riley says with an abundance of confidence.

*I get it.* She's a girl with a crush and she's soaking up these last few minutes with Elias before the night ends. It doesn't change what happened and what could happen, though.

"I don't like this."

Elias stops walking, still holding Riley's hand tightly. "Don't you think if someone wanted to get to you, they would have by now?"

"I...I guess so." *Fuck. I don't know.* Maybe it's time to be honest with Riley and Elias. They're my closest friends here and it might help if they knew what's been going on. I nod toward the stairs in front of the library. "Can we skip the snacks and sit? There's something I need to tell you both."

"You okay?" Riley asks while at the same time Elias says, "Yeah. Sure."

I bite my lip, taking a seat on the bottom step. My legs stretch out in front of me and I twiddle my thumbs in my lap, trying to figure out where to start.

"Help!" someone shouts in the distance, grabbing all our attention.

I'm back on my feet, my heart racing. "What was that?"

"I don't know. It sounded like a girl," Riley says.

We look around, waiting for someone to show their face, when the harrowing sound of a girl's screams ring through the small-town square.

Riley begins walking steadfastly toward the sound and I shout after her, "Don't go, Ry. You don't know who's out there!"

Elias jogs to her side, trying to stop her. "Someone's in trouble," Riley hisses, throwing Elias's arm off her hip. "We have to try and help."

I'm shaking uncontrollably. Frantic. Terrified. Unsure whether I should go with her or stay behind. I'm too scared to make a decision.

Before I have to decide, in the distance, someone stumbles out of the woods. Riley and Elias rush to her side while I press my fingertips to my temples, not knowing what the hell is going on.

"Who is it?" I shout, too scared to find out for myself. *Is she hurt? Is she alive?*

"It's Melody," Riley hollers back.

Pulling myself together, I jog over to them and see Melody sitting on the ground, hugging her knees to her chest. Her face is smeared with a mixture of tears and dirt. Her hair is a mess and her white jacket is ripped on the sleeve. "Oh my god, Melody," I bellow, dropping to her side, "are you okay?"

She shakes her head, crying. "Someone grabbed me. He's out there."

"Out where?" I ask. "In the woods?"

She nods, body trembling. Her eyes pin to mine and her expression shifts to one of deep fear. "He wants you, Scarlett."

"Me?" I sputter. "Why would you say that? What did he say?"

She holds her hand out to me and unravels her fist. Sitting in her palm is a small piece of folded paper. "What is that?" I ask, although I can clearly see what it is.

"He told me to give this to you."

Reluctantly, I take the note from her with a shaky hand.

"Open it," Riley urges me as she consoles Melody with a hand on her shoulder.

I look from person to person, not so sure I want to know what this note says.

"What the hell are you waiting for? Open it!" Melody pushes, and I can see she's returned to her normal bitchy self.

Slowly, I unfold it. My eyes pinch shut, and when I open them, I read the words in my head.

*It was supposed to be you.*

Shuddering, I let the paper flutter to the ground. I fall back on my ass in the snow. "No. No!" That's all I can say because I can't think coherently enough to form a full sentence.

Riley picks up the paper, reads it, then hands it to Elias as she looks at me with terrified eyes. "What does that mean? *It was supposed to be you?*"

Melody snatches the note from Elias, then balls it up and throws it at me. "It means my best friend should have never been attacked. It should have been her. Of course this is all your fault."

"No," I shake my head, "it's not my fault."

"It is so and now Hannah is hurt because of you."

"Shut up, Melody," Elias grumbles. "How the hell was Scarlett supposed to know Hannah would be hurt in those tunnels?"

"Wait," I say, mid-thought, "what if he's not referring to Hannah, but Lucy instead? Someone grabbed Lucy in my room, but when she screamed, he pushed her away and took off. What if he was trying to kidnap me?"

Melody scoffs as she climbs to her feet. "Well, either way, it's your fault. I say you give yourself up to save anyone else from getting hurt."

Something just isn't adding up here. How is Melody suddenly involved in this, anyway? Better yet, why is she?

I look at her, scowling. "Why should I believe anything you say? For all I know, it's you doing all of this. You hate me, so why not?"

She laughs. "Oh yeah...and I just decided to bang my best friend's head into a wall. Do you hear yourself?"

*Melody's schedule.* Another piece of evidence that comes into play.

"I've got a question for you, Melody? Where is your class schedule?"

She scoffs. "Hell if I know."

"I do. I found it on the library floor after someone dropped it. Now I'm thinking that someone was you."

"Me?" She chuckles sarcastically. "In the library? Now you're really sounding crazy."

"You would have been disguised. So yeah."

"Someone please tell this girl she has officially lost her mind."

"Maybe I have. But why don't you tell us what this mystery person in the woods was wearing, *Melody*?" I enunciate her name, adding a punch of my own sarcasm.

"Umm. A black robe with a hood and a black ski mask."

*Exactly what I saw in the library.*

"Did he talk to you?"

"No, Scarlett. He used sign language to tell me to give you this note. Yes, he fucking talked to me."

Man, I really wanna punch this stupid bitch. But I won't. Not yet. "And did you happen to recognize his voice?"

"Don't you think if I recognized his voice, I would tell you who it was?" She sweeps the snow off her white jeans. "I have to go. Elias, will you walk me to my dorm, please? Really don't wanna be alone after what just happened."

Elias shares a glance with me and Riley before saying, "Yeah. I guess you can walk with us?" He looks at me. "That okay with you?

I shrug my shoulders. "Whatever."

On the walk back, I'm lost in my thoughts. What if I really am the one this guy wants? People are getting hurt in the process, all so he can get to me.

Maybe Melody's right. Maybe I do need to give myself up. But before I decide, I need to know what I'm up against. Part of me hopes it really is Melody, so I can finally hit her where it hurts...right in the fucking jaw.

# TEN

## JAGGER

Last night after Crew picked up Scar, she filled us in on a situation that involved Melody Higgins. Things are getting really messy, and if we don't do something soon, we're going to lose complete control over the student body. If that happens, the Elders will be forced to step in and the guys and I risk losing all our authority.

"Maybe I should skip the game," Crew says, pacing my bedroom floor. His eyes are pinned to his feet; he's been deep in thought all morning.

I shuffle through the hoodies in my closet, searching for my favorite one. "And what good would that do?"

"Scar needs extra protection. She's downplaying this too much, and I don't think she realizes the danger she's in. If I skip the game, I can stay with her."

My hands drop to my sides when I remember I let Scar have my Essex High hoodie last night. I'm pretty sure she lent it to the frantic chick on the deck. I'm not sure she ever got it back.

"Look. Neo and I will keep an eye on Scar. She'll be fine."

"Neo?" Crew laughs. "I wouldn't trust that fucker with a goldfish, let alone my girl."

*His girl.* Is that what she is?

"Do you trust me?"

There's a beat of silence before he says, "Of course, I do."

*But does he really?* "You mean that?"

"Shouldn't I trust you?"

I snatch a random hoodie from a hanger and hold it up —a black one with the teal BCA logo. Once I pull it over my head and slip my arms in, I turn to face Crew. "Depends on what we're talking about. In regard to keeping Scar safe, of course."

"And," he drawls, glaring at me, "in regard to something else…?"

"Then no. You probably shouldn't."

When I look back at him, he's glowering. He tips his head to the side. "Care to elaborate on that?"

I had no intention of drudging this up right now, but we're alone and it's time some shit is said. "You know I like her." My words come out as smooth as a casual conversation over morning breakfast.

"No shit. But you know we're together now. Apparently that doesn't mean shit, though. Does it?"

"Didn't know you and Scar had a label on your relationship, but either way, I don't wanna come between you two, if that's what you're thinking."

"So what?" He laughs wryly. "You just want me to share her with you? I'm not Neo, and this isn't some random chick."

We've all shared girls more times than I can count, but that's not what I'm asking for. If I'm being technical, I'm not asking for anything. I don't need Crew's permission, but out of respect, I'm letting him know where I stand.

"This isn't about a one-night fuck and you know it."

"Then what is it about? Humor me, *best friend*." He puts emphasis on the title, dropping down into my desk chair. The arms in his veins protrude as he clicks his jaw.

"Did Scar ever tell you about her first kiss?"

His brows pinch together and he huffs. "No. Why the hell would I care about her first kiss?"

"It was me." I press my lips together, watching him intently for a reaction.

His shoulders draw back, chest tight. "Bullshit."

"It's true. Four years ago, to be exact. I was also her second, third, fourth—"

"Shut the fuck up. Even if this is true, it doesn't matter. What matters is her last kiss. Which will be me."

I click my tongue on the roof of my mouth. "We'll see about that."

The next thing I know, Crew is on his feet, lunging at me. When I go to push him back, not wanting to do this shit again, he grabs my waist and takes me down to the floor. My back hits with a thud, knocking the wind out of me. "What the fuck is the matter with you?" I growl at him, nose to nose.

"I lost her once and I won't lose her again because you've suddenly decided you've got a crush on my girl."

We exchange blows as he tries to grab me by the throat. "This isn't a sudden crush. I've had feelings for Scar for years."

"Liar! I know you, Jagger. You don't get feelings for girls. You wanna fuck her and leave her like you do every other girl."

When he makes a wrong move, I get the upper hand. In a swift motion, I kick my leg up, flinging him off me and onto his back. With both his wrists pinned in my hands against the floor, he doesn't stand a chance. "Maybe I let go of all the other ones because I was waiting for her."

"Well, brother, you waited too fucking long. She's with me now."

"I know she feels something toward me. You know it, too. If you didn't, you wouldn't feel so threatened by me."

"I don't see shit and I sure as hell don't feel threatened."

He squirms, trying to break free, but I slam his wrists hard on the floor. "Then give me a chance with her. Worst-case scenario, she doesn't reciprocate my feelings, and she stays with you."

"She won't do it. There's no way in hell."

He says the words, but the pique in his expression tells the truth—he's worried.

"You don't know that."

Crew surrenders and turns his head, looking to the left. When he looks back at me, he curls his lip. "What do you want from her?"

It's simple really. "I just want a chance."

I let go and climb off him. Crew stands, rolling his wrists as he grinds his teeth. "Give it your best shot. But don't expect anything from her in return. She won't give it to you." With that, he walks out of my room, slamming the door hard behind him.

"You know," Scar begins as she takes a bite of her hot dog. "Normally I'd argue that I'm fine and don't need your protection, but after yesterday, my pride is taking a back seat." Her arms wave around the kitchen, hot dog in hand. "I welcome all security from this point forward."

I pick up my empty paper plate from the table and push my chair back. "Good. Because I have no intention of letting you out of my sight. It's you and me tonight, girl."

With a full mouth, she points her half-eaten hot dog at me. "It's a date."

*If only.*

"So," I continue, "the plan is to go to the game, then back here for a chill night. We've put a temporary curfew in place until we catch this guy. Everyone is in their dorms by eleven o'clock this weekend."

She laughs, finding humor in the situation. "If you really think everyone is going to abide by that, you're delusional."

"Honestly. I don't care about everyone else. I only care about you."

She's mid-bite when she stops herself. "Crew said the same thing last night."

"I guess Crew and I think alike."

*More so than I care to admit.*

I step on the lever for the trash can and drop my plate inside. "Kickoff is in ten minutes. We should probably go."

Scar stuffs the rest of her hot dog in her mouth, filling her cheeks as she chews. I chuckle at her, warranting a glare. "What?"

"Just admiring your dinner etiquette."

She points to her mouth, chewing and speaking. "It's a hot dog. Hot dogs don't require etiquette."

"Good point." I extend my hand to her, and she takes it.

We're walking through the kitchen when Scar stops at the fridge. "Would the almighty Lawless leader penalize me if I were to sneak a little drinky drink into the game tonight?" She bats her lashes, trying to woo me—and it's working.

"That depends. Do you plan to share with your almighty Lawless leader?"

"Absolutely." She nudges me with her elbow. "We're friends now, right?"

*Friends.* The word is like a knife straight to the gut. *We're just friends.*

She pulls out a half-empty pint of fireball from the fridge, which is fitting for this cold night.

"Yeah," I say, "we are." I hook an arm around her shoulder and lead her out of the kitchen. Once we're by the door, I drop my hold on her. She steps into her snow boots and pulls on her winter coat—stuffing the pint of booze in the inside pocket of her jacket—while I lace up my black combat boots.

We're halfway out the door when the cold air hits me, so I reach back in and grab a jacket off the coat hanger. It's Neo's, and he'll probably raise hell over it, but it beats freezing my ass off in just a hoodie.

It's not snowing right now, but there's at least an inch on the ground, and when the wind picks up, flakes fall from the trees.

I lead Scar over to my sled and hand her the helmet that's coated in snow. She brushes it off and says, "Good thing I didn't do anything special with my hair today." Then she slips it on.

Once we've both got our helmets on, I start up the engine and take off. This is the second time in twenty-four hours Scar has ridden with me, and I'm starting to get used to the feeling of her body pressed to mine. Now, when she's not there, I'll miss the warmth rolling off her. For someone who's cold all the time, she sure does emit a lot of body heat.

I pull right up to the bleachers at the football field, turning a few heads. Or all of them for that matter.

A glance around the area proves that Neo is not here, and I'm not the least bit surprised. Lately, his time is spent digging into the mystery surrounding us. It's consumed him, much like Maddie's case did. That is, until it was closed, but even then, he kept digging and came to the conclusion that Scar was at fault. There's no saying where his mind will lead him this time.

Scar and I both climb off the sled and hook our helmets on the handlebars. "Not a bad turnout," she says. "With a madman on the loose, I figured more students would stick close to their dorms."

"Eh. I doubt most of them take this shit seriously. As far as they're concerned, this is just another game."

Scar gives me a quizzical look, as if she's questioning it herself. She can rest assured that it isn't. "You need to know this isn't one of our games, no matter what we've done."

"I know," she says. "Can you blame me for considering it, though?"

I shake my head. "No. Not even a little bit." I look around at the crowd—the football players, the scenery. Everyone at this school has an agenda, even me. *Especially me.*

"Hey." She smiles, the dents in her cheeks pronounced. "Meet me under the bleachers." And with that, she takes off, walking steadfastly and leaving me in her shadow.

Biting my lip, I look around again, making sure no one's watching—not sure why I care—and jog after her.

When I catch up, she's pulling the pint from her jacket. "Here," she says, handing it to me.

I side-eye her, smirking. "You trying to get me drunk?"

"Maybe I am." She flashes me a flirtatious grin that has me questioning that whole friends' statement she made earlier.

With the bottle in hand, I unscrew the top and swallow down a shot's worth. The powerful pinch of cinnamon rolls down my throat, igniting my esophagus. I hand it back to her and she takes a baby sip. "Oh, come on. If I'm getting drunk, so are you."

She grimaces, pressing the bottle to her soft pink lips. What I wouldn't give to be that bottle right now. *Fuck.* I want to devour her mouth. Scratch that. I *need* to devour her mouth—and her body. I want it all. Every last bit of her. Her tears after a hard day. Her smiles when she's happy. Even her attitude when she's in a mood. I'll savor it all. Crew will never appreciate those small moments the way I will. He can never fully give himself to her because he's so hung up on his place in the Society. At least, that's what I've always thought. I'm starting to wonder if he realized she's worth the loss and the backlash from Neo, too.

"Jagger," she says, shaking the bottle in front of me. When I look down, I realize it's only a quarter full.

"Holy shit, girl. You're not messing around tonight."

"We're getting drunk, aren't we?"

I take the bottle, tipping it back for another swig, then snatch the top from her hand. "It's best if you pace yourself. You're not used to drinking."

"Says who?" She huffs. "You been watching me?"

Twisting the top back on, I bite down on a smile. "Maybe I have."

"Seems to be everyone's M.O. here."

"We don't all have the same motives, though. That, I can assure you."

Hugging her coat to her chest, she asks, "What's your motive? What do you want from me, Jagger?"

*It's not what I want from you, but with you.*

"Your safety. That's all I care about." It's not a lie.

Scar's eyes burn into mine, and I'm wondering if she's expecting me to say more. I hand her back the bottle, slicing through the tense moment. "Here. One more won't hurt."

After a few minutes of awkward small talk about the weather, the alcohol begins to take hold. "Jagger," Scar says apprehensively.

"Yeah?"

"Can I trust you with a secret?"

That seems to be a heavy topic lately among the four of us. But there has to be a reason she's asking this. "Sure. You can tell me anything."

"Good. Because I'm going to be brutally honest with you." *Oh shit. Here it comes.* "I didn't plan to tell you, but I'm going to the tunnels tonight."

"Like hell you are!" The words fly out of my mouth without any thought process behind them. "Are you insane?"

Completely unaffected by my outburst, she draws her shoulders back. "I'm going, and you can't stop me."

Her determination is cute, but I'm not giving in. "I can and will stop you, even if it means tying you to your bed."

"Kinky. But no. I'm going to the tunnels and checking out that room you and the guys found."

"Then I'll be forced to let Crew and Neo in on your plan."

Her forehead creases, brows tight. "You said I could trust you."

Dammit. Why is she putting me in this position? My head drops back and I'm staring blankly at the tin bleacher seats above me. "Fine," I spit out. "You can go." Her eyes light up, but I'm not finished. "But I'm going with you."

"Okay."

"Okay?" I'm a bit surprised she agreed so quickly.

"Didn't really wanna go alone anyways. Now if someone comes for me, I can use you as bait." She elevates her chin, and when I scowl at her, she laughs. "I'm fucking with you. In all seriousness, I was a little scared at the idea of going there by myself."

"As you should be. This shit is no joke, Scar."

"Ok then." She stuffs the pint back in her pocket. "Let's do this." Her arm hooks around mine, and she skips us out from under the bleachers, her buzz obvious.

Before we duck out, I slouch down and look both ways. There's a group of students gathered to the left, but no one I need to be concerned about. The person I'm looking for is likely still not here—Neo. If he sees Scar and me getting on my sled and leaving together, he'll ask questions. Crew's on the field, so I don't have to worry about him. Once I'm sure the coast is clear, I unhook my arm and take her by the hand, leading her out. "Straight to the sled. Talk to no one."

"Are you good to drive?" she asks, and I realize that alcohol also makes her loud.

"I'm fine," I whisper.

Laughter escapes her. "Why are you whispering? No one can hear us over the game and all the people here."

I take her hand, staring straight ahead. "You don't

understand how much shit I'll be in if anyone finds out about this. So, just play it cool."

She laughs again, and I can see that her courage has skyrocketed with just a few shots.

We get to the sled and I'm shoving the helmet at her, hoping she hurries this along. When I say I'll be in some serious shit if Neo and Crew found out, I'm not exaggerating. That room is full of conspiracy theories, threats, and secrets. Not to mention, everything pertaining to Scar's life over the last couple years.

"Calm down, *Dad!*" She laughs again, and I curl my lip at her.

"For fuck's sake, don't ever call me that again."

I climb on the sled, and she's back in her place behind me. We've got a good hour before the game's over, and we just need to get back before anyone knows we left.

Not wasting any time, I drive out of here at full speed, causing Scar to hug me even tighter. There's nothing quite like being between her legs, but I'd prefer to be facing the other direction with my face down. *Fuck.* The thought has my cock twitching in my pants.

When I take a sharp right, Scar mumbles under the shield of her helmet. "Where are you going?"

I raise my voice and shout, "Different entrance."

If we go in through the Eldridge Mountain entrance, it won't be as long of a walk through the tunnels.

She settles back in place, resting her chin on my shoulder. Even through my helmet and the cold breeze, I can still smell her. Or maybe her scent is so ingrained in my mind, it never really leaves—vanilla and lavender—and damn, does she smell good.

Ten minutes later, I'm coming to a stop on the east side

of Eldridge Mountain. There's an old door that leads to a staircase that will take us right into the tunnels. It's not often we use this entrance, but it's how I entered the last time I went to that room and it cut about ten minutes of walking time.

I turn the key, shutting the sled down, and Scar swings her leg over the side and gets up. I take her helmet from her, hanging it on the handle, then do the same with mine. "Let's make this quick," I tell her.

As we're walking, Scar pulls out the bottle of booze and takes another swig. She passes it to me, lifting a smile. "Liquid courage?"

Against my better judgment, I grab it from her and drink the last drop, then toss the empty bottle to my right.

My tongue sweeps across my lip, taking up the excess liquid. "This way. It's just a small trek to the door."

"So," she begins, looking at me with serious eyes, "it's a little late to ask this, but do you have protection if we need it?"

I stop walking, eyes wide. *Did she really just ask me that?* "Umm, yeah. I always have protection."

"Good. We can't be too safe."

Is she insinuating what I think she is? Crew told me to give it my best shot, but I had no idea it would be this easy. Not that sleeping with Scar is what I was referring to when I said I just wanted a chance. But if she's down, there's no way in hell I'll deny her.

We approach the door and my mind is anywhere but on that room. Each step has my heart racing, and each beat has my erection throbbing. I've tasted Scar's mouth before—felt the tightness of her pussy with my fingers, all the while dreaming about what it would feel like to bury my cock inside her.

"Wait," I say, grabbing her by the waist and pressing her back to the old door blanketed in ivy vines. Her eyes peer up at me, wondrous and full of lust.

"What is it?" she asks, tone placid.

I'm not sure if it's the booze or her words playing on my emotions, but I need to find out if Scar reciprocates my feelings.

*Give it your best shot.*

My hands move to her head, cradling it in my palms like a breakable object.

When her eyes dance across my mouth, I know she feels the tension coiling between us.

Slowly, I bring her lips closer to mine. My tongue drags faintly across her bottom lip, the sweet taste of cinnamon igniting something inside me.

"Jagger," she whispers, the heat of her breath sending chills throughout my body.

I know she wants this as much as I do. I can feel it in my bones. But, this isn't just any girl—it's Scar—and I need her approval first. But once I get it, I'll never ask for it again.

With our noses brushing, my eyes burning into hers, I beg her, "Tell me to kiss you."

When she hesitates, my posture slackens, and all hope is lost. This was my chance, and I blew it. Now, it can never happen again.

She clears her throat, her words crackling. "What about Crew?"

"He told me to give it my best shot. Probably didn't think I'd actually do it. But here I am." I swallow hard. "So again...tell me to kiss you, Scar."

Scar sweeps her fingers through my messy hair. "Okay, then. Kiss me."

My eyebrows hit my forehead. "Really?"

She nods, her beautiful mouth lifted at the corners. "If you don't, I'll kiss you." Before I can react, she grabs my face, pulling my lips to hers.

It's raw and natural, like we've done it a thousand times. Our tongues tangle together, and if I wasn't certain before, I am now. I'm crazy about this girl.

My fingertips graze softly against her cheeks and her hands move to my waist, holding me in place. I move one hand to her hip, sliding it beneath all the layers in search of her soft skin. When flesh meets flesh, I growl into her mouth. "Fuck, Scar. You have no idea how long I've waited for this."

I fall into her, my chest heaving against hers. Letting her go, I press my hands to either side of the door, my fingers getting tangled in the webs of ivy. Her head rests back, eyes closed, and I trail my lips down her neck, sucking and kissing.

I draw in a deep breath, inhaling her. The scent of her hair, paired with a crisp, woodsy aroma, flood my senses and my entire body fills with heat. This time, I'm certain the hot whiskey has nothing to do with the flames dancing in my stomach.

"We should go inside." She hums in my mouth. "What if..."

Her words trail off, but I know what she's thinking. *What if someone sees us?* She might not regret what's happening, and she knows Crew's aware of our situation, but there has to be a part of her that feels uneasy about us in the public eye. Not that there is any foot traffic out here, anyway. We're all alone, but to appease her, I cup her ass and lift her up. Her legs wrap around my waist, and I already miss the taste of her tongue on mine.

Holding her up with one arm, I reach into my coat pocket, pulling out my keys. When her mouth finds my neck, and she peppers it with kisses, I'm tempted to throw her down and take her on this blanket of snow.

Once I've got the door unlocked, I kick it wide open and carry her inside.

CHAPTER

# ELEVEN

SCAR

DON'T OVERTHINK THIS, *Scar*.

It's been a long time coming. I know it. Jagger knows it. And most importantly, Crew knows it. He said to tell him if anything changes between me and Jagger, and I will tell him. I'll tell him everything.

The salty taste of Jagger's skin wets my lips while the aroma of clove and his cologne invade my nostrils. Heat rolls off his body, warming every inch of mine. I hold him tight, not wanting to let go because I fear I'll never have him in my arms again.

Everything about this is wrong, but God, it feels so right. The moment Jagger's mouth met mine, I came alive. I'm alive with Crew, but it's different with Jagger. My connection with both of them is equal, yet still, so different.

Jagger gives the door a swift kick, and it slams shut. I break away from his neck, already missing his taste when I ask, "Should we lock it?"

Like a crazed beast, he growls. "No one's coming."

My back hits the brick wall of the tunnel, my legs still

118

snug around his waist. Jagger grumbles into the crease of my neck, "I need you. Now." His voice is raspy and hungry and I want more than anything for him to feast on me.

"Take me. Devour me. I'm yours."

He pulls back, eyes beaming into mine with a bleak expression that tells me he doesn't believe me. "You mean that?"

"Right now. Yes."

It's like something shifts inside him and aggression takes hold. "Then I'm going to savor every fucking second of it."

*Yes. Please do.* I've wanted this for so long. For years, I've wondered where Jagger's feelings stood with me. After every secret date at the treehouse—every shared kiss—I was certain he was falling for me. Then the treehouse was gone, and so was he. Not in the real sense, but emotionally, he checked out. Eventually, I did the same. There was no point holding on to someone when they already let go.

Now here we are. Back where we started.

Jagger drops his hands from my hips and my feet land on solid ground. The zipper of my coat flies down and he peels back the shoulders. Panting with each breath, I pull my arms out.

My coat hits the ground, and before any other articles are shed, Jagger kisses me again. This time, passion sizzles. Electricity rushes through me, hitting every nerve with a desperate need. *More. All of it. All of him.*

No matter how close he is, it's not enough. I return the favor, taking his coat off for him, our lips never parting. Once he's free of it, he pulls off his hoodie and drops it. My hands shimmy up his shirt, pawing at the rigid cords of his abs. It's too hard to see him, so I use touch, taste, and smell as my only senses. And right now, I'm loving what I feel. Jagger has been many things to me: a friend, a secret, an enemy, and a thief, but the one thing that has been constant is the physical attraction I feel toward him. He, Crew, and Neo are three of the most gorgeous guys I've ever laid eyes on, and I would never deny that, even through months—years—of hostility.

Our lips glide together with ease while sexual frustration sears to the point of combustion. I grip the hem of his shirt, lifting it up and breaking our kiss. With a toss, it lands somewhere in the dark. Next, my shirt leaves my body. Then my bra. Cold fingers teeter with the button of my jeans, popping it off. The only sound is our heavy breaths before Jagger says, "Turn around."

I do as I'm told, turning to face the wall. He takes one hand, pressing it to the cold brick. Then the other. I keep them in place as he tugs down my jeans and panties, letting them pool around my ankles. My body shivers in response, and it's definitely not because of the cold temperature. Every feeling inside me is due to Jagger and what he's doing to me —and what he's not doing to me.

When his jeans drop, a smile creeps across my face.

This is really happening. I might be acting like a whore right now, fucking Crew's best friend, but deep down, I know Crew saw it coming and I've convinced myself he won't mind. I knew since that day on the Ferris wheel; it was inevitable.

Jagger's fingers dust my inner thigh, sliding up farther and farther until he stops at the slit of my pussy. His other hand sweeps my hair to the side and his hot breath on my neck sends goosebumps spilling down my back.

"I'm gonna fuck you, Scarlett." His words are a song in

my ear. "I'm gonna fuck you so hard, you'll be walking bowlegged for days. Then, I'm gonna fuck you again."

*Holy shit.* My body trembles, legs shaking as if they have a mind of their own.

When his fingers dabble at my pussy with a small amount of pressure, I become desperate. "Do it. Now." My words come out in anguished pants.

He laughs a menacing sound. "Patience, baby."

My legs part, back arched as I grant him entrance. I'm not above begging at this point, and if he doesn't give me what I need soon, I'll take it for myself. "Please," I whimper.

Trailing his fingers backward, they glide between my ass cheeks. In feverish circles, he rubs at my hole, and it's another thing I've never felt before. I've only been with one guy my entire life, and while Crew is incredible in bed, he's not aggressive—aside from the hate-sex we've had, which was insanely fulfilling.

Oddly enough, it feels good, so I let Jagger use me the way he wants. "Have you ever been fucked in the ass, Scarlett?" The way he's saying my given name and not the nickname they labeled me with is sexy as hell right now.

"No," I tell him honestly.

With his chin on my shoulder, he whispers smoothly in my ear, "Good. Save that for me. I'm taking it next time."

He moves his hand and I'm back to groveling. "Do something. Anything."

His mouth draws in the skin of my neck, teeth grazing the sensitive flesh. A moan of desperation climbs up my throat, and I've had enough.

I spin around, hands planted on his chest, and I walk him backward, until his back is pressed to the stairwell wall. I can't see his face, but I can feel the resistance in his body, though he doesn't fend me off. "If you won't give me what I want, then I'll just have to take it." I reach down, taking his cock in my hand, and I audibly gasp. My God, he's huge. I guess that explains his big ego and the reason so many women fall at his feet. I'm not sure my mouth could even open wide enough to fit it all in.

"Is there a problem?" Jagger asks, and I'm speechless. "You said you'd take what you want, so go ahead. Take it." His hand presses to the top of my head and he forces pressure until I'm kneeling in front of him.

"Not exactly what I had in mind," I sputter. "But okay." I give him a few pumps, unable to even wrap my fingers around his full girth.

Jagger presses on the back of my head, guiding me toward his monstrous cock. I swallow hard, lick my lips, and open wide.

He slides in with ease, and while he fits, my teeth drag across his head. I take him as far as I can, feeling him hit the back of my throat. My hand pumps in sync with the motions of my mouth, giving attention to the other end of his cock.

When he fists my hair and grunts, pleased with my performance, I'm given a boost of confidence. I reach between his legs and cup his balls, caressing them in the palm of my hand.

"Mmm. You're doing so good."

Taking him out of my mouth, I drag my tongue down his length then suck him from the side as I work my way back up. Saliva coats his erection, and I slop it with my hands, stroking him back and forth.

Jagger maneuvers himself so that he's back in my mouth, his hand regulating my every move. He thrusts deep, causing me to gag, but I keep going because each whimper from his mouth has me starving for his rapture.

"My dick loves your mouth, baby."

His words appease me, and I pick up my pace, his hand dragging through my hair, knotting strands around his fingers. Just as I feel him swell against my cheeks, I pull my mouth off him. He jerks my head back so that I'm staring up at him, though I can't see his face.

"Hands and knees. Now," he barks the order, and I do as I'm told.

The next thing I know, Jagger's on his back and his head is between my legs. The wispy strands of his hair prickle against my inner thigh, and he says, "Sit on my face."

I hesitate, feeling a little self-conscious and inexperienced when it comes to this position. When I don't move, he pinches his fingertips into each of my ass cheeks and pulls me down.

"Oh, fuck," I cry out. I wasn't expecting that. His teeth nibble at my clit and I blink away the stars flickering in my eyes.

Two fingers shove inside me and there is nothing gentle about the way he's working them.

Knuckle-deep, he curls his fingers, pumping them continuously. I can feel my arousal dripping from me, and he uses his tongue to clean up the mess I'm making. "Damn. You are soaked."

He sucks harder, then resumes flicking his tongue as I bite hard on my lip. My chest rises and falls in rapid movements, hips swaying.

When he pulls his fingers out, I grumble. "Don't you dare fucking stop."

"Someone's bossy." His laughter vibrates against my sex. "But I'm in control here and you won't come until I let you."

"Nice try, but no one controls me." I push myself up on my hands until my back has only a slight arch, and I roll and grind, leaving him no choice. The short stubble of his chin grates against my pussy, and I cry out in pleasure.

Two hands land on my inner thighs, pinching with tenacity and bringing blood to the surface, and I know to expect twin bruises from it. Jagger pushes up, pulling me away from his face.

"What are you doing?" I ask, breathless.

"Whatever I want."

He comes up from behind me, his chest ghosting my back. One finger presses to my chin and he lifts. "You tell me if it's too rough, all right, baby?"

I nod against his touch.

"Good. Because then I'll fuck you harder. I wanna hear you scream, Scarlett."

*I'm screwed—literally.* Who am I and since when do I let any man control me like this? It's out of the norm for me, but damn if I wouldn't crawl on my knees, begging at this point.

I draw in a deep breath, preparing myself, but before I can even exhale, Jagger is plunging his beast of a cock inside me.

My lungs deflate on impact, and my body jolts forward, nails scratching into the surface of the concrete floor beneath me.

Two hands land on my hips, fingers burying into my skin. Jagger pushes me out, then pulls me back in, filling me up completely. My stomach bulges with each thrust, where his cock settles inside me. He rolls his hips left and right, molding me for him, and while there's a bite of pain, I won't make him stop. I'll never make him stop.

"Does it hurt?" he asks, his voice heady and gruff.

"No," I tell him on an exhale.

Not satisfied with my response, he grabs a fistful of my hair, pulling back and exposing my neck. I gasp, while he thrusts deeper—harder, faster. My ass ricochets off his pelvic bone, and my knees grind against the floor, small pebbles of concrete embedding itself into my kneecaps.

"And now?"

I'm my own worst enemy when I grit back at him, "No."

He jerks harder, and my hair follicles are on fire. When he wraps a hand around my throat, squeezing, I gulp. I whimper. I moan. I cry out. I manage to get out the words, "Oh god, Jagger." My entire body seizes up. My blood pumps faster. My heart racing, and the pulse in my neck pounding against his palm. My walls clench, squeezing his cock— until he slows his motions to nothing more than a steady in and out. His hands drop back to my hips, and I internally beg for him to choke me again.

"Did I say you could come, yet?"

"Finish me off, dammit." My words are laced with intent because, if he doesn't, I'll pin him to the ground and ride his cock until I'm squirting all over his stomach.

"Since you asked so nicely." He pounds into me again, his hand slapping at my pussy while he growls an animalistic sound. I bridge my back and meet him, thrust for thrust, as I reach the height of my climax. I can feel the head of his cock expand right before he grunts and releases inside me.

My mouth falls agape as I exhale all the pent-up air in my lungs.

A couple more pumps, and he pulls out before I drop straight to the ground, completely naked. My mind is in an altered state; I'm unable to think clearly.

"That was…intense," I finally say through dry vocal cords and cracked lips.

I can feel him leave my side, so I push myself off the cold floor, wiping off the grit and dirt from my body the best I can.

"I'll definitely need a shower—"

Before I can even finish my sentence, his lips are on mine. Fingers rooted in my hair, once again. Only this time, it's soft and gentle, and it's the Jagger I know.

I reciprocate the kiss and wrap my arms around his neck. "Thank you," he mutters into my mouth.

"For what?"

"Giving me a shot." He kisses me again, and I smile against his lips.

I'm not sure if I'll ever regret what we just did, but I hope Crew can forgive me for wanting to do it again.

# TWELVE

JAGGER

AFTER SCAR and I caught our breaths and got dressed, I took her hand and led her through the tunnels. I wasn't able to see her face in that room where I corrupted her body, but I can see her now and the smile on her face reflects the one on mine.

This moment, right here, is everything I've been waiting for. The sex was fucking amazing, but sex can be had with anyone. It's her hand in mine and me being the reason for her smile that I've longed for.

"Hey, Jagger?" she says, and I snap my eyes to hers. "Remember yesterday when you took me to the Ferris wheel and told me you wanted to tell me something?"

I respond with a, "Yeah."

"What was it?"

My thumb grazes the soft spot between her thumb and index finger. I crack a smile. "Doesn't matter now."

She halts. "Oh, come on. You took me all the way out there, even when we thought the student body was under attack. It had to have been important."

We're standing under the dim light of a sconce, her eyes wide with regard. "You really wanna know?"

"I really do."

I take her other hand, pulling her close, then draping her arms over my shoulders. Face to face, I ask, "Do you remember the last time we kissed? The night before the treehouse burnt down?"

She nods, so I continue, "I never wanted it to be the last time. It just...made sense to put an end to our meetups. Ya know?"

"Because of Neo." It's not a question but rather a statement.

"Yeah. Neo. And Maddie. And even Crew." The day of the fire, I realized the odds were against us. Scar and I met up every night at the treehouse after that first night. After two weeks of meetups and making out, I went there one day to find the treehouse on fire. Scar came seconds later, and it was too late. Neo burnt it to the ground. He lashed out at me for going to Scar the night his mom died, instead of being there for him. I guess it served as a reminder of the day he got that call.

"Besides," I continue, "we were only fourteen, and if I remember right, you accused me of being a...what did you call it? A player?"

She chuckles. "Yeah. I did say that. And every day after that. I really thought you were. I've watched you. Saw the way you pulled girls in then pushed them away after you got what you wanted."

"And now?"

"Now I'm starting to wonder if maybe you never kept any other girls close," she bites her lip, considering the possibility of whatever she's thinking, "because of me."

Her blue eyes burn into mine, and for the first time ever, we're on the exact same page. "It was. No one ever measured up to you, and I guess part of me was waiting to see if we might get our chance again."

There's a pang in my chest when I remember she's taken. This evening has been a dream, but it's not reality. Crew's made a home inside her heart, and even if we have this moment, where do I fit into her life? Am I still her old crush, turned enemy, turned friend? Or am I more? I sound like a fucking pussy, but I've got no problem owning up to how I feel.

Scar squeezes my hand, noticing my apprehension. "What's wrong?"

Eyebrows pinched, I tell her, "Everything." I let go of her, looking down and running my hands through my hair. "Did we just fuck up, Scar?"

"No," she huffs, and my eyes lift to hers, "we didn't fuck up, Jagger. I have no regrets, if that's what you're thinking. Crew knows I have feelings for you. I'm not sure what those feelings mean, but they're here and they're real."

Just like that, the weight on my chest feels lighter. "Come here." I grab her by the hand and pull her body flush to mine. "I don't know what any of this means either, but whatever happens, I'm all in."

"You do realize, I have to tell him, right?"

"Yeah. I figured you would. And if you didn't, then I probably would."

She nods, biting the inside of her cheek.

"Are you worried?"

"Little bit," she admits. "I do care about him a lot."

My fingers intertwine with hers. "I know you do, and so do I."

We start walking again, engaging in small talk about everything from the football game to Maddie, and when we approach the door to the secret room, our conversation shifts to the BCA Stalker—that's the name we've decided to give him.

"So this is it?" she asks, referring to the door.

"Yep," I say, eyes straight ahead.

"How do we get in?"

I take a few steps and run my fingers down the lock. "When Crew and I found it, we had someone come down and help with the lock. I assisted, so I was able to get the code to get in. After that night, we made a pact to stay out of here until we had a lead. If this person knows we've found their lair, they're likely to respond. Could be a threat. Could be a dead body. Or it could be a trap that throws us off his trail."

Scar side-eyes me, brow lifted. "But you came back, didn't you?"

I start turning the dial to enter the combination. "You know me too well." She's watching intently and I'm sure it's to memorize the combination. I also know her well.

Once the lock clicks, and I turn the handle, I look at Scar. "You sure you wanna do this?"

She nudges me out of the way and pushes the door open. "Hell yes."

I follow behind her, patting my pockets for my phone. "Shit," I grumble. "I think I forgot my fucking phone."

Scar's eyes widen, and she scoffs. "You what!"

"I was caught up in the moment at the house before we left, and I must've left it on the kitchen counter."

"Dammit, Jagger. We'll have no light. And what if we need to call for help?"

"No. We'll be fine. Let's just make this quick. See what you need to see and we'll get the hell outta here."

"How do you expect me to do that with no light? Once that door closes, I won't even be able to see you."

I rack my brain for the answer to that question, but the only thing I can come up with is for her to hold the door while I search for a flashlight, a lighter, or a candle. "Stay here," I tell her, gesturing to where I stand. "Hold the door while I look around."

Once she's got the door, I move my hand and tread deeper into the room. There's a beam of dim light that casts across a small space, but it doesn't do much good since the shelves run along the walls. I keep straight ahead, reaching out so I don't bump into something.

"Find anything yet?" Scar asks, her voice raised as I move farther and farther away from the door.

"Nothing yet."

The slamming of a door has my eyes snapping to the left, right where the sound came from. "What the fuck was that?"

It was a definitely a door. There must be another one over there, possibly another entrance. Which would mean someone knows we're here. It also means the tunnels don't end here.

"Jagger! Please tell me that was you."

I look in her direction, finger pressed to my lips. "Shh." Turning back around, I follow the sound but trip over something on the ground. "Son of a bitch." I kick what sounds like an aluminum can out of the way. So much for being quiet.

"Jagger, I'm getting a little scared. Why don't we do this another time."

Ignoring her plea, my curiosity gets the best of me. Slapping around on a shelf on the far wall, I search for anything that feels like a flashlight or lighter.

My eyes bolt over my shoulder when I notice some of the light has diminished. "Scar?"

When she doesn't respond, I panic, rushing back over to the door. Once I'm there, I notice it's propped open with a foot-long copper pipe. *Fuck.*

I pull the door open and breathe a sigh of relief when I see her. "What the hell are you doing?" I ask as she slams her hand into the fixed sconce on the tunnel wall.

"Something we should have done in the first place. It's battery-operated, right?"

*Holy fuck, my girl is a genius.*

I hurry to her side, bumping her out of the way. "Hey," she hisses, "I almost had it."

"I know you did, but we have to do this quickly. Someone was in there, and if we hurry, we can catch them."

"What?" She gasps. "Have you lost your damn mind? We can't try to catch them. What if they kill us?"

With both hands, I thrust upward, knocking the light free. "If they wanted to kill us, they would have done it by now. I get the feeling, death is not their endgame. At least, not with us."

"I dunno, Jagger. Whoever this is seems pretty smart. I think this is a bad idea."

"Come on, Scar. You're one of the most badass girls I know. If you can jump off a mountain, onto an antique Ferris wheel, you can do this. Besides, I'd never let anything happen to you."

She hesitates, and it's time we can't waste. Finally, she

says, "Okay. Let's do this, I guess. I'm just glad you brought protection."

I'm cradling the fixture like a delicate baby as we go back through the door. "Shit. I'm sorry, Scar."

Of course! I never used protection like she asked. She either doesn't know I didn't use it, or she's taking a jab at me because I didn't.

"Why are you sorry?" She chuckles. "You said you have something to protect us with if we get ambushed, right?"

I stop walking, eyebrows pinched tightly. "Wait. You did mean *protection,* protection, right?" I've never felt like more of an idiot than I do right now, and the look on her face says she'd agree with me. "You meant a weapon of some sort, didn't you?"

"Yeah. What did you..." She bursts out a laugh. "You thought I meant a condom?"

"No."

She swats me playfully as I continue into the room. "You did so. But if you did have a condom, why didn't you use it?"

I blow out a heavy breath before giving her the truth. "Heat of the moment. It's crazy because I've always used condoms, but with you, it totally slipped my mind. You mad?"

"I'm not mad. I have an IUD so we're good there."

*Whew.* I was sure she'd be pissed.

We're in the middle of the room when Scar stops and looks around. Her wide eyes take it all in, while I shine the light through the open area, exposing newspaper clippings, old photographs, and family trees of the Elders.

"Oh. My. God." She gulps. "Crew wasn't kidding. Whoever did this is completely obsessed with the Blue

Bloods." She looks at me, her eyes curious with a glint of fear in them. "Where's my room?"

I take in a deep breath, really hoping she's prepared for this. When I tip my head to the right, she follows my line of sight. "Over there?"

I nod, walking toward the other door. "A quick look then we search for another door. I'm almost positive there's another exit, or entrance."

Her hands rest on the handle, and we share a look before I nod with approval. She pushes it open, and I watch her face the entire time.

As soon as her eyes land on the wall in front of her, she clasps her hands to her chest. "Who is this monster?"

She takes the light from my hands and holds it up. "This is sick, Jagger. So fucking sick."

I don't say anything, but I agree with her. Whoever this person is has some sort of sick obsession with Scar. The crazy thing is, it doesn't appear to be a sexual obsession, but more of a scorned one, as if this person blames her for something—similar to Neo's obsession with revenge on her because of Maddie.

When Scar reaches for a picture, I blurt out, "Don't touch anything!" Her hand jerks away, and I lower my voice. "I'm sure he knows we're here right now, but he might not know we found this room."

Crew went on a rampage, ripping down pictures of Scar, and we did our best to hide the evidence of our findings, but we're still not sure if we were inconspicuous enough. Either way, we don't want to piss this person off any more than we have by being here in the first place.

A loud thud has both our eyes shooting in the direction of the sound. "What was that?"

I press my finger to my lips. "Stay here," I whisper.

"No. No, no, no," she repeats to herself.

Looking around on the floor, I spot another piece of old pipe, this one with a sharp end that could slice someone in half. I crouch down and pick it up, then tell her again, "Stay. I mean it."

She nods her head in rapid movements, and I hope she means it.

Soft, slow steps lead me back out into the main room. When my eyes land on the door, I roar, "Son of a bitch!"

In two seconds flat, she's at my side, light in hand. "What happened?" She spots the door, seeing what I see. "It's shut. What does that mean, Jagger?"

"Let's hope like hell it means nothing." I hurry over to it, Scar hot on my trail. When I grab the handle and turn it, it's confirmed...we're locked in.

"Is it locked? Tell me it's not locked," she chirps in my ear with her head nuzzled against my back.

My hands drop to my sides, letting the pipe fall to the ground. "It's locked. And unless we find another exit, we're stuck in here."

# THIRTEEN

SCAR

"STUCK!" I blurt out. "No. There has to be another way out." I look around the room, but I only see four walls with shelves running the width of them, and the door to "my" room.

Jagger turns around, facing me. "Don't worry, we'll find a way out. This creep can't keep us down here forever."

His words do nothing to settle my unease because we have no idea what this lunatic's plan is. We have no food. We have no water. And when the sconce begins flickering, I realize, it's only a matter of time before we have no light.

"Let me see that." He reaches for our only light source and I hand it over. I follow closely behind him while he searches for another exit. I'm so close to him that the toes of my boots hit the back of his with every step we take.

After minutes of pacing the room, we've found nothing. I finally stop tailing him because I'm certain no one else is down here. If there was, we would know by now. We might be stuck, but at least we're safe, for now.

With my back pressed to the door to the adjoined room, I slide down to the floor. Knees bent, I hug my legs to my chest. "This is pointless," I tell Jagger, who is still searching for some sort of miracle. "We're not getting out until we're let out."

"Fuck that. We're getting the hell outta here."

I like his confidence, but I can also tell he's getting really pissed at the situation, as am I, but stress has also exhausted me. So for now, I'll sit here and let him figure this shit out.

More minutes pass. I'm not sure how many, sixty maybe. I'm thirsty. I'm hungry, and I'm tired. The game has to be over by now and Crew is probably losing his mind, trying to figure out where I am.

*Why was I so stupid?* I should have never come down here in the first place. Then again, I'm glad it happened this way because had I not told Jagger, I would have tried doing this all on my own. I like to think of myself as a strong girl, but I think the Academy is starting to break me little by little.

My head lifts when Jagger taps his knuckles to a wall. "What are you doing?"

"Someone slammed a door in here when we were in the other room. There has to be another exit somewhere."

I really hope he's right because the idea of being stuck down here, for even a night, has my stomach twisting in knots.

While Jagger puts his detective skills to work, I look around at some of the documents on the desk. I pick up a newspaper article dated back to 1963. My eyes skim over the words that focus on the murder of a lady named Betty Beckett. Nothing about it rings a bell, so I set it back down and pick up an old photo of a couple. It's in black and white, but I smile at the sweet gesture of a man kissing the woman's cheek. Time changes so many things, but at least love still exists today.

"I think I found something," Jagger says, and I drop the picture and head his way. He's only a foot away with the light held up.

My gaze snaps over to him and he's no longer looking at a wall; instead, he's looking up.

One big step and I'm beside him. I follow his gaze to a square outline in the ceiling, where it looks like there's some sort of an insert. "Do you think it's a door?"

He kicks an old box, and I assume it's to see if it's sturdy enough for him to stand on, but when his foot goes through it and it gets stuck, I bite back laughter.

"Motherfucker!" He kicks it off, getting himself all worked up. He looks at me and I roll my lips together. "Something funny?"

"Not at all."

Out of the corner of my eye, I see a footstool sitting under the desk I was just at. I walk over and grab it, then hand it to a fuming Jagger.

Finally, he cracks a smile and passes me the light. Before he puts the stool to use, he swoops an arm around my waist and pulls me snug to his chest, the light serving as a barrier between us. His eyes land on mine before he kisses me, making all my worries disappear momentarily. "Thanks."

"You're welcome."

He sets the stool down right beneath the cutout in the ceiling and steps on it. His fingers slide along the ridges. "I don't think I can get a good grip on it." He looks down at me. "See if you can find a crowbar or anything I can shove in there to try and pry it open."

The light begins to flicker even more and I can tell we're running out of time. Carrying it close to my chest, I search the room for anything that might help us.

"Hey," Jagger says, his palm pressed to the ceiling, bracing himself, "grab me that pipe I had earlier. I set it on the shelf over there." He tips his head to the right.

Hurried steps lead me over to it.

"Quickly," Jagger says, rushing me along.

Picking up my pace, I get back to him and hand him the pipe. "Someone's pushy tonight," I tease, only finding humor right now because I'm hopeful this will be our escape.

"We need to get the fuck out of here before Crew and Neo realize we're gone." He shoves the pointed edge of the pipe into one of the cracks. "All shit will hit the fan if we don't."

"Ya know. I've never understood that statement. When does shit ever hit a fan?"

"I don't know either, but it's fitting." He pushes harder, then bends, causing the pipe to dent in the middle. "Come on, you damn thing." Using his forearm, he wipes away the sweat beading on his hairline.

The next thing I know, a three-foot square in the ceiling is opening and Jagger is jumping off the stool so it doesn't hit him.

My arms fly around him. "You did it!"

Finally, the tension in his expression fades. I'm swept up in his arms and he spins me around. "Hell yeah!"

As soon as he sets me down, he goes back over and looks up. "There's a pull ladder." He steps back on the stool, reaching up. Once he has a good grip on the rope, he jumps off the stool, pulling the ladder down with him.

"This is insane. Where do you think it goes?"

His brows hit his forehead. "Don't know, but we're about to find out. Come on." He nods toward the ladder. He goes up a couple steps then offers me his hand. My fingers wrap around his, while I cradle the light under my other arm. We ascend together, me directly behind him.

As we're going up, Jagger drops something. "Wait," I tell him, bending down and picking up the folded square paper and holding it out to him. "You dropped this."

"Just put it in your pocket and you can give it to me later."

The light flickers again, and this time, it goes completely out. "Oh no!"

We're left in complete darkness, on a ladder that extends from a secret room in a tunnel to God knows where.

It doesn't matter, though; we're getting the fuck out of this place.

# FOURTEEN

## CREW

"Where the hell are they?" I kick up a mound of snow on the tracks near the bleachers, flinging it off my boot before doing it again.

"They were definitely here. No one else rode a sled to the game."

"No shit they were here. But what I wanna know is where the fuck they are now! Have you heard back from Victor?"

"Not yet. I've got six guys doing a sweep around the Academy grounds. Victor should be getting to our place anytime."

"We can't wait for him to get all the way back here. Who knows what could happen if we wait too long. I swear to God, if Jagger put her in harm's way, I'll fucking kill him."

Neo sits back down on his sled and rests his elbows on the dash. "Calm your cranky ass down. I'm sure they're fine. Probably just off screwing somewhere, getting it out of their systems."

My jaw clenches, nostrils flared. "Fuck off."

"I'm just saying. Jagger's got a thing for your girl."

"Yeah. No shit. Everyone's got a thing for my girl. Wouldn't surprise me if you treated her like shit, just to hide that you're simping on her, too."

Neo throws his hands up, shaking his head. "Not a chance in hell. I hate that fucking—"

"Don't say it." I shake my finger at him, side-eyeing him with a scowl. "Don't you dare fucking say it."

"I'll say what I wanna say and when I wanna say it, but right now, we need to find those assholes before they get themselves killed and we have to explain to the Elders why Kol Sunder's daughter was found dead."

"You've really got a way with words, ya know that?"

He grins, pleased with himself. "Thanks. I think so, too." With the twist of his fingers, he brings the sled to life. "Get on."

"Try calling Jagger's phone again first."

Sighing, he pulls his phone out, taps into it, then presses it to his ear.

*And I wait.*

"Voice mail. Again." He swipes out of the screen and puts his phone back in the inside pocket of his coat.

Neo's a fucking prick, but right now, I need him on my side. I go to swing a leg over the seat, directly behind him, and just as I do, the fucker takes off, sending me backward and falling into a pile of snow.

"Dickhead!" I shout, arms in the air.

He whips a one-eighty, laughing his ass off as he returns for me.

"Let's try that again," he says as he comes to a stop beside me.

With a balled fist, I punch him hard in the shoulder, and

he continues to laugh. I jump back on, stretch my arms behind me and take hold of the grab bars.

Neo doesn't have any helmets with him because he thinks his ass is invincible, but I'm not a fan of shit flying in my face, so I've always got a helmet or two on hand.

We start to slow down and Neo raises his voice over the rumble of the engine. "We'll follow his tracks and hope they lead us to them."

*Where the hell did you take her, Jagger?*

Him taking her someplace is the scenario I'm going with because if I let my mind wander elsewhere, I'll lose my cool. He said he'd keep her safe and I should trust in that, but with all this weird shit going on, I'm not sure anyone is safe here.

CHAPTER

# FIFTEEN

SCAR

Jagger has been pounding on the trap door for a good ten minutes, fuming and cursing, while I sit on the step below him. We're both beyond exhausted at this point and my inner thoughts have become a transcription of a goodbye letter...

*To whoever finds this,*

*We tried our damnedest to get out. We almost made it. But Jagger Cole's continuous shouting and swearing drove me batshit crazy. So I killed him and ran away.*

*Don't look for me,*

*Scarlett Sunder*

"Got it!" he says, and I jump to my feet.

"You did it!" I hug his legs, grinning from ear to ear. "I never doubted you for a second."

*The note thing will be our little secret.*

I need to get off this ladder. I'm officially losing my mind.

As he goes up, I follow his lead. Any hope I had for light quickly diminishes when I don't see any, but getting out of that tunnel is progress, so we'll take what we can get.

Once Jagger's feet are on the ground, he reaches down and takes my hand. As soon as I'm out and off that ladder, I breathe a heavy sigh of relief. "Where are we?" I ask, looking around.

There's a glint of moonlight shining through some windows, offering a small glimpse of the area. "We're in a house."

"Yeah. Looks like someone's cabin." Jagger pulls on the rope, raising the ladder, and once it settles in place, he closes the trapdoor. "But we're out of that dungeon, so that's a victory all on its own."

*My thoughts exactly.*

I walk over to one of the windows. "Jagger," I say, peering out at the yard in front of me. "We *are* in someone's house." It looks like there's a porch out front and a yard with a short lamppost that isn't on. "Oh my god." I gasp. "There are footprints. Fresh ones."

Jagger comes up behind where I'm standing in front of the window. His hands press to the wall on either side of me, caging me in. "I figured. Told ya I heard someone slam a door shut. If I had to guess, that fuckwad was getting ready to come down and heard our voices, so he slammed the trapdoor closed. He must've gone around to a different entrance and came down to lock us in. Probably didn't think we'd find his house."

Panic sets in. I spin around, facing him. "We need to go. Like, right now."

Jagger reaches out, cradling my face in his hands. "We're safe now. I won't let anything happen to you." His lips press to mine and my nerves slightly settle. When he pulls back, he says, "We need to look around. This could be our only chance at finding a clue to who's doing this."

I nod against his hands.

"All right. Start searching for a light switch."

We both run our hands along the wall. Bypassing the outside door, I find a switch. I flip it up, then down, then up and down again. "Either the bulb is burned out or there's no electricity."

"Dammit," he huffs when he finds and flips another switch and nothing happens.

"Maybe it's an abandoned cabin and it's just some homeless person who likes to torment people."

"Doubtful. He's got some sort of connection to the Beckett family and that room below. You're not just a random target."

The thought leaves an unsettling feeling in the pit of my stomach. I look out the window again and whisper to myself, "What does he want from me?"

I'm snapped out of my thoughts when a beam of light hits the side of my face. I look up to see Jagger with a wide grin and a flashlight in his hand. "Yes! Yes! Yes!" I chant. "Okay. Let's do this."

I lock my arm around Jagger's, our hip bones crashing together from my tight grip on him. My eyes follow the beam of the flashlight, as he moves it around the room. "It's furnished."

"Yeah. Everything is old and dusty as fuck, though."

"Bad housekeeping?"

"Either that, or it's been vacant for a while. I'm not so sure anyone lives here now, but someone definitely did at one time."

There's a brown floral couch that looks like something

you'd see in a TV show from the late nineties. A tall grandfather clock, covered in dust, that sits against a wall and isn't ticking. "Ugh. Disgusting." I cup my hand around my mouth and nose when I see flies swarming over a sink of moldy dishes.

"I think you were spot on with the bad housekeeping."

Jagger points the light at a table soiled in grime. Old newspapers are thrown about with old, crushed beer cans. Something glimmers on the table and catches my eye. "Wait. Go back with the light." I walk over to the table and pick up the charm. "No fricken way." I reach into my jacket pocket, bypassing the paper Jagger dropped earlier, and pull out the other half to the heart. With one in each hand, I hold them up together—a perfect fit.

Jagger leans over my shoulder, observing the heart halves. "Where'd you get that?"

"I found it at the library on Thursday. The day you met me on the trail then walked with me. Ya know?" My eyes sweep lazily over him. "The day you sent my study partner away to fetch a keg for you, which we need to talk about, by the way."

"Oh, that day. I do remember that. Any idea who dropped it?"

"No. It was on the floor near the table I sit at."

He reads the inscriptions out loud, "I'm with you wherever you go—Kenna." And the other, "I'm with you wherever you go—Jeremy."

"Kenna and Jeremy?" I repeat the names. "My mom once mentioned a Kenna. I'm pretty sure it was her roommate during her stay here."

"No shit?"

"Maybe I should call and ask her. It might be some kind

of clue as to who's been screwing with us." Fisting the charms, I drop them into my coat pocket.

"Wouldn't hurt. But you'd have to downplay it, so you don't raise suspicion."

"I'd need your phone."

Jagger pats his pockets as his way of reminding me he doesn't have it. "It'll have to wait."

The sound of an engine drawing close has Jagger's eyes, and mine, bolting to the door. My heart jumps into my throat. "Shit. I think someone's coming." I go left, then right, in a panic-driven state. "Where do we go?"

Jagger kills the light and grabs me by the waist, nodding toward the couch. "Let's hide back there. We might actually get to see this person's face."

"Yeah," I gasp, "then they might murder us!" I shuffle toward the door again. "We have to leave this cabin, Jagger!"

He reaches out and grabs my hips with both hands, pulling my back to his chest. "No. We need to hide."

"My heart is going to explode out of my chest."'

He leads me over to the couch and I slide back before he follows. "Dig deep for Badass Scar. I know she's in there somewhere."

I slouch down with him, my knees knocking. "Badass Scar is in bed sleeping, where I should be," I whisper.

Jagger takes my hand, pulling it between his crouched legs. "Let her sleep then. I've got you."

For the first time all night, I feel safe. Even as we're hiding from a madman, who could walk in that door any second—Jagger's got me.

At least, he did. As quick as he took my hand, he lets go.

"Stay here," he demands as he stands up and slides out from behind the couch.

"Jagger! Get back here!"

His response is a hushed, "Shhh."

"Damn you!" I peek my head around and watch as he tiptoes into the kitchen. He pulls open a drawer, then another, and when his hand comes up, I catch the glistening tip of a butcher knife.

My eyes widen in fear when he walks over to the door, knife in hand. His back presses to the wall beside it, and he rests his head back.

Each passing second has my breaths becoming more and more laborious.

"Jagger," I seethe, but he doesn't respond.

A GLANCE out the window has him dropping his guarded stance. "What the fuck! That's my sled. That shithead must've hot-wired it to get it here."

I jump up, hands gripping the back of the couch. "Your sled? Can you see who it is?"

"Come here." He waves me over with the knife. I slip out from behind the couch, and he keeps waving his hand. "Hurry up."

I huff out a heavy breath. "I'm coming."

Once I'm at his side, he pulls open the door. "Show your face you fucking coward!" he screams, knife still in hand.

I keep glancing at it, hoping like hell he doesn't need it.

When no one responds, Jagger steps outside into the accumulating snow on the porch. "Did you hear me?" he wails. "Show your fucking face."

I look at his sled that's parked in the middle of the yard,

fresh footprints surrounding it. "There's more footprints," I point out. "And they lead to the woods."

One step forward has Jagger pulling me two steps back. "Whoa. We're not looking for trouble tonight." He reaches into his coat pocket and pulls out his keys. "I'm getting you home safely, then me and the guys will track this fucker down."

Normally I'd argue that no one tells me what to do, but right now, home sounds nice.

Jagger tosses the knife to his side and it sinks into the snow on the porch. He grabs my hands, taking me with him. "Let's get the hell out of here."

We're walking across the yard, the only sound the jingling of his keys, when I see something out of the corner of my eye. "What was that?" My eyes snap to the right and I see someone running. Jagger holds up the flashlight, flicking it on, and that's when I see her. A girl. At least, I assume it is. "There!" I point to Jagger, but it's too late, she's gone.

"Where?"

"Over there!" I jab my finger in the direction of where the girl went. "Jagger...it was a girl. I saw blonde hair flapping out of the hood of a black robe." I repeat myself. "A girl. It's not a guy doing this; it's a fucking girl!"

"Come on." Jagger pulls my hand as we run to his snowmobile.

At this point, I'm positive my heart has fled my body, while all the blood has drained from my face.

We get right on, noticing that the helmets aren't here and bringing the engine to life.

"Go after her!"

Jagger takes off so quickly that my body flies back and I almost fall off. He's at full speed, ripping down trails and dodging trees. At this point, I'm certain my death is imminent, and it won't be at the hands of that bitch who's been tormenting me. No. Jagger is going to kill us both.

I want to shout at him to slow down, but I'm hell-bent on catching this girl. As fast as we took off, we stop, engine off now. "What are you doing?"

Jagger turns his head and whispers, "If she stayed on the trail she took off running on, we should be meeting her any second."

*Holy shit.* This is really happening. It's all gonna end tonight.

Jagger slowly swings one leg over the sled, then the other, as he gets to his feet. I slide up to the front and grab the handlebars. "What are you doing?" I ask, tone hushed.

He doesn't respond. Instead, he crouches and walks silently and carefully through the snow. The next thing I know, he's running as fast as he can, ready to pounce.

My heart jumps into my throat and I flee from the sled, chasing after him. "Who is it?" I yell, hoping I didn't fuck up his attack, but my patience is getting the best of me.

His body lunges straight to the ground, and by time I reach him, I see that he's lying on top of someone. "You caught her!"

The girl squirms and kicks, but doesn't say a word, being careful not to give up her identity. It doesn't matter, though. We have her now.

With her arms restrained and Jagger straddling her back with his legs on either side of her, she buries her face in the snow.

I walk around to her side, press my knee to the ground, and grab the hood of her robe. I don't even have to see her face to know exactly who it is. But I turn her head with both hands anyway, and when my guess is proven to be true, I gasp. "Melody!"

"It's not what you think. I swear to you. I had to do it." Words fly out of her mouth that I don't even comprehend because I'm too shocked, though I shouldn't be. She sputters and kicks, finally surrendering when she realizes she's not going anywhere.

My head shakes repeatedly in disappointment—with her, with myself. "I should've known." *How did I not see this?*

Jagger flips her over, still holding her down in the snow. He gets right in her face, jaw locked, and grits, "Fun's over, Melody. At least for you. For us, it's just begun."

"I swear to you both, it's not me. He or she or someone made me do it. I don't know who it is."

Jagger, who I hope isn't believing her bullshit lies, presses for answers, "Who made you do what?"

"I don't know who it is. I got notes. I was blackmailed. Told if I didn't do exactly what I was instructed, my secrets would be exposed."

It's taking everything in me not to press my boot to this bitch's head, but I refrain because I want to hear what she has to say.

"What secrets?" Jagger asks, steam streaming from his flared nostrils due to the cold temperature.

"Stuff that can't get out. Like my dealings at the Academy...and other things."

Her secrets are the least of my concerns. I just need the truth. I'm not sure if she's giving it to me, but I humor her anyway. "Sit her up," I tell Jagger, and when he does, he takes her hands behind her back and holds them tightly. I move directly in front of her, hoping I can sniff out her lies. "What tasks did you carry out for this person?"

"Umm." She licks her lips then blows a piece of hair from her face, biding time.

"Out with it!" I shout. "I'm tired. I'm hungry. And I'm really fucking angry, so if you don't answer my questions right now, I'll have no problem dragging you into that cabin and dumping you in his lair, so he can torture the fuck out of you."

"Okay. Okay. It was only a couple times. Mostly just leaving you notes."

"When?" I grind out.

"Just a couple times. I was supposed to leave one in the library, but you saw me before I could, so I took off, that's when I dropped my schedule."

"And yesterday, when you ran off the trail?"

"I never really saw him, but I acted like I did." She takes a moment to catch her breath, and I'm getting really fucking impatient. "I wrote the note because I needed to eliminate any suspicion that I was part of it."

"What about Hannah? How does she fit into all this?"

Melody chokes up. Tears begin streaming down her face before she's full-on ugly crying. "That wasn't supposed to happen." She sniffles and snorts, her chest shaking with each breath. "It was never supposed to happen."

"What the hell did you do to her?"

Her head drops back and she closes her eyes, tears falling. "She shouldn't have been down there."

"You did it, didn't you? You're the one who pushed her?"

Bringing her head back down, she opens her eyes. "She was really drunk. She saw me in the mask and the robe and was trying to pull it off, so I had no choice. I had to do something before she realized it was me."

"Your best friend!" I shout, "You knocked out your best friend, just so you could keep your stupid secrets?"

She swallows hard, nodding. "Yeah, I did." Her expression shifts, her eyes becoming sinister, and she curls her lip. "And I bet you'd do the same exact thing."

"Never! I'd never hurt my friends like that."

"Oh yeah? Then why'd you push your best friend off a cliff?"

Her words are like a punch to the gut, but when I repeat them in my head, I lose it. "You fucking bitch!" Both hands lunge out and I grab her by the throat, squeezing with tenacity.

"Stop it!" Jagger hisses. "This isn't the time, Scar." I hear him, but I don't listen as I throw my body into hers, causing us both to crash into Jagger.

"Why would you say that?" I seethe, the blood in my veins running hot. "Who told you that?"

Melody is at my mercy when she finally says, "He told me in a note. That's why I did what I did to you without an ounce of remorse. And you know what, I'd do it all over again."

I pounce on her again, going straight for her pretty blonde hair.

"Not now!" Jagger snaps. Letting go of her, I fall back onto my ass in the snow. I don't get up; I just bend my legs and drape my hands over my knees while I try to compose myself.

"I didn't want to hurt Hannah." Melody continues with more cries of desperation. "She's my best friend and I love her."

Jagger takes over, squeezing her wrists and keeping her in place. "Why'd you come here tonight?"

Melody looks down at her lap, licking the tears from her lip. "A note was slid under my door tonight. I had to skip our final game for this bullshit. I was told to go into the tunnels and close the door to a room you were in, then take your snowmobile that was already running for me and bring it here. That was it. I was leaving to go back to the dorms when I saw the two of you."

Jagger and I share a look, and I can tell he's buying it. Regardless, she won't get away with what she's done.

"Even if we do believe you, it doesn't change what you did," I say, speaking to Melody before looking at Jagger. "I think she needs to reap the consequences of her actions."

He nods at me in agreement. The sinister look on his face mimicking mine. "Every choice does have consequences. What do you suggest?"

I shrug my shoulders, smirking maliciously. Melody has always been a bitch to me, and now I get the chance to do whatever the hell I want to her. "Jagger, what's a girl's most prized possession?"

Jagger lifts his shoulders. "Her pussy?"

I shake my head. "No. Her hair."

Melody goes to flee, but Jagger pulls her back down. "No. Please. I'll do anything. Don't touch my hair."

I grab a handful of her luscious locks and glance at Jagger. "Do me a favor?"

"Name it."

"Could you go in the cabin and fetch me a pair of scissors?"

"You evil fucking bitch!" Melody cries. "You're insane. You're both insane!"

Jagger gets up and I grip Melody's hair tighter. If she

tries to run, she's running with a bald spot on the top of her head.

"Maybe I am insane, but did you ever stop to think that maybe it's because of bitches like you?"

"Scarlett, please." She looks at me with sorrow in her eyes. "I didn't want to do this. I had to protect my secrets."

"By exposing mine?" I shout. "By taunting me? You act all innocent by flaunting everyone else's flaws, but you're just as insane as the rest of us. And now, you're gonna learn your lesson about sticking your nose where it doesn't belong."

Jagger returns a minute later with a pair of rusty steel scissors. They look dull as fuck, but they should do the trick.

Balling Melody's hair in my fist, I pull her head down and position the blades right above my hand, ready to chop off a good four inches. "Take this as a warning, *Melody*," I emphasize her name. "Next time you fuck with me, or my friends, you will pay."

Then I cut until her gorgeous, silky blonde strands fall into my hand. I take her palm, open it, and give her the chunk of cut-off hair, then close her fingers around it.

Her cries ring through the air, echoing off the trees surrounding us.

Jagger grabs her by the arm and lifts her to her feet. "Go back to your dorm room and do not leave until one of the Lawless members gives you permission. I don't care how many fucking notes you get, you do not leave. Do you understand me?"

Her palm slides up her snotty nose and she sniffles some more. "Am I getting kicked out? Are you going to report me to the Elders? Tell my parents?"

He repeats himself, enunciating each word. "Do you understand me?"

She nods in response.

"Good. Now go."

There's no hesitation as she climbs to her feet and flees for the woods, sobbing and carrying her hair with her.

I toss the scissors into the snow and close my eyes. Drawing in a deep breath, I attempt to process what just happened. As I open my eyes, Jagger comes to my side, putting an arm around my shoulders. "Damn, girl. I did not see that coming. Remind me to never get on your bad side."

Lifting an eyebrow, I smirk back at him. "Oh, you have been. Just not quite like that girl."

"So," he begins, "do you believe her?"

"Really don't want to. I'd love nothing more than to stick it to that bitch, but yeah. I think she's telling the truth."

"Guess we're back at square one?"

I rub my temples aggressively, hating that this whole mess tonight was a waste. "Seems so."

We sit there for a couple more minutes in silence, both lost in our own thoughts, before Jagger says, "Let's get you home."

# SIXTEEN

CREW

"Still mad at me?" Scar asks, pouting from where she lies on my bed.

I'm staring at the ceiling, arms folded over my bare chest. "You know my answer to that question." I drop my pissed-off stance and roll to my side to face her. "How can I be after everything I've done to you? That will *always* be my answer to that question."

With her hands pressed between her cheek and the pillow, she lifts a smile. "You're allowed to be mad at me, Crew. I'm pretty mad at myself."

"Good. I'll let you be mad at yourself for both of us."

Scar changes the subject quickly, likely trying to ease some of the discontent. "I still can't believe Melody is this fucker's henchman."

"Yeah. I'm pretty surprised at that, too. Melody's a pansy. I just can't imagine that girl running out in the woods alone at all hours of the night."

We both start laughing at the thought and it's the first time Scar's smiled all night. "I'm just glad you're home and safe." I throw an arm around her waist and pull her closer. Her face nuzzles into my chest, and I press my lips to her forehead.

"So, what are you guys gonna do about her? Is she getting kicked out?"

"Not really sure. Neo wants to fry her ass, naturally. Jagger thinks we can use her to lure this guy out. As of right now, this person doesn't know we're on to Melody."

Her eyes peer up at me, and she asks, "And what do you think?"

"I think you're the one who had to endure the most pain from her actions, so it should be your choice."

"Me?" She chuckles. "I'm in no position to make authoritative decisions."

My fingers run through her damp hair. "Sure you are. You live here, don't you? You're like the first unofficial Lawless female."

She blows out a heavy breath of laughter. "Probably best if you never let Neo hear you say that."

"Fuck Neo."

She lifts her head, looking at me. "You've really been going above and beyond proving that guy no longer has a hold on you."

"That's because he doesn't. I'll stick to our pacts and promises, but in my personal life, Neo can fuck off."

Ever since he caught Scar and me together after Maddie's accident, Neo's made me feel inferior to him. For a while, I put up with it because my guilty conscience told me I should. Not anymore. His days of being in control of me are done. Hopefully soon, Jagger has the same mindset as me, and we can both knock him off his high horse.

*Jagger.* Another person I need to talk to Scar about, but I haven't been able to bring myself to do it. I could entertain the thoughts in my head and just straight out ask her if anything happened, or I can wait for her to tell me, if and when something does. Either way, once I know, there's no forgetting it—even if I could potentially forgive it.

"Well," Scar says, leaning her face over mine, "I really hope one day, when everything is settled and out in the open, you all can repair the parts of your friendships that were broken. I'd hate to see it all be for nothing."

Lifting my head off the bed, I make the conscious decision to end *this* conversation. Just for tonight, I want to pretend no one else exists but the two of us in this room. My hand presses to the back of her head and I pull her mouth to mine. "No more talking."

"But I wanted to hear about your game I missed."

I inhale her words as they roll into my mouth. "We won and it ended, now kiss me."

And she does. Her mouth parts slightly, making enough room for me to slip my tongue between her sweet lips.

Scar climbs over me, straddling my lap. My fingers clench her waist beneath her shirt and I raise my hips, grinding against her.

With her hair draped around my face, I drag her scent straight to my lungs, wondering how I went so long without it. All those wasted years when she could have been mine, but I let my guilty conscience get the best of me. If I could go back, there are so many things I'd do differently, like kissing her every chance I got.

I pull her face closer to mine, our noses touching. As she opens and closes her mouth against mine, I drag my teeth along her bottom lip, remembering the time she bit me. Crazy how far we've come. "On your back."

She shakes her head no. "I wanna ride you."

My cock pulses, threatening the fabric of my pants. "All right. Ride me, baby."

I fold my arms under my head, giving her complete control. She lifts up, a grin on her swollen lips. Straightening her back, she pulls her sheer white tank top over her head, freeing her tits. I want to reach out and grab them and suck on her nipples, but I refrain. Instead, I just watch her in perfect form.

Lifting up, she pushes down her boy short underwear, then brings them to her ankles and kicks them off.

"Fuck, Scar." I growl. "Being this sexy should be a sin."

She bites the corner of her lip before sliding down my body, popping the button on my pants and freeing me of them. I decide to help her out a little and I rip my shirt over my head, then toss it on the floor.

Two hands plant on my chest and she shoves me back down. "Mmm. I like when you take control. Where's this coming from?"

Shouldn't have asked that question. *Don't go there, dumbass. Don't you dare fucking go there.* To shut off the thoughts threatening to invade my mind, I grab two handfuls of her ass, squeezing and hoping to leave an imprint for any other guy—namely Jagger—who might look at what's mine.

"Hands off," she tsks, grabbing my hands and placing them at my sides.

I lick my lips, hungry for any taste of her I can get. "Let me lick your pussy first."

She shakes her head no.

"Then let me finger you."

Another no.

"We gotta get you wet somehow."

Her hands run down my chest and the lustful look in her eyes has me wondering if she might want to do the job herself.

My heart races at the thought. I don't think there could be a more beautiful sight than my girl pleasuring herself. I go to grab her hand, but she pulls away. "Ah ah. Hands to yourself," she demands, and holy fuck, it turns me on.

"Touch yourself, baby."

Her forehead creases, cheeks flushed. "I can't do that."

"Sure you can. Lean back, spread your legs, and just play with yourself. It's just me and you."

There's some hesitation, but I can tell she wants to. There's no way in hell Scar hasn't touched herself before, and if she says she hasn't, I'll call her bluff. Hell, if I were a chick with a pussy that tight and bare, my fingers would live inside it. I'm sure any guy would agree.

Eventually, with some persuasion, she leans back, keeping herself up on her elbow pressed into the mattress. Her legs fall open and she brings one hand between them. My eyes immediately land on the double bruises on her inner thighs but I won't allow myself to wonder how they got there—not right now.

"That's my girl."

Her eyes lock on mine, never faltering as she massages her clit.

"Holy fuck," I grumble, my voice raspy and thick.

She twitches, liking the pleasure she's bringing to herself. Her fingers rub faster, mouth agape, while her eyes remain cemented to mine.

I break our stare, needing to see exactly what's right in front of my face. "Come for me, Scar. Come all over me." I reach down, taking my erect cock in my hand, and I pump the shit out of it. My head dabs at her entrance with each stroke as she rubs vicious circles at her sensitive nub.

If I die tonight, I'll die a happy man. I've never seen anything more beautiful in my entire life. The way she pleasures herself while letting me watch—it's every man's dream.

When her hand curves, fingers crooked, she dips two inside her pussy, I lose it. I prop myself up on one elbow, getting a better view, and I fist my cock and pump faster.

Dropping her head back with her mouth wide open, sounds of ecstasy rip through her vocal cords.

"Crew," she whimpers, bringing her head forward and locking her eyes with mine again.

"You're so fucking sexy, Scar. Come, baby. Come on my cock." I hold my dick at her entrance as she releases, squirting proof of her orgasm all over me.

A heavy groan rumbles my chest. "Jesus Christ." Her arousal seeps out, coating her fingers, and I come undone. Pumping through my own orgasm, cum shoots out, soaking her pussy.

Her legs twitch while beads of cum roll between her folds. When she brings her legs together, I grab her hand and pull her down beside me. "That was no doubt the hottest thing I've ever seen."

"Really?" She lifts her head, gaping at me in a breathless state. "You've never watched a girl do that before?"

"Nope." I lift my head, kissing her lips. "You did so good, baby."

Scar curls under my arm, her head on my chest. This was exactly what we needed after the shit day we both had.

It's been three days since Scar and Jagger were locked in the tunnels. Three days that Melody has been confined to her room and sworn not to speak to a soul. And three days that I haven't asked about the details of that night in regard to what went on with Scar and Jagger.

I know the gist of it. They got locked down there. Scar found a charm that connects to another one. And Melody was working with the BCA Stalker.

What I don't know is what happened between Scar and Jagger for those hours they were alone. With all that idle time, I know something happened. How could it not? She likes him; he likes her. Not to mention, the bruises on her thighs are a telltale sign that Jagger sunk his fingers into her skin.

The really fucked-up part of this, I'm not even sure I want to know. The only thing that's eating at me is the fact that neither of them has come to me with the information. I shouldn't have to ask. They owe me that respect.

"It's like dawn of the dead in this place," Jagger says, looking around the cafeteria before setting his lunch tray down and taking a seat across from me.

I follow the trail of his gaze, noticing that it is unusually quiet. "Think Melody said something?"

"Bitch better not have."

Scar joins us, taking the seat beside me. "Why so serious?" she asks, tapping a straw to the table and pulling it out of the paper wrapper.

"We were just noting how quiet everyone is today. Seems strange, right?"

Before sitting down, she looks around at the students, a

few who are whispering and gazing our way. "Yeah. Something is definitely off." Her straw slips in the opening of her orange juice carton and she takes a sip.

Neo, who's been quiet this entire time, shoots back in his chair and jumps up. He looks out at the group of students and shouts, "What the fuck is going on?"

I look at Scar, scratching the top of my head. "Guess we won't be wondering for long."

She scoops up a spoonful of her soup and blows on it. "Leave it to Neo," she whispers before taking her bite.

No one answers Neo, so he gets more aggressive. "Someone better fucking tell me what all the whispering is about right now or the Halloween dance will be canceled."

My eyes widen, Scar's mirror mine as she looks back at me. "He's fucking with them, right?"

I nod subtly, lips pursed.

The sound of a chair scraping against the floor has me looking over my shoulder. To all of our surprise, it's Hannah who gets up. Aside from the gash on her head, she's also sporting a black eye and a swollen cheek from the impact against the wall. "I'll tell you what the whispers are about," she says, walking toward us.

Neo takes a dominating stance: chest puffed out, shoulders drawn, arms folded against his chest. "Spill. Now."

Once Hannah is at our table, we all turn to face her. She looks each of us in the eyes, stopping at Scar. "Rumor has it, Scarlett is the one who pushed me, and we're all wondering what the hell you boys plan to do about it."

"Whoa." Scar jumps up defensively. "Where the hell did you hear that?"

I slide my chair back and get up, too, followed by Jagger.

We all gather on one side of the table to hear what Hannah has to say, knowing it's all fabricated lies.

Hannah pulls back the side of her brunette hair, exposing the row of stitches on her scalp. "Do you see that?" She lets her hair go, eyes glowering at Scar. "She did it!"

The rest of the four dozen students begin stirring and whispering in their seats, so I silence them. My hand cuts through the air. "Everyone, quiet!"

They settle down, and I return my attention to Hannah. "Tell us where the fuck you heard these bullshit lies from now or you'll be brought forth for defamation and slander."

She gasps. "Me?" Nodding toward Scar, she wears a look of shock. "What about her?"

"Now!" Jagger reinforces. "Tell us where you heard it."

Hannah draws in a deep breath, her nervousness apparent. On her exhale, I ask, "Was it Melody?"

I swear to all that is holy, if Melody spoke to anyone about this situation and fabricated her own spin on the story, we'll destroy that girl. Keeping her secrets safe will be the least of her worries.

"No," she finally says, "it wasn't Melody. It was Victor Hammond."

When I take notice of Scar's flushed skin and her flared nostrils, I put an arm around her. "We'll deal with this."

"Victor," Jagger hollers across the room, "get your ass over here."

This he-said, she-said bullshit is getting old. Of course there will be rumors flying, but they shouldn't involve Scar.

Scar jumps to her own defense, ready to squash these lies. "I swear to you, Hannah, Victor is lying. I'm not sure where he heard that or why he said it, but the girl who pushed you—"

I squeeze Scar's hip while Neo and Jagger tense up. She peers up at me and I shake my head. "Don't."

"You say it wasn't you, but it was a girl then?" Hannah questions. "Who? Was it Riley? Why would she want to hurt me?" Hannah becomes frantic, almost inconsolable. "Why would anyone want to hurt me?"

Scar takes it upon herself to put an arm around Hannah's shoulders, stepping out of my hold. "It's not you they want to hurt." She steers her to the left. A glance over her shoulder has me giving her a look of warning, and I'm sure she knows why. She can't say anything, or it'll ruin any plans we have for Melody—whatever those plans might be.

Victor comes forward like a dog with his tail between his legs, his head is hung low, his eyes avoiding contact. "It was a stupid rumor. I didn't mean anything by it."

Neo grabs Victor's head with both hands, lifting his eyes. "Explain to me right now why you said what you said. No lies, Hammond."

Victor gulps. "The other night when I was walking Scarlett and Riley back to the Foxes' Den from the Ruins, I...I handed them over to that Elias kid. I wanted to make sure they were safe, so I followed quietly behind them. The next thing I know, Melody was running out of the woods saying she was attacked." Neo grips his head harder, the veins in his hands protruding. "I couldn't hear the whole conversation, but I heard Melody shouting at Scarlett that her best friend getting hurt was all her fault. That's it. That's the whole story."

"And with that information, you decided to open your disgusting mouth and spread lies?"

"I didn't mean any harm. We were talking in gym class and it came up."

Neo gives Victor's head a shove back. "Next time, think before you speak. Or better yet, don't speak at all. Now bend the fuck over!"

Grinning, I egg Neo on. "That's right. Kick his ass."

Victor's wide eyes look questioningly at Neo, and when he doesn't do as he's told, Neo spins him around by his shoulder and shoves him down until he's on all fours. "Listen up," he raises his voice for everyone to hear, "let this be a lesson when you open your mouth and spread lies." He grabs Victor by the waist and rams his knee into his ass.

Everyone gasps, a few hoot and holler. I cover my mouth, fighting back the laughter brewing inside me. Neo is fucking ruthless.

Victor falls forward and Neo barks at him. "Get back up. I'm not finished with you." As soon as Victor returns to his hands and knees, Neo presses the sole of his boot to his back. "Twenty push-ups. And go."

Victor tries to lift his body, but Neo forces more of his weight on Victor's back. He finally rises, the muscles in his forearms strained. "One."

His chest hits the ground and Neo humiliates him further. "Come on, you fucking pussy. You wanna talk shit and try to be cool, yet you're lying on the ground like a little bitch. Does everyone see what a little bitch Victor Hammond is?"

Everyone watches for a good fifteen minutes, and finally, Victor gets his twenty in. Once Neo removes his boot from his back, Victor drops to the ground in a puddle of sweat.

Neo crouches down beside his head, grabs his hair, and lifts. "You're not to talk to a single student at the Academy until I tell you to. Got it?"

Victor nods his head in Neo's hand then it's shoved back.

Well, as of right now, it seems we have two students muted. Wonder who's next in line?

"This bullshit is getting outta hand." Jagger huffs, spinning around and walking straight to where Scar is consoling Hannah.

I watch them, as Hannah cries into Scar's shoulder, and it's obvious nothing was brought up about Melody. Jagger joins them, placing a hand on the small of Scar's back. Instead of reacting, I let it play out. See if she'll step away from him. But she doesn't. Once Hannah walks away, she turns to face him and sweeps her thumb across his chin, giggling like he had a smear of something on his face.

Jagger returns her giddiness with a flirtatious smile while his hand caresses her hip.

"Still think nothing's going on between them?" Neo asks, his voice a buzzing sound in my ear.

"Nope. I think you're right. Something is definitely going on." I turn back around and snatch my tray off the table and cross the cafeteria, neither Scar nor Jagger noticing my absence. When I reach the door, I drop the whole thing in the trash. "Evan," I say, grabbing his attention from the doorway, "fish my tray outta the trash and put it in the dirty stack."

With that, I leave—my girlfriend and my best friend none the wiser.

# SEVENTEEN

## CREW

SCAR SETS her American Lit book on the table and sits down beside me. "What happened to you at lunch?"

I run my fingers through my hair, eyes on my open textbook. "Just needed some air."

"Crew?" She grabs my hand, lowering it to her lap. "What's wrong?"

Tangling my fingers with hers, I force a smile, because the last thing I want is for Scar to feel any more emotional turmoil. "Just in my head too much today."

"Do you wanna talk about it?"

Before I can answer, Jagger drops his books down with a thud on the other side of Scar. "What a clusterfuck lunch was today."

Scar doesn't acknowledge him, just keeps her focus on me. Squeezing my hand, she asks again, "Crew? Do you wanna talk about it."

"Talk about what?" Jagger butts in, and suddenly, I'm not in the mood to talk about anything. I drop Scar's hand and turn back around in my seat.

"Nothing now," I mumble, and I realize I'm behaving like a spoiled child. I shake away the thoughts invading my mind—of Jagger and Scar and how neither of them has come and talked to me about whatever went down between the two of them.

Mr. Collins begins his discussion on modernism, and I manage to block his voice out completely. "You okay?" Scar whispers, her hand on my leg.

"Yeah. Just following along with the lecture."

It isn't until Scar reaches over and turns my textbook the right way, that I realize it was upside down. My eyes lift, and I see her grinning, and it's hard not to do the same. Why is she so alluring? So perfect? Does Jagger see how amazing she is?

*Fuck. I can't do this!*

I slam my book shut, push my chair back, and get up. Leaving all my shit on the table, I walk quickly behind the back row of students and straight for the door.

Without looking back, I pull it open and leave the room, slamming it shut behind me. The glass pane in the middle rattles and I'm thankful it didn't shatter. Then again, I wouldn't give a flying fuck right now if it did.

I'm halfway down the hall when I hear her voice. "Crew!"

My feet stop moving, but I don't turn around. Shoulders drawn, I drop my head back and close my eyes, waiting for her to catch up.

Once she does, she starts poking again. "What the hell is going on?" Her hand lands on my shoulder and she turns me around to face her. My head comes down and I open my eyes, a blank expression on my face. "Baby, tell me what's bothering you?"

I could just lay it all out there. Tell her I know something is going on with her and Jagger and that she broke her promise to let me know if and when that time came.

My only response is a deep exhale, so she tries again. "Is this about Jagger?"

Finally, she mentions his name. Maybe we're getting somewhere, after all.

"Why would it be about Jagger? Is there something you need to tell me?"

"Actually," she bites the corner of her lip, and I'm sure it's a tactic to soften the blow, "there is something I need to tell you. I was planning to wait until this whole thing with Melody blew over, but it's been gnawing at me the last couple days."

"All right," I say, tone flat, "out with it."

*Here it comes.* The truth that I can't deny. She's fallen for him and I'm history.

"This really isn't the place. But as soon as we get home, we really need to talk."

*Of course.* More time spent living in misery.

I nod, accepting her response. "Okay then. Can't wait." I spin around, feeling like my entire world is an hour away from shattering. Once she dumps me, I'll probably pack my shit and leave this place. There'll be nothing left for me here.

*No! Screw that.*

I'll fight for her. I refuse to give up that easily, especially when it comes to keeping what's always been mine.

"Crew!" Scar snaps, grabbing me by the arm. "Would you stop? You're acting like a brat."

*It's true, I am.*

"I'm sorry, baby. All this shit is just getting to me. I don't mean to take it out on you."

"I know." She grabs my hands. "It's been hard on all of us. I'm not surprised we're all a little wound up after everything that's happened. How about a nice, quiet night at home? Just you and me. No distractions."

"Sounds perfect."

The final bell rings and students rush out of their classrooms, filling the hall.

"Hey," Jagger says to Scar in passing, "meet you out front?"

"Actually," I voice, "football is done for the season. I'll walk her home from here on out."

Jagger and Scar share a look, and I can see the disappointment in his eyes. "Well, how about we all walk together then," Scar says, now looking at me for approval. "Is that okay with you?"

*No. Fuck no. It's not okay.*

"Actually," Jagger says before I can respond, "if you're good, I need to take care of some stuff after school."

"Oh. Okay." Scar nods, looking far too disappointed herself.

"See you both at the house." Jagger waves goodbye and disappears into the mix of students.

Scar and I go into the classroom to grab our books. Mr. Collins is sitting at his desk and doesn't dare say a word about Scar or me walking out a few minutes ago.

We make a quick stop at each of our lockers, then we head out for a walk back to the house.

# EIGHTEEN

## SCAR

"ANY WORD on when your snowmobile will be fixed?" I ask, making small talk before we dive into the deep stuff.

"Uh. Yeah." Crew runs his hand down the back of his head. "Should have it back tomorrow."

"Good." I nod.

And he nods.

And this is really awkward.

Finally, I just blurt out, "You already know, don't you?"

Crew looks at me, a sour look on his face. "Yep." Then he resumes staring straight ahead.

I stop walking, grab his arm, and look up at him. "You have to know I had every intention of telling you. It's not like I was trying to keep this a secret. We've all just been so preoccupied with everything else."

He doesn't say anything. Not that I'm sure what I want him to say. That he still wants to be with me, maybe? Or, that nothing has changed between us?

"Say something," I urge him. "Anything. Yell at me. Call me a whore. Just please say something."

"Did you like it?"

My mouth drops open. "That's it?"

He shrugs a shoulder and the tranquility in his reaction is unnerving. "Well. Did you?"

"Look. I know you're pissed—"

"I'm not pissed," he says, interrupting me. "Did I say I was pissed?"

My stomach twists in knots, my heart aching. He won't even look at me. Tears prickle the corners of my eyes, and I blink them away. "I'm sorry."

His eyes drop to mine. They're soft and warm, and it hurts even more looking into them because it's proof of the pain I've caused.

Without a word, he sweeps his fingers across my cheek, then grabs my hand, the dampness of my own tears seeping into my skin.

"I'm not mad at you," he finally says. I'm not buying it, though. Lately, Crew is always telling me what I want to hear because he feels so much guilt about the nasty things he's done to me.

I call his bluff. "Yes, you are."

His head shakes in slow movements, his fingers gliding between mine. "I'm not. Disappointed? Yes. Hurt? A little. But mad? No, I'm not."

"I never wanted to hurt you, Crew. I told you I was questioning things with Jagger, and I guess I should have been more upfront with my feelings. He just sort of took me by surprise, much like you did."

"Listen, Scar," he cups my face in both his hands, "I've gone over this shit in my head a thousand times. I've tortured myself. I've played out every scenario, and in the end, it all comes down to me losing you. As long as that doesn't happen, I can cope with what you and Jagger did. What's done is done. It's out of your system and now we can all move on."

"Out of my system?" The words fly out of my mouth as a question, and I immediately wish I could take it back because they are only going to destroy this moment of clarity for Crew. Except, it's not a moment of clarity for me. Part of my heart is still back in those tunnels with Jagger. When we left, we were forced to go back to normal, but every minute of every day has me wishing we could go back and live in that moment a little longer.

"Yeah. You and Jagger caught a thing for each other. You fucked and now it's done, right?"

The force of my eyebrows pinching together so prominently gives him my answer, without me having to say a word.

"Tell me it's done now, Scar," he demands, needing to hear me say it.

*But I can't.*

"It's not done."

Have you ever looked at someone and saw the exact moment that their heart broke? Have you ever loved that person so much, you felt their pain inside your own chest?

I have.

As Crew pulls away, his posture slumped, I grasp my own heart and shed tears for his pain. "Please, Crew." I'm not sure what I want to say, but I have to say something.

He turns away, unable to even look at me. The toe of his boot digs into a bare spot on the ground and he kicks up a chunk of moss and dried leaves. "Fuck!" he shouts, fisting the hair on the sides of his head.

I should approach him, try to calm him down in some way, but right now, I can tell he needs space.

The crunching of leaves in the distance has my head snapping in the direction of the sound. Elias and Riley come into view, holding hands and smiling from ear to ear. They're so cute together, and I'm envious of Riley for knowing exactly what her heart wants.

I look over at Crew, who pays no attention to their impending presence.

"Scar," Riley hollers, her hand in the air waving. It's so weird hearing her call me by the nickname the guys gave me. Before the end of the school year, I'll probably be Scar to everyone here.

I give her a low, subtle wave back and force a smile. "Hey, Ry."

"What am I, chopped liver?" Elias teases, and I chuckle.

"Hello, Elias."

"How are you holding up?" Riley asks. "I heard Victor Hammond spread a rumor, saying you're the one who pushed Hannah."

"Yeah," I sweep my hand through the air, "just students talking about something they know nothing about. Everything's fine. Hannah knows it wasn't me."

Riley notices Crew out of the corner of her eye. His palm is pressed to a large linden tree and his head is hung low. She leans close and whispers, "Did we interrupt something?"

"We were just...having an important conversation."

"Oh shit. I'm sorry, girl. Let us get out of your way." She takes a step forward, Elias a shadow at her side. Then she takes a step back. "Oh, hey. Me and a couple girls are decorating the Square after dinner. You should stop by. Catch up, ya know?"

"Yeah." I nod. "For sure. I'll be there."

Her brows perk up. "Yay. I'll see you then."

With that, they continue on their way. Once they're out of sight, I approach Crew. "Can we finish?" I ask him.

He gives me a lazy sweep over his shoulder, the expression of sadness on his face now one of disdain.

*Oh, the many moods of Crew Vance.*

Being the manipulative, pain in the ass I am, I try out a reverse psychology tactic. "Okay then. I have some studying to do and I'm not sure if you heard, but I just made plans with Ry. So I guess I'll catch you at home."

I start walking, knowing damn well he won't let me leave. My steps start off quick, but when he doesn't come, I slow down a bit. A glance over my shoulder has my heart splintering.

*He's gone.*

"Crew," I holler, moving my feet down the trail and hoping for any sign of where he might be.

The next thing I know, I'm staring straight at a snowmobile coming right at me.

*This has to be Neo.*

Unintimidated, I plant my hands on my hips and stay right in his path. When he doesn't slow down, my heart begins rattling against my rib cage.

He comes closer, and closer, and it's confirmed Neo is the driver. A war is waged in my head. *Death or pride?*

I choose pride as he comes right at me, only swerving seconds before taking me out. He whips around, spraying me with a blanket of snow. "Asshole!"

Slowing down, he pulls up beside me. "Get on," he barks the order as if he expects me to obey.

I flip him my middle finger, teeth clamped down. "Fuck you!"

"Quit being a pain in the ass and get on the damn sled."

"I'd rather trek up a mountain in the middle of a blizzard at midnight than take a ride from you. Besides," I glance around the wooded area, "I'm looking for Crew."

"You're not gonna find him. He went home. Asked me to get you there safely."

If he thinks I'm going to thank him and hop on, he's wrong. "What's the catch?"

He smirks. "Just doing my duty as a member of the Lawless and helping a student in need."

"Bullshit. You don't help anyone."

Getting bored with this conversation, he scoots forward, making room for me. "Would you just get the hell on? I have better things to do than argue with you right now."

Once again, choosing pride as my virtue, I drop my hands from my hips and continue walking back to the house.

Doesn't mean Neo leaves, though. Which actually surprises me. Instead, he edges me, standing up, back arched while he drives. "Might do ya some good to quit being so fucking stubborn all the time. Maybe then your boy wouldn't be mad at you."

Gripping the strap to my backpack, I glower at him. "Don't talk to me."

"Point proven."

"This isn't me being stubborn. This is me disliking you and refusing to accept anything you offer. I don't trust you and I never will."

"Feelings are more than mutual. At least we have that in common."

Why won't this asshole just go away? I can literally see the house right in front of me. He knows I'm safe—not that he really cares. Hell, he doesn't even give a damn about Crew, so I'm not sure why he'd do him any favors.

"So what's the deal with you and Jagger? You fucking him, too?"

I stop walking, and Neo stops his sled. The grin on his face appalls me, almost as much as his ungodly sexiness does. No one should be allowed to look this good and act so inhumane. "What I do is none of your fucking business, Neo. Why don't you just continue sticking your dick inside whatever pussy invites you in and leave me the hell alone."

"Oh, but you're wrong," he tsks. "You see...those boys are my friends, and at one time, we were all really fucking close. And here you are, once again, trying to break apart a bond we've had since birth."

His words hit me like a knife to the gut. Not because I care about what he thinks, but there is some truth to what he's saying. I'm stepping between two friends and pulling them further and further apart.

I start walking again, and Neo starts creeping at my side...again. "You know I'm right."

"You're wrong!"

"Then why are you so affected by what I said?"

"Go away!" I shout, not giving him the satisfaction of looking at him while I beg for his exit. When he doesn't leave, not that I expected him to, I say what needs to be said. "For the record, aside from my relationship with those guys, I've never done anything to come between your friendships."

"Sure you have. Let's see," he begins, "it all started the night my mom died. I had to hunt Jagger's ass down, so we could go to the movies. Turns out, he was with you. Did you know my mom was the ride we got after Jagger's sister couldn't take us?"

*I didn't know that. No one ever told me.* I steal a glance at him, searching for any hint that he's lying.

He catches my quick look and continues, "Yep. She was gonna come right home and take us, but I told her I had to track down Jagger, so she ran some errands first."

Chills break out over my entire body. Why didn't anyone ever tell me this? Is he implying that if Jagger didn't come to meet me, his mom might still be alive? Does Neo blame me for his mom's death, *and* his sister's fall?

"Neo, I swear. We never meant to hurt you. Is this why you hate me so much? Is that why you burned down my treehouse?"

"It's unfortunate you weren't inside. Might wanna watch your back. What goes around, comes around." He says the words so casually that I'd prefer he shout them at me instead because his listless tone makes my skin crawl.

Neo speeds up, taking off and leaving me in a dust of snow behind him.

Suddenly, I see everything clearly. Neo blames me for every bad thing that has happened in his life. But does he put any of that blame on Jagger? Or even on Crew? Deep down, does he really hate us all?

# CHAPTER
# NINETEEN
### JAGGER

Bottled water in hand, I trek behind the couch, en route to the basement to lift weights.

The front door swings open, grabbing my attention, and Crew comes in. Snow falls in plenty from his boots, and he peels off his coat, hooking it on the coat rack. One look at his face and I'm certain he knows. Lifting might have to wait because he's gonna have a shitload of questions, no doubt.

"Everything all right?" I ask him, unscrewing the top to my water. I hold it in one hand, the bottle in the other.

"No!" he huffs. "Everything is not all right."

I roll the cap between my fingers, not saying anything, because he needs to get out his feelings on this first.

"Ya know, maybe if you didn't walk around this damn house shirtless all the fucking time, you wouldn't be turning her head in the first place."

Normally I'd take that as a compliment, but not this time.

Still not saying anything, I just stand there.

He drops his backpack on the floor right beside his

snow-covered boots. "I should kick your ass right now." He punches his fist into the palm of his hand, sneering. "Pound my fist into your face until it's so dismantled she doesn't even wanna look at you."

All right. I expected that. Knew he'd be mad. I curl my fingers, motioning them toward myself. "Keep it coming. I deserve it."

"Damn right you do. It's one thing to kiss her. Another thing to fuck her. But to make her catch feelings for you? Did you really have to fucking go there?"

It's a question, so this time, I have to answer. "None of it was planned, man. I swear. I tried to just step aside and let you two do your thing."

"Do our thing?" he shouts. "We're not just *doing our thing*. Scar and I were building on a relationship that started years ago behind closed doors. We were finally out in the open and ready to be together. But you couldn't allow that, could you?"

"That's not what I meant."

He steps up to me, nostrils flared. "Then explain. Tell me exactly what you want from her?"

"It's not just about fucking, if that's what you're thinking."

"No shit! If it were just fucking, I might be able to let it go. What. Do. You. Want. From. Her?

I take in a deep breath, filling my lungs, and on the exhale, I tell him the truth. "I want it all, man. I want the parts of her that she doesn't give to you."

Crew shakes his head and looks down, running his hands through his hair. "Of course you do."

Before I can respond, the door flies open again. Neo trudges in more snow, but it's his expression that catches me off guard. Looks like we're about to have one, big blowout that's been a long time coming. "Your girl is a royal pain in the fucking ass." He slams the door shut and it has me wondering where Scar is.

"Oh." Crew lifts his head, expression stoic. He points between him and me. "Are you talking to me or Jagger? I can't tell because it seems we're fucking sharing her now."

His condensing tone has me shaking my head. "Come on, man. It's not like that."

"It's not? Then tell me how it is. I'm with her. I'm not fucking going anywhere until she tells me to, so where does that leave you?"

And the door flies open again. I breathe a sigh of relief when I see that she's okay. But, once again, I'm greeted with a scowl. She juts a stern finger at Neo, before even relieving herself of her bag and coat. "Your friend here is a grade-A asshole!"

I scratch the top of my head, wondering what the hell is going on. "Well, isn't this a nice little family reunion?" Everyone looks at me as if I'm the one who's lost his mind. "Tough crowd."

Scar gives us all a lazy sweep then asks, "What did I just walk in on?"

Neo, being the instigator he is, takes it upon himself to address her question. "If I had to guess, I'd say they're discussing whose dick fits better. My vote's for Jagger. Guy's hung like a horse."

"Dude. Really?" I scoff.

His shoulders rise, then fall. "Just saying."

Scar ignores him, and me, and walks over to Crew. "Can we talk? Please?"

Crew rolls his neck, eyes landing on mine. "Actually. I think we should all have this conversation together."

Scar tugs his arm. "Please stop."

"You two talk," I tell him. "I'll be in the basement with Neo if you need me."

"Why the fuck do I need to go in the basement?"

"Because you and I need to discuss the matter of Melody Higgins." I screw the top back on my water bottle and pull open the basement door, leaving it open behind me. When I don't sense that Neo is following, I glance at him over my shoulder. "Let's go."

To my surprise, he actually comes. I step aside, letting him go down first, then I close the door. Once it's latched, Neo jogs back up the stairs he just went down. "What are you doing?" I ask him.

"Listening. Isn't that what you planned on doing?"

"No, dumbass. I was gonna lift while we figure out a plan for Melody."

"No shit? You don't care what's being said up there?"

"Sure, I care. But it's not my business. Scar and I will talk later."

With a scoff, he heads back down. "Jesus, that girl must have a gold-plated pussy. Might need to tap it myself, just to see what all the fuss is about."

"The fuck you will."

We reach the bottom and I go straight to the bench. I don't give Neo's statement any more attention because I know damn well he'd kill Scar before he'd fuck her.

I lie back, craning my neck under the bar, and once it's set in my palms, I lift, and I talk. "I was thinking we'd set a little trap, using Melody as our bait to lure this fucker out. What are your thoughts?"

Neo begins curling two fifty-pound dumbbells, his veins bulging. "I was thinking we could tie your girl to a tree butt-ass naked. He's sure to come for a taste."

Once again, I don't humor him with a response. Bringing the bar down an inch from my chest, I lift up, feeling my muscles strain against my skin, and repeat the action. "Assuming this fucker isn't onto us," I blow out a breath, "we could put up cameras outside Melody's room. Watch 'em like a hawk, then pounce when we're given the opportunity."

"Or, better yet, you could just stay in Melody's room with her, and as soon as he shows up, you take him down."

"Fuck that. I'm not staying with that whiny bitch. Why don't you stay with her?"

"Hell no. I'd stay in a room with Scar all night before I'd enclose myself in a room with Melody."

This is the second time he's brought up Scar in the last ten minutes. What I don't understand is why she's so heavy on his mind. "Hey. What happened with you and Scar before you got home? Things seemed heated."

He sets the dumbbells down and rips off his shirt before picking them back up. "She wouldn't let me give her a ride, so I toyed with her a little. Nothing she's not used to."

"But *how* did you toy with her? You must've said something that got under her skin."

"When am I not under that girl's skin. All I told her was *what goes around, comes around.* It's the truth. She'll get what's coming to her eventually."

"Are you still on this trip about your sister? Come on, Neo. You have to know Scar didn't have anything to do with Maddie's fall." I'm not usually this forward with Neo when it comes to Maddie because he's extremely defensive, but enough is enough.

"I don't know that. In fact, I don't think for a second she didn't have something to do with it."

I lift the bar over my head and drop it in the bench hooks. Sitting up, I grab my towel from the foot of the bench and wipe the sweat from my face. "What's it gonna take for you to let this go?"

He sets the dumbbells down and takes a seat on a metal folding chair. "My sister waking up and telling me the truth."

I don't see that happening anytime soon, but I don't tell him that. "Well, then I guess we keep hoping for the best."

"Enough of this. I'll deal with my bullshit and you deal with yours. Besides, you've got enough on your plate with Scar and Crew. So tell me, if it comes down to kicking his ass, would you do it?"

"You're a damn idiot." I chuck my sweaty towel at him, but he dodges left and it misses him.

The sound of footsteps on the stairs has Neo standing. "Looks like that time might be now. Later, fucker." He snatches my towel off the floor and throws it back at me. I catch it in midair, just as Crew shows his face.

"Ready to deal with this shit?" He grabs the chair Neo was in and spins it around, then drops in it, straddling the backrest.

"Yeah. Let's lay it all out there. I'll start." I take a seat on the bench, the towel hanging from my hand between my legs. He nods for me to go ahead, so I tell him, "I'm not going anywhere. If Scar wants anything from me, I'll be there waiting for her."

I watch as his Adam's apple bobs in his throat. "All right. And I'll tell you that I'm not going anywhere either."

"Then I guess we got that out of the way. Now, what does Scar want?"

He takes in an audible breath, head dropped back as he stares blankly at the ceiling. When his eyes come back down, he says, "She said she won't choose. That she can't, and if she's forced to, she'll have to choose neither of us."

I anticipated that. Her choosing neither of us has always been an option that weighed heavily on my mind. "So what are we gonna do?"

His shoulders rise, then fall. "May the best man win." He pushes the chair forward, dropping his feet to the floor.

I jump onto my feet, too. "This isn't a fucking football game, Crew. This is Scar we're talking about."

"Says the guy who's worried he'll lose."

"No! Fuck no! I'm not competing with you for her. You're still my boy."

"Then let her go."

"Also, no!"

Crew tosses his hands in the air, huffing and puffing. "Then what the fuck do you want, Jagger?"

"Her. Same as you. We both want her."

"Are you suggesting we share her?"

"Do I like it? No. But we've shared before, and it's never gotten in the way. This time, it's just more than a body, a heart is involved, too."

"You've lost your fucking mind."

"Maybe I have. She makes me crazy and irrational, and it's exactly why I'll do whatever it takes to have her."

"Look," he says, tone serious, "you do what you need to

do and I'll do what I need to do. In the end, she'll make the best choice for herself."

I'm not sure what he's saying, but if he's giving me permission to pursue her, I'll take it. Not that I need it.

"And you won't try and get in my way or make her feel like shit for her choices?"

"I won't interfere as long as you don't try and fuck up what I have going with her. If that happens, I'll do more than get in your way. I'll toss your sorry ass *out* of the way."

"I've told you before, I don't wanna come between you two."

"Good," he deadpans, "let's keep it that way." He stalks off, fuming, and while it wasn't the exit I wanted him to make, at least we've got an understanding. It's a start and that's more than we had before coming down to this basement.

"Thanks for walking with me to the Square," Scar says. "I figured it was best this way, so we could have some time to talk, ya know?"

"Not a problem. There is a lot we need to discuss."

One of the biggest things on my mind right now is whether or not she's feeling any regret over what we did. I have to know. If she is, then maybe my time with her is up. If she's not, it could have only just begun.

Before I can ask, Scar takes my hand, pulling me to a stop. "I'm not sorry for what happened between us. I hope you know that."

She said it before, but hearing it now puts everything into perspective. There's still the matter of Crew, though. I take her hand, lifting it to my shoulder, then the other, until she's hugging my neck. "So what are we gonna do?"

"I told Crew I wanna explore my relationships with both of you. I know it sounds selfish of me, but I can't choose. Not yet, anyways."

"He didn't seem too happy with that idea when I brought it up."

"It's the choice I've made. And if he wants to make the choice to let me go, I have to let him. Same with you."

"He won't. Crew will never let you go."

Her head leans toward her shoulder, eyes on mine. "And you?"

"You're stuck with me as long as you'll keep me."

A smile lifts her cheeks. "You have no idea how insanely happy that makes me."

"I guess we just let things play out and happen the way they're meant to then."

Her eyes dance to my lips, tension sizzling between us, and I use this opportunity to my advantage. Just as she goes to speak, I crush my mouth to hers.

"I guess so," she mutters against my lips, her hands fastened behind my head.

I cradle her cheek in my palm, parting my lips slightly and slipping my tongue between hers. It's a soft, quick kiss, but it definitely leaves me wanting more. "We should go. Riley is waiting for me."

Taking her hand in mine, we continue down the trail. It's sort of surreal walking out in public like this. It should feel weird since she's with Crew, but instead, it feels right because now she's with me, too.

# TWENTY

## SCAR

"Oh," I blurt out, remembering that I need to call my mom, "do you have your phone with you?"

Jagger pats the breast pocket of his coat. "Yeah. Do you need it?"

"I've been meaning to call my mom, but with everything else going on, it slipped my mind. I still need to ask her about Kenna."

Reaching into his pocket, he pulls it out and hands it to me. I hold it up, then sulk. "Dammit. No service."

"It'll pick up once we're off the trail."

We reach the end, and I can already see the girls stringing orange and black lights around the lampposts.

"This is nice," I say. "Do you all decorate here for Christmas, too."

"They do. I sure as hell don't."

"How come? Not into holidays?"

"The holidays I'm fine with, it's my decorating skills that aren't up to par. You see, if that was me with those lights, they'd already be sliding down that pole."

"Hmm. Well, maybe we should work on improving those skills."

Jagger shakes his head. "Uh-uh. The deal was, I drop you off, and Crew picks you up. No one said anything about me decking the halls for Halloween."

I mope, stopping him at the entrance of the trail. "Not even for me?"

He sighs heavily. "Damn you and that pouty face." His finger swoops under my droopy lip, and I smile.

We're holding hands, walking again, when I warn him, "Now, just so you know, my decorating skills aren't exactly something to brag about either. In fact, I hate it probably as much as you do. But I'm doing this for Riley."

His phone vibrates against my palm and I lift it up. "Oh. You got a text from Crew." I'm able to see the first half of the message which begins...

**Crew: Tell Scar I'll be there to pick her up on foot around...**

I hand the phone to Jagger, letting him read the rest. "Crew says he'll be here to get you at eight."

"And on foot," I add, knowing this since I saw it.

"Actually, he can borrow my sled. Neither of you should be out walking after dark."

My heart swells. "Really? You'll let him do that?"

"Of course. He's still my boy." He squeezes my hand, and my heart officially doubles in size, making room for both of them.

Jagger hands me his phone back. "You wanna call your mom before we're up there?"

"Oh yes!" I completely forgot, once again. "Prepare yourself," I tell him, "she's gonna give me hell for using a phone here. She's certain I'm going to endure the wrath of the Lawless if I break the rules."

"She has no idea, does she?"

I waggle my brows. "Not a single one, and I intend to keep it that way. At least, for now." I dial her number and press the phone to my ear. Jagger uses this opportunity to coerce me by walking me back into a large tree. He plants one hand above my shoulder against the dried bark, and the other drapes at his side.

She picks up on the third ring. "Hey, Mom."

Immediately, she starts screaming in my ear, so I pull the phone away. It's loud enough that Jagger can hear, and he fights back laughter.

"Everything is fine, Mom. No. I'm not going to get kicked out. I'm actually—"

More screams and demands to end the call and toss the phone into the river.

"It's not my phone to throw in the river. It's Jagger Cole's."

"Yes, Cain's son, Jagger. What other Jagger Cole is there?" I shake my head in annoyance. "Would you just listen to me? I have to ask you about someone."

And more shouting, so I cut her off. "Mom! Do you know a girl—or a lady, rather—named Kenna?"

Suddenly, the shrills stop.

"Mom?"

I decide to put the phone on speaker, so Jagger can hear; that way, I won't have to relay the message.

"I heard you, Scarlett. Why are you asking about Kenna?"

"Wasn't she your roommate?"

"Answer me. Why are you asking about Kenna?"

"Well, I think I found something of hers." I reach into my pocket, pulling out the heart halves. "It's a charm, but there are two."

"What kind of charm?"

"I don't know. A best friend one but for a couple. One half says, *I'm with you wherever you go—Kenna.* And the other half says the same thing, but with the name Jeremy."

"Say that again."

"One half says—"

"No. The name of the boy. Did you say Jeremy?"

"Yeah. Do you know him?"

"Where did you find them, Scarlett?" Her voice is frantic, which has my wide eyes looking at Jagger.

"In a cabin outside of BCA property."

"At your father's cabin? What were you thinking leaving the Academy grounds?"

"What?" I look at Jagger, brows raised. "Dad has a cabin here?"

"It's abandoned and we haven't set foot in it since you were born. But yes, he owns the cabin and the surrounding property. Scarlett," she says my name in warning, "you haven't been roaming around in those tunnels, have you?"

I look at Jagger, wondering if I should tell her the truth. When he shakes his head no, I lie, "No. Only as far as the Gathering room, why?"

"Keep it that way. It's easy to get lost in those tunnels. Now, about these charms. You need to throw them away and forget you ever found them. Do you hear me?"

"Yes, Mom. I hear you, but why?" I chuckle. "They're just charms."

"Just do as I say."

Jagger and I share a look, and while we might not have gotten any answers, the fear in my mom's tone says that these charms might be more of a clue than we thought.

"Before I hang up, can you tell me what happened to Kenna?"

There's a beat of silence before I hear her gulp. "Kenna passed away seventeen years ago, only days after she gave birth to her son, Jude."

"Jude," I say the name out loud, hoping it rings a bell to Jagger, but he shrugs his shoulders in response. "I'm sorry to hear that, Mom. I imagine if you were roommates, you were pretty close at one time."

"Time is the bard of truth, Scarlett, and I hope you never have to understand exactly how true that statement is."

"Hold on, Mom." I cover the speaker with my hand and move it to my side, so she can't hear me. "What else should I ask her that could help us?"

Jagger whispers back to me, "Ask her where this Jude kid is now? And how Kenna died?"

I nod before putting the phone back to my ear. "Sorry, Mom. Students were passing by and I had to hide my phone. "Mom," I say with a softness in my tone, "how did your friend Kenna die?"

"Are you alone now?" The desperation in her tone is unsettling.

"Yeah," I wince, "it's just you and me."

"Kenna was murdered in her home, but no one will ever admit that. They'll all say she took her own life, but I know the truth. He did it."

"He, who?"

"Jeremy Beckett."

Chills skate down my spine at the sound of that last name hitting my ears. "Did you say Beckett?"

"The sworn enemy of our kind, Scarlett. You need to promise me you will never go near one of them. They will pretend to be your friend. They will mask themselves, and they will lure you in. Once they've got you, they will do everything in their power to destroy you. Just like they did with Kenna."

"Whoa, Mom," I laugh, though there is nothing humorous. "No one is after me." It's a lie, but after this conversation, I have a pretty good idea where to start digging to find out who it is. There's no doubt in my mind now—it's definitely a Beckett.

"Secrets lurk in the shadows at BCA, and they aren't only Blue Blood secrets. Be safe, honey. Don't leave the school grounds, and remember what I said, never go out alone at night."

"Wait. I have to ask you one more thing before we hang up. What ever happened to this Jeremy guy?"

"He's passed away and his son was put into foster care."

"Okay, Mom. I should get off now. Give Dad a hug for me. I love you."

"Promise me you'll be in touch if you have any trouble at all. The Becketts aren't a threat to us anymore, but we can never be too safe when it comes to that family."

"I promise."

"Be safe. I love you, honey."

I end the call and hand the phone back to Jagger. "Well, that was an earful. She might think the Becketts aren't a threat to us, but I think she's wrong."

"Very wrong."

My brows dip, the wrinkles in my forehead prominent. "Are you thinking what I'm thinking?"

"The son?"

"Bingo. It would make sense that he'd have his parents' charms as proof of their love for one another."

"Eh. I wouldn't say love. Didn't you hear your mom? She thinks this Jeremy guy murdered Kenna."

"True. But she doesn't know that for a fact. It's all speculation. Like many things at BCA. And plot twist, my dad owns that damn cabin. How the hell did I not know that?"

Jagger shrugs. "Seems they aren't planning any family vacations there anytime soon."

"Or ever."

"All right, we have to look at this from all angles. I should probably fill the guys in."

I nod. "Yeah. I'll help Riley and you go back and talk to them. I'll let you off the hook this time."

Jagger presses his lips to my cheek. "Thanks. I'll see you back at the house."

Warmth rides through my stomach as I walk away, feeling the giddiness of a thirteen-year-old girl with a crush. How did I get so lucky to have not only one, but two of the most gorgeous guys in existence?

When I reach Riley and the group, I wave goodbye to Jagger. He disappears back on the trail, and I focus on being present for Riley. I haven't been there for her much and I've got a lot of guilt about it.

"You made it." Riley beams in her 'always chipper' tone. Her arms fly around me, of course, and this time, I hug her back. I, *really,* hug her back.

"I've missed you," I tell her, warranting a look of panic on her face.

"Are you okay?"

I laugh at her concern for me. "Of course I'm okay."

"Why are you being warm and fuzzy? That's not like you."

"Ry," I drawl, "I'm not always cold and heartless."

"Yes, you are. Now tell me what's going on and why you were holding Jagger Cole's hand when I saw you coming down the trail."

I wince. "You saw that?"

"Mhmm. I take it things aren't going well with you and Crew?"

"No, actually. Things are great."

Her posture slumps, a look of confusion on her face. "How is that working out then?"

"It's just a casual thing among us three. No need to think too much into it." What I'm feeling is anything but casual. Riley doesn't need to know that, though. The last thing I need is judgment.

"Oh, okay. I was about to bow at your feet thinking you were bagging two guys at once."

My cheeks flush, and I say, "Never said I wasn't." I bite my lip and Riley's mouth drops open.

"Holy shit. You dirty little slut. I love it."

"Come on," I throw an arm around her shoulders, "let's darken up this place with ghouls and goblins, while you tell me how your one-man relationship is going."

"Ugh. Boring," she singsongs, and it has me stopping.

"Really? I thought you were madly in love."

"Oh no. I am. It's the one-man thing that's boring. Why can't I have two? Or even three?"

"Consider yourself lucky. It's confusing as hell. I just...

don't wanna let either of them go." I puff my cheeks out, then exhale the pent-up air. "Is that selfish of me?"

Riley straightens the hat on a standing witch, then moves to another. "Nope. You gotta do what feels right. You know I'm not a fan of those guys, but I can tell they have your best interests at heart—now that the games are done, that is."

"Yeah. Crew and Jagger have been great these past couple weeks."

"And Neo." Her words are a statement, rather than a question, and it has me turning my head.

"Neo?"

"Yeah. He might be the biggest dickhead I've ever met, but I notice the little things he does."

"Oh yeah?" I chuckle. "Like what? Because I don't see it."

"You will." With that, she walks over to Hannah and takes some spiderwebbing from her, then weaves it through the witches gathered around a cauldron.

I'm watching them decorate, knowing I should offer my help, when I spot Melody. Her hair is now shoulder length, and evenly cut. Even after chopping off a good four inches with rusty scissors, she managed to fix it up and look as beautiful as ever.

She catches my look and quickly turns away. It's ironic, really. A girl like her with soaring confidence suddenly living in fear and trepidation.

Using this time while Riley is busy, I greet Melody, who has recently been ungrounded from her room. "Anything from *him* yet?" My words come out a whisper, but she hears me.

"Nothing. I told the guys I'd let them know if I heard anything and I will."

"You better, or it's your ass that'll be sitting in that cauldron."

"Don't threaten me, Scarlett."

"Oh," I snicker, "it's not a threat, *Melody*." I enunciate her name. "It's a promise." I swing back around and go help Riley.

I tossed out a couple plastic spiders on a web, shimmied up a lamppost to replace a bulb in the mini lights —it was literally only a foot off the ground—and watched Riley and some of her cheer squad act a fool to the Michael Myers theme song. Turns out, tonight has been pretty fun. And we didn't even have to run from any monsters. Except Elias, who came running through the Square wearing a werewolf mask. Riley freaked, then a second later, they were making out like teenagers—which they are. Sometimes I forget, we all are.

Doesn't feel like it, though. I haven't felt like a careless teen in a while. Dealing with stalkers and adult issues has sort of sucked the innocent life out of me. I stand back, watching everyone laugh and chat without a care in the world, and I wonder if this is all still a game to them. Why wouldn't it be? The BCA Stalker isn't after them; he's after me.

"Looks like your ride is here," Hannah says, and I follow her gaze to the snowmobile coming down the trail. The rider is wearing a helmet, so it relieves any suspicion that Neo came to get me.

As he comes closer, he pulls his helmet off, and I can clearly see that it's Crew.

Riley stirs to my side, whispering, "Dropped off by one. Picked up by another. You lucky bitch."

I nudge her shoulder with mine, grinning, because I do feel pretty lucky.

Crew doesn't slow down until girls are jumping to the side, at which point, he bumps into one of the five-foot-tall witches, knocking her to the ground.

"Crew!" Riley bellows, bending down and picking her up, "you knocked down Winnie!"

He flings his leg over, helmet tugged under his arm, eyes on me. "My bad. Just trying to get to my girl." He reaches for my hand and I take it.

*Oh my god.* I can feel the heat in my cheeks, and I'm thankful it's dark out.

Three of the four girls stare longingly at Crew, swooning at his words. It's not often they hear a man of his stature talk so sweet. Riley, on the other hand, is battling a witch that keeps tipping over.

"Damn you, Winnie! Stand your ass up!"

"Crew, would you mind?" I nod toward Riley, asking him to give her a hand.

"I can call in a Rook."

Sighing, I swat his arm. "Just help her."

"Fine." He drags out the word, snatching the witch by her hat. "But don't tell anyone. I've got an asshole reputation to uphold."

I chuckle in response. "Your secret's safe with us."

Once he's got Winnie in place and Riley is pleased, we say our goodbyes and head to the house.

It's a cold, quiet ride, and I'm so tired, I could have easily fallen asleep against Crew's back.

Stopping directly in front of the steps to the house, Crew

shuts off the engine. He gets off first then takes my hand and helps me off. A big yawn has me covering my mouth.

"Tired?" he asks as we walk in the house together.

"Very. I'll definitely sleep good."

Once we're inside, he closes the door and takes me by the waist, walking me back until I'm pressed against the door. "Did you have fun tonight?"

"Yeah. I actually did. It was a nice escape for a couple hours."

His lips press to mine. "Good. You deserve it."

This is still so surreal. Crew kissing me. Crew being kind. Sometimes I still feel the need to pinch myself.

"What about you? Did you and the guys work through some of your issues?"

His head wavers from side to side as he clicks his tongue on the roof of his mouth. "Eh. I wouldn't say that, but we did come up with a plan regarding Melody. Jagger and I are gonna keep watch tonight outside of the Foxes' Den in hopes of a delivery."

"Oh, wow. Tonight? What if he doesn't show? It'll be a waste of a whole night."

"Then I guess we'll try again tomorrow."

"Crew, that's insane. It could take days and you and Jagger need sleep."

My head tilts instinctively when he peppers kisses on the nape of my neck. "I won't sleep until I know you're safe."

Goosebumps spill down my body, and I close my eyes. "But who will keep me safe while you're both gone?"

His eyes lift to mine, and I already miss his hot breath against my skin. "Neo."

I blow out a heavy breath of annoyance. "Neo? Really? He'd feed me to a pack of wolves, given the chance."

"She's not lying." His words hit my ears before I see him, but when I do, I want to smack him.

Standing there in nothing but a pair of black boxer briefs that hug his hips to perfection, is the most arrogant guy I've ever met.

Crew turns around, one hand resting lazily on my waist. "Thought we talked about this shit?" His words are directed at Neo, who's chomping on a toothpick.

"We did. But I couldn't pass up an opportunity to be an ass."

I chime in, voicing my indignation. "Of course you couldn't."

"What?" He brings his hands to his bare chest, covering the broken crown tattoo on his breastbone. "Don't act like you wouldn't throw me to a pack of wolves given the chance too."

"Oh, I would. I most definitely would."

"You see. We have something in common. We're practically friends now."

I mumble, "Yeah, right."

"Well," Crew cuts in, "if we're done with this little moment of truth. I need to go change and load up on the layers. Gonna be a cold one tonight. Neo," he continues, "I trust that you'll leave Scar alone unless she needs you."

Neo holds up two fingers. "Scout's honor."

I cough, covering up the sound of me muttering, "Bullshit."

Crew takes my hand and we pass by Neo. As we do, Crew says, "It's three fingers dumbass."

"Damn. Jagger must've really loosened her up, but okay, if she insists on three."

Crew was referring to the Scout symbol, while Neo is just being the vulgar idiot he always is. He and I both know I wouldn't let his fingers anywhere near me.

"Ignore him." Crew squeezes my hand as we head up the stairs.

"Always do."

# TWENTY-ONE

## SCAR

AFTER CREW AND JAGGER LEFT, I took a shower, brushed my hair for a good twenty minutes while staring at myself in the bathroom mirror, thinking about all the ways this thing with Crew and Jagger can go wrong.

The last thing I want is to ruin their friendship, but so far, they seem to be handling everything fairly well. After all, they're working together tonight to try and catch the BCA Stalker. In a perfect world, they'd catch him, or her. I never once assumed it was a girl, but after seeing Melody in that black robe with her blonde locks hanging out, all I picture is a girl now.

My mind is a mess tonight and I attribute it to exhaustion. Jagger got some sleeping pills from Melody at the beginning of the school year when he said he couldn't sleep at night, and he left one on my nightstand in case I needed it.

Lying in bed alone, the down comforter tucked snuggly around me, I stare at the ceiling, thinking I should probably take it.

It's been a few days since I've gotten a good night's sleep and, even then, it was only because Crew was holding me and I felt safe.

Tossing the blanket off me, I scoot up. The glow of my nightlight plugged in beside the bed offers me enough light to see, so I grab the single pill sitting on my nightstand. I pop it in my mouth, pick up my glass of water, and take one big gulp...and down it goes.

Once I'm comfortable again, I close my eyes.

I'm not sure what time it is when I spring up in bed at the sound of footsteps coming down the hall. Feeling groggy and disoriented, I close my eyes while in a sitting position, ignoring whatever I heard.

*Sleep. I just need sleep.*

Even as my bedroom door comes open, I only crack a lid, my mind unable to process what's actually happening.

*It's all a dream. Go back to sleep.*

Unable to hold the weight of my head, my neck tilts to the side.

"Is someone there?" I grumble, smacking my lips and peeking through a half-open eyelid.

My head rolls to the other side and the dark shadow of a figure comes toward me. "Who are you?" I ask through dry vocal cords and sleepiness. I see a flash, then another, and another. "Are you taking pictures?"

He comes closer, and closer, and this dream has suddenly turned into a nightmare.

*Wake up. Do something.*

I straighten my back against the headboard, lifting my head and looking into the cutout eyes of the masked figure. My hand reaches out to grab his face, but my wrist is captured in a black, leather glove.

"That hurts." I try to pull back, but he squeezes harder, and harder, snapping me out of the nightmare and into reality.

My mouth opens to scream, but no sound escapes, and that's when I realize, his other hand is a barrier for my voice.

I kick and scream and squirm and try to get away, but he only strengthens his grip. He's strong, but I won't give up.

Lifting one leg up, my flexibility allows me to curl my foot under his arm, and I extend it out, moving his hand away from my mouth long enough to scream as loud as I can. "Help!" Then he puts it back in place, silencing me again.

"What do you want?" I try to say, but I'm speaking into a palm of leather.

*This can't be happening.*

*I'm going to die.*

*He's going to kill me.*

Tears fall recklessly down my cheeks, splattering against the glove.

Finally, I surrender because, whatever he wants, he's going to get.

Then, when I least expect it, hope returns. The masked figure removes his hand from my mouth, eyes burning into mine, but I can't make out the color in the darkness. I go to scream again, but before I do, a note is dropped on my chest.

I lie there, frozen in place—unable to think...unable to move—as I watch him walk out the door.

Once the shock of the situation has worn off, I shout at the top of my lungs. "Neo!"

While I wait, I pick up the note, folding back each bent corner.

Neo comes barreling into the room, rubbing his tired eyes. He hits the light, before hurrying to my bed. "What the fuck are you screaming about?"

Tears continue to stream down my face as I hold the note out in front of me. "He was here. He took pictures, and he held me down." I cry some more, choking on my words. "He left this." I hold up the note with a shaky hand, showing proof of the BCA Stalker's visit to my room.

Before I can hand Neo the note, he flees from the room. I tear the blanket off me and get to my feet, feeling woozy and off-balance. My head feels like it holds the weight of a bowling ball and it's official, I will never take another sleeping pill as long as I live. "Neo," I holler, my voice cracking as his name leaves my lips.

I take one step, then another, before losing my balance and crashing to the floor.

*That must've been a primo sleeping pill.*

I'm not sure how much time has passed when I open my eyes and see Neo kneeling beside me. Somehow I manage to get out the words, "Did you catch him?"

"No. The bastard got away."

I attempt to sit up, but the spinning in my head sends me right back down. "Whoa." Neo grabs me. "Did he hurt you?"

I shake my head. "I took a pill. I don't feel so good."

"Come on." He lifts me up, and when I flop around like a fish, he stands, grabs me by the waist, and throws me over his shoulder.

I'm upside down, my chin pressed to his back. "Why are you being nice to me?"

When he tosses me on the bed with force, I laugh. "I take that back."

"I could always throw you back down on the floor and leave you."

I'm curled up against the headboard and he grabs my foot, pulling me down so that my head is resting on the pillow. "I feel weak, Neo."

"Stay here. I need to get my phone and call the guys."

"No!" I blurt out. "I don't wanna worry them." I pat the mattress beside me. "And I don't wanna be alone. Stay with me. Please."

I can't believe what I'm saying. In a strange turn of events, it seems I'd rather be in Neo's presence than die. At least, high me would. Who would have thought?

Neo looks around the room, and it's strange because he seems uncomfortable. It's not often I get that vibe from him, if ever.

With a deep inhale, he sits on the corner of the bed and says, "Go to sleep so I can leave."

I shift to my side and curl my legs up. "You're so charming." My eyes blink a few times and while my body is telling me to sleep, my mind is still wondering if this is all a fucked-up dream. "Did someone come in here?"

"Yeah, Scar. Someone did come in here and he got away. What the fuck kind of pill did you take?"

"Sleeping."

"You took a sleeping pill?"

"Mmhmm. Jagger left it for me." Only the slits of my eyes show and everything around me is hazy as I pat the mattress beside again. "Tell Jagger to come here."

Neo grabs me by the shoulders, pinning my back to the mattress. "Snap out of it. Jagger isn't here."

My eyes shoot wide open. "Where'd he go?"

Now holding a glass of water, he shoves it in my face, but I turn my head. "I don't want another pill."

"Just drink the goddamn water. In fact, you might wanna eat something. I can guarantee whatever you took was not a sleeping pill."

His words raise red flags in my head, and I feel myself suddenly snapping out of whatever trance I was in; yet, my brain is still a thick blanket of fog. "What was it?" I scoot up, taking the water from him and pressing the glass to my lips.

"Did he actually hand it to you and watch you take it?"

I shake my head no, splashing water over my face. After I wipe the back of my hand across my mouth, I tell him, "He left it on my nightstand while I was in the shower."

"Son of a bitch! I bet that fucking creep was in here all night. Probably switched out the pill for something else. Wouldn't surprise me if he watched you in the shower."

My pulse races. "You think he watched me?"

"If he was here, I'm sure he did. No one would pass up that opportunity."

*Was that a compliment coming from Neo?*

I'm processing things slowly when I remember he said something about food. "Don't leave me to go get food."

He glares at me from one eye. "I'm not fucking leaving you. Get some sleep and the guys and I will handle this."

"Yeah," I laugh, "same way you handle everything else."

"What's that supposed to mean?"

"In layman's terms, it means you all suck at handling things. We're nowhere closer to catching this guy than we were during the Ladder Games."

"Some of that blame can be placed on the Guardian." His words come out as a peeved mumble, but I heard him.

"Did you say guardian? What's that mean?"

"Nothing. Forget it. Go the fuck to sleep."

My body shoots up, water spilling all over me. "Oops. I forgot I was holding that." I laugh, but the angered look on Neo's face says he doesn't find it funny at all. One glance down at my shirt reveals the bud of my nipples showing through my, now soaked, white tank top.

My mouth draws back. "Umm. Don't look."

"As if there's anything to look at." His words don't match his actions when I catch him staring at my chest.

"Then what are you looking at?"

He grumbles. "Nothing special, I can promise you that."

I scowl at him, eyebrows knitted. "Why are you so mean?"

Gripping the hem of my shirt, I lift up and pull my tank top over my head.

"What the fuck, Scar!" He grabs a pillow, shoving it to my chest. "Have you lost your damn mind?"

"Actually, yes. I do feel like my mind is lost. But what's the big deal? It's nothing special, so you shouldn't care."

Neo jumps up and goes over to my dresser, pulling open a couple drawers before he finds a shirt. He tosses it to me, but it lands on the end of the bed, so I drop the pillow and crawl to it. "Thanks, Neo. Aren't you just a ball of sweetness."

As I'm pulling it on, I catch him watching me, and when my eyes drag down to his crotch, I see his erection growing. A smile tugs at my lips. He can pretend my tits are nothing special, but his dick thinks otherwise.

Once I'm in a dry shirt, I lie back down. Minutes pass of Neo standing in my room, watching me, and waiting for me to fall asleep, so he can leave.

But I can't sleep. I suddenly feel a burst of energy and I, too, am convinced I didn't take a sleeping pill. "What do you think the pill was?" I ask Neo, who's deep in thought.

"Hmm?" He snaps out of it. "I dunno. Mood stabilizer, maybe?"

I move to my side again, so I can see him while I speak. "He probably tried to kill me and failed."

"If he wanted to kill you, there are easier ways to get rid of you."

"Sounds like you've thought about it."

He raises a shoulder. "A time or two."

"Neo?" I say his name as a question. "Why do you blame me for everything bad that happened in your life?"

He breaks eye contact with me, turns around, and begins messing with something on my dresser. "Because you are to blame."

I sit up, bringing the blanket with me. I don't want to open old wounds, but this is the first real conversation I've had with Neo in years, and it might be the last for years to come. "I'm not, though."

He picks something up off my dresser, a note, maybe, and he unfolds it. Spinning around, his demeanor has completely shifted. Shoulders drawn back, nostrils flared. "Where the hell did you get this?"

"I dunno. What is it?"

"It's mine! That's what the fuck it is! And I wanna know where you got it." He charges at me, fingers spiderwebbed as he reaches for my throat. I pull back, my head pressed firmly against the headboard.

"I don't know how it got here. I swear, Neo." Fingertips dip into the flesh of my neck and I stare into eyes laced with hate and intent. My throat tightens, the pulse in my neck pounding against his palm.

"Liar!" he shouts. "You've known all this time I had the proof and you thought you could steal it from me, didn't you?"

I swallow, feeling a ball lodge in my throat that won't go down. Neo shoves me back, apparently not wanting to end my life tonight. For a second, I was certain he'd kill me with his bare hand.

I cough and sputter, then finally shout, "Get out of my room!" The words sting as they climb up my throat. "Get out!" I cry carelessly, rubbing the sore spot of my neck. "You're demented! Who does this shit?"

"I do!" He jabs his thumb to his chest. "I do, because you've pushed me to do it. Ya know," he shakes his head, "for a second, I thought maybe, just maybe, I was overreacting, that it was all a coincidence. Then I find this." He holds up the paper and I can only assume it was planted here, whatever it is.

"Wait!" That paper. It's the one Jagger dropped on the ladder going up to the cabin. "I know where that came from. Jagger dropped it and it was in my coat pocket." I immediately eat my words, hoping I didn't incriminate Jagger in some way.

"Why the hell would Jagger have my sister's investigation report?"

His words take me by surprise. "Investigation? I didn't know there was an investigation. Maddie fell."

"Did you read it?"

I shake my head, while trying to process all this.

Neo bolts at me, shoving the paper in my face as he seethes. "Did you read it?"

"No," I answer honestly, "I never even opened that paper. I took it out of my coat and sat it on my dresser." But now I want to. I go to snatch the paper from his hand, but he pulls it back, causing it to rip down the center.

"Now look what you've done!"

"Fuck you! And when we catch this asshole, I'm asking him for some of those mood pills for you, so you can start acting like a normal human being! Now give me the damn paper."

"You don't deserve to read this. You don't even deserve to breathe the same air as Maddie."

His words hurt, but it doesn't stop me. I get off the bed and grab for the paper again. He doesn't give in, so I grab him by the arm and clamp my teeth down, biting into his bicep. He curses and shakes me off, but the harder he fights, the harder I bite. "You rabid little cunt!"

Finally, my teeth drag off his skin, the taste of his blood seeping onto my tongue. I gag a couple times, but while he's babying his wound, I snatch the paper from him and I run like hell to my bathroom, slamming the door and locking it before he can get to me. His fists immediately begin pounding and as my body slides down the wooden door, I can feel each thrust against my back.

I spit out any leftovers of Neo's bodily fluids and grab a dirty shirt off the floor, rubbing it across my tongue.

Once I can't taste him anymore, I read.

**COY COUNTY POLICE DEPARTMENT**
**CRIMINAL INVESTIGATION REPORT**

| **OPENED:** 12-19-2020 | **CLOSED:** Remains under investigation |
|---|---|
| **RELATED DOCUMENTS:**<br>Criminal Investigation Report<br>Medical Analysis<br>Witness Statements | **VICTIM:**<br>Madeline Carian Saint |

On December 19th of the year 2020, Madeline Carian Saint was found unresponsive on the east side of Coy Mountain.

Madeline Saint was found by a local climber at approximately seven-thirty pm. Madeline fell at least 100 feet from the top of Coy Mountain during a ski trip with a group of friends (see witness statement 03D)

Medical attention was received immediately and she was airlifted to the nearest hospital.

Findings presented from Detective Ann Lindon: Coy County Police Department and The Coy County Forensics Team:

It has been determined in the case of Madeline Saint, 16 years old of Essex, Co, further investigation is necessary. Our findings are due to the trajectory of the body going outward and no indication of her body sustaining injury from sliding down the side of mountain. Had she fallen without force, she would have endured marks and bruising to a severe extent covering a great deal of her body. The lack of such indicates force from behind, sending her into the air before hitting ground at which time, she was located.

Several pieces of evidence are noteworthy. (See evidence file 9F2)

CCPD will maintain the investigations reporting procedures.

"No," I whisper, "this can't be."

My hands tremble as I hold the paper out in front of me.

*Maddie was pushed?*

Neo finally stops pounding, knowing it's too late.

"Why didn't you ever tell me?" I choke out, loud enough for him to hear me.

"Because you already knew."

I lick away the tears falling on my lips, fighting for breath. "You think I did this? All this time, you thought it was me?"

He doesn't respond, but I keep talking. "You blame me for Maddie's accident. You blame me for your mom's death. And now you blame me for the broken bonds between the three of you guys. You think it's all my fault."

The door rattles, and I feel him near. His response, a confident, "It is all your fault."

I ball the paper up in my hand, tossing it across the bathroom. "I'd never hurt her, Neo. I'd never want anything bad to happen to anyone in your family—even you. How could you ever think I would?"

"You wanted her gone. She was the only thing standing in the way of you being with Crew."

"That's really what you think?"

"It's what I know."

"Yes. I left Maddie at the top of the mountain to come down herself. All this time, I thought you blamed me for her injury because I didn't go down with her. But that wasn't it at all."

I may not have pushed Maddie, but according to this report, someone did.

Wiping my tears away, I get to my feet and unlock the door. Just as I pull it open, Neo gets up from where he was sitting on the other side. His hand extends to me, giving me a small black coin purse. "Found this. Stalker must've dropped it on his way out. Looks like the sleeping pill you should have taken, and Crew's stolen key. This must be how he got in." He stalks into the bathroom and snatches the crumpled paper off the floor. Snarling, he steps past me and leaves the room.

I hurry to the doorway, pressing my palms to each side. "Neo," I holler, and he stops but doesn't turn around, "I didn't do it. But someone did and I'd like to help you find out who that person is, if you'll let me."

He keeps walking, pulling his bedroom door open, then he slams it shut.

# TWENTY-TWO

SCAR

"Hey," Jagger says, sliding under the blanket with me. My eyes are wide open and haven't shut all night. "I heard about what happened. I can't believe no one called us."

"Neo wanted to, but I didn't want you guys to worry. Besides, Neo ran him off."

"Doesn't matter. He swapped your sleeping pill and you could have been seriously hurt."

Jagger curls his fingers, running them down my cheek, and I catch a glimpse of dried blood. I take his hand in mine and hold it in front of my face. "Oh my gosh, Jagger. What happened?"

I sit up, bringing his injured hand with me, and that's when I see his swollen left eye.

"You got in a fight!"

"I'm fine. But you should see the other guy."

"This isn't funny. Who were you fighting?" I run my fingers over his knuckles, smearing some of the fresh blood, and that's when I realize this wasn't last night, it had to have been this morning. "It was Neo, wasn't it?"

"Is it any worse than you taking a chunk out of his arm?"

I cringe at the thought. I did that. I smack my tongue around in my mouth, searching for his taste. Fortunately, it's gone. "In my defense, I was under the influence last night. I'm surprised I didn't strangle him after he choked me…"

My words trail off, knowing I spoke too soon.

Jagger shoots up, getting onto his feet. "After he what?"

"No. It's okay. I'm fine. Really. He didn't hurt me."

Grabbing my chin, he turns my head left, then right, searching for any sign of Neo's fingerprints. His lip curls up and he drops his hand before walking thunderously to my open door.

"Jagger. Wait!" I holler, throwing the blanket off me and getting to my feet. I don't make it far before my head begins pounding. It feels like my brain is caught in a tornado, and it's slamming against my skull. I grip both sides of my head then sit back down. "Jagger!" I try again to no avail.

Crew's walking past my door when he gives me a double take. "Whoa, babe." He hurries to my side. "You okay?"

"Just got up too fast. I'm fine. Will you go after Jagger before he kills Neo? Please."

"Neo's not here. He left."

I lift my head and drop my hands in my lap. "Where'd he go? School doesn't start for another hour."

"Not sure. He just walked out the door, got on his sled, and took off."

"Is he pissed because of his fight with Jagger?"

"Because of his fight with both of us. He deserved it, Scar. He's run his mouth enough. He needed to be put in his place."

I grab Crew's hand, searching for signs of injury, but I see none.

"I didn't fight him with my fists. I fought him with my words."

My chest pangs. It's an odd feeling. I can't stand Neo, but I hate what's happened to his friendships with Crew and Jagger. I feel so selfish.

"Hey." He tips my chin. "You're worth it all, okay?" It's like he read my mind, but did he hear the part where I said I'm selfish? Because if he did, he might agree.

"We have to fix this. I'm not Neo's biggest fan, but he has to be feeling some sort of way over all this."

"Like, sadness? Or, helplessness? No," he shakes his head, "Neo doesn't feel those emotions. If anything, he's feeling an abundance of rage and he's devising a plan of attack against us all. Don't feel bad for him."

*But, I do.*

Jagger comes back into the room, huffing and puffing. "He's gone."

Crew fills him in and Jagger relays what I said about him choking me, which leaves them both pleased with Neo's exit and a hope he doesn't return. Am I the only one that sees how wrong this all is? These guys are all best friends.

An idea surfaces, and I think I know exactly where to find him.

I shoot to my feet, interrupting whatever conversation they're having. "We should get ready for class."

When I get lightheaded again, they both take notice and each holds me up—one on each side. "I'm fine," I tell them.

"You're not fine," Jagger says. "Whatever you took last night is still working its way out of your system. You need to stay home today. I'll stay with you."

"I agree," Crew cuts in. "But you should go to your classes, Jagger. I'll stay with her."

They begin to bicker, so I throw my hands up and shout. "Stop!"

I can't take any more of this. First Crew and Neo, then Jagger and Neo, and now Jagger and Crew. They're all fighting, and it's all my fault. "I'm going to school and that's the end of it." I push past them and go to my bathroom, not giving them a chance to argue with me.

MY HEART HAS BEEN HURTING all morning.

Feelings are getting stronger and with them comes choices that I'm not ready to make.

Crew is the one I always swore was *the one.* Jagger stole my first kiss and in that moment, he stole a piece of my heart, too. The last thing I want is for Crew and Jagger to lose people because of me. Whether it's their families or their friends.

Everyone hates Neo. In fact, I'm positive Neo hates himself, and he wants us to all hate him, too. Which is good because I'm pretty sure I do. Hate is a strong word, but I've never felt so much rage toward another human being.

My conscience won't allow me to just sweep this all under the rug. I have to try and fix things with these guys. Putting all my anger aside, I think I can. Which is exactly why I'm sneaking out the door of the cafeteria while Crew and Jagger are at our table having lunch.

I managed to snag Jagger's keys from his pocket when I gave him a hug before going to my creative writing class. It felt sneaky, but it was necessary, so the guilt is minimal.

I'd give it about ten minutes before they frantically begin searching for me, so I have to go now. On a good note, they have to find me on foot because Crew's sled still isn't fixed.

I run around the building, snow seeping under the leg of my jeans and dropping into my boots. Once my eyes are on Jagger's sled, I bolt to it.

I've watched the guys drive their sleds many times so it shouldn't be too hard.

Without a second thought, I jump on, start the engine, and hold down the throttle. I take off faster than I expected, causing me to fly back on the seat, but a couple seconds later, I've got it under control and I'm moving at a leisurely pace. I'm in no position to try and show off, so I take things nice and slow and head back to the house.

My plan is to follow the tracks leaving the house this morning, in hopes that they'll lead me right to Neo.

Fortunately, they're fresh and clear and easy to follow.

By the time I start on his trail, I know Crew and Jagger have probably started questioning where I'm at. They'll probably ask Riley, and maybe even Elias. But no one will be able to give them the answer they want.

I take a left and my hands become clammy, even in the fifty-degree temperature. My shoulders tighten and unease pools in my stomach. It's that unearthly feeling that someone is watching me. I've felt it time and time again and my intuition is always on target.

Picking up my speed, I try to get to Neo faster. A right on his tracks has me guessing where I'm going because, from here, it's a straight shot to the Ruins. Neo must have gone there to clear his head.

When I arrive, I'm relieved to see his sled parked under the overhang beside a large pillar.

I turn off the engine, pull out the key, and drop it in my pocket.

My eyes immediately land on the open trap door to the tunnels and unease brews again. Last time I was dumb enough to go down there, Jagger and I got locked in. Instead of heading down the ladder, I stick my face in the hole and shout, "Neo!"

The next thing I know, I'm being pulled back, screaming as loud as I can. "Let me go!" Like a rag doll, I'm tossed aside. My shoulder crushing against the concrete pillar before I collapse to the ground.

Neo stands there, scowling at me. He's sporting a swollen eye, similar to Jagger's, and a busted lip that still has fresh blood seeping from it. With a black beanie on his head, a leather jacket, and boots to match, he stands tall and unaffected by my presence. "Why the hell are you here?"

I pick myself up off the ground and punch him hard in the shoulder. "Asshole!"

"Bitch!" he snaps back.

"So what if I am?"

"Oh, I know you are. And a stupid bitch at that. Are you insane coming out here by yourself?"

I roll my eyes at him, not responding because I am insane for coming out here by myself.

"I take it Crew and Jagger don't know you left?" He tips his head to Jagger's sled. "Or that you stole a ride?"

"Nope." I pop the P. "Because for the first time in a while, I'm making a decision for myself."

"You realize it's a stupid decision, right?"

"I do." I blink a few times, looking up at the clear sky. "But I had to try."

"All right," he waves his hand over the opening to the

tunnels, "go on down. You wanna get yourself trapped again? I won't stop you."

"I didn't come here for the tunnels." I take a step toward him. "I came here for you."

"Whoa." Hands fly up. "Not interested."

*Damn. That was harsh.*

I shake away the ego-stomping words. "I came here to *talk* to you."

"Again. Not interested." As he spins around, I grab the sleeve of his leather jacket, suddenly remembering how his hands felt around my throat last night, and once again, realizing how much of an idiot I am. Still, it doesn't stop me.

He shakes me away with a growl. "Hands off, home-wrecker."

"Would you drop the asshole act and just listen to me?"

"Trust me, baby. It's not an act."

"Ugh," I snarl. "Please don't call me that again. It's appalling coming from you."

"And yet, I'm the asshole?"

I click my tongue, raising my shoulders.

"Go back to school, Scar." He starts walking toward his sled again, but I jump in front of him.

"Not until we hash this out. All of it!"

He sits down on his sled, hand in the front pocket of his jeans, one leg extended, the other bent. "Fine. Talk. Doesn't mean I'll respond."

"I didn't push Maddie."

"Next subject. We're not having that conversation."

"Fine." I reason with him. "I'll save that for later." Have his eyes always been that pretty? They're the prettiest shade of olive I've ever seen. I blow out a heavy breath, suddenly forgetting why I'm here.

"Are you done?"

"No." Swallowing hard, I continue, "You have every right to call me a homewrecker because, right now, I feel like one. You, Jagger, and Crew have been best friends for as long as I can remember and right now, you're all fighting because of me—"

"That, we are," he cuts me off, and it seems he's eating his words about not responding.

"Okay, now that we're clear on that. I need you to know it's not what I want. I can't stand you, Neo. No one has ever treated me as awful as you—"

"Are you sure about that?" he cuts me off again, and it's starting to annoy me.

"Yes, I'm sure."

"So, I've treated you worse than a stalker who is taunting you and probably hiding in these woods, watching you at this very second?"

"Yeah," I spit out honestly, "that person might scare me more than you do, but there's no doubt you've caused me more pain."

He leans back, one elbow pressed behind him on the seat. He reaches into the inside pocket of his jacket and pulls out a toothpick, popping it in his mouth. "Good." He smirks around it, pleased with himself.

"See what I mean? That!" I point at him with both hands. "That arrogant-ass attitude you have."

"Don't like it? Then leave."

I stomp my foot to the ground beside his sled, cursing internally. "You're so infuriating. There is no reasoning with you, is there?"

"Nope." He moves forward, straightening his back, and starts the engine.

"Neo!" I huff. "Don't you dare leave. I'm not done."

He lifts a smirk and accelerates right in my direction, then circles me. "If you know what's good for you, you'll get back to school."

Then he takes off, leaving me furious and ready to strangle him. I have never met someone so maddening in my entire life.

# TWENTY-THREE

## SCAR

I'M a statue standing in Neo's dust of snow. At a loss for words, I just watch, half expecting him to come back because, who the hell does that?

More than one person has made a claim that Neo would protect me if needed; yet, he leaves me here, alone, with the tunnel door still open?

Anyone could climb up that ladder right now and drag me to my death. The truth is, Neo doesn't care, and they're all blinded by their own issues with him, they don't see the death wish he has for me.

I turn around slowly, eyes on the opening to the tunnels. Anyone can come up, but also, anyone can go down.

Walking toward it, the voices in my head battle.

*Don't do it, you stupid girl.*

And...

*Go. Search for answers. Find out anything you can about Kenna, Jeremy, and their son.*

Or better yet...

*Find proof that this monster had his eyes on me even at a*

*twenty-thousand-foot elevation. That he had the means to push Maddie from that cliff.*

I could clear my name while bringing this person to the Elders, and there's no doubt in my mind they'll kill him—if I don't first.

I'm already halfway down the ladder when the choice is made for me. It's as if my body knows what to do without my mind even telling it.

It's a long walk, but I make the trek because Maddie is worth it—because my life is worth it.

It won't be long until Neo tells Crew and Jagger where I am. They'll see Jagger's sled, and with any luck, they'll come down, too. At least then I won't be alone. Although, as I walk these tunnels, I really hope I *am* alone.

One minute turns to many. And many minutes turn to almost an hour when I finally reach the door.

My shaky fingers grip the dial and I begin turning the combination. It's engrained in my memory from my trip down here with Jagger.

*Eight, thirteen, nineteen, eight, four.*

Wait.

*Eight, thirteen, nineteen, eight, four.*

As in...August 13, 1984

My mom's birthday.

The hairs on my arms stand tall as my limbs quiver. *It has to be a coincidence.*

It just has to be.

Once the lock clicks, I turn the handle and push the door open.

Taking care not to make a sound, just in case I'm not alone, I move slowly. Before I step fully inside, I poke my head through the crack and look around. I'm surprised to see a beam of light coming from a lantern and it's a warning that someone is here.

Movement catches my eye, and my heart drops.

Just as I go to close the door, I see two hands holding a stack of papers. A black hood pulled over his head.

If I could just see his face. That's all I need. *Show me your face.*

He turns to the left, setting down the papers on the desk and sifting through them. My eyes drag to the fingers turning the pages and like a knife straight to the back, I see something I can't unsee.

Neon orange nail polish. Polish I painted on those fingers.

This is a girl.

But not just any girl—*it's Riley*.

I close the door as quietly as I opened it, and once it's latched, I take off running through the tunnel, back the way I came.

How could she? Or is she? This could be the same situation Melody was in. But why wouldn't she tell me? Either way, I can't wait to find out. On the off chance that Riley is working with the BCA Stalker, I need to get the hell out of here and go tell the guys.

Unable to mentally process what I just saw, I refuse to think. Right now, I just want out of here. My mouth is dry. I feel faint. I'm breathless, and I'm almost positive I pissed myself.

Tears pool in my eyes, clouding my vision. I stumble over my own feet, catching my fall by pressing my hands to the cement wall.

*How could I have been such a fool?*

I feel betrayed. I feel sick. I stop walking and curl over,

throwing up everything in my stomach. I haven't eaten much today, so fortunately, it's not a lot. I spit and sputter and cry some more then pull myself together and keep on moving as quickly as I can.

The sound of voices rings in my ears, but I can't tell if I'm imagining it, or if they're real.

As I approach the exit, the voices come closer and closer until I'm full-on sprinting toward Jagger and Crew, who are running just as fast to me.

"It's Riley!" I blurt out, the taste of vomit on my tongue. "I saw her."

Neo comes up behind them with a slow swagger, taking no care to hustle. "Ah. There she is."

He must have gone and told them I was down here. Did they not hear me? "It's Riley," I say again.

Then my eyes catch hers. Behind Neo, walking toward us with a perplexed look on her face. I point my finger and shout, "She's behind you!"

*She's going to kill them. She's going to kill all of us.*

"It's okay, baby," Crew says, wrapping an arm around me. Jagger comes up to my other side and does the same, until I'm only standing with their help.

"It's not okay! I saw her." I shift my attention to Riley. "I saw you, you lying, deceitful little—"

"Scar," Jagger cuts me off, "it's not what you think."

I know my head is a mess. My mind has been working overtime. But how is it not what I think?

Words fail to escape me as Jagger continues, "She's not the BCA Stalker, and she's not working for him."

"But I saw her there. She was going through papers. I know it was her. Her nail polish. That black hoodie..."

"It was me," Riley finally speaks. "But I'm not working with him. I'm working against him. We all are."

"I...I don't understand."

Riley comes closer, but I take a step back, bringing Crew and Jagger with me.

"Do you remember when you asked me about the term *Guardian*?"

"I remember. You said you never heard of it in regard to the Society."

"I lied."

*None of this is making any sense.* "Why would you lie?"

"The Blue Bloods is comprised of dozens of watchmen, or watchwomen. They're the protectors of the Society. They go through extensive training and the majority are descendants of prior Guardians. My father is a Guardian. My grandmother, and great-grandfather. And I'm now training to be one, too."

"What?" I look from Riley to Jagger and from Jagger to Crew, then finally to Neo. "Why didn't I know this?"

"No one does," Neo says, kicking his foot on the wall and staring at the wall opposite him. He pops another toothpick in his mouth, or maybe it's the same one. "And you're not supposed to either."

Riley continues, "You're not supposed to know until the final initiation after graduation from BCA. If students knew, we wouldn't have a job. They'd be extra leery of us and hinder our ability to complete tasks. We're here to keep you all safe, not just on the inside, but on the outside, too. Which is exactly why you can't tell a soul. If word ever got around that a student outside of the Lawless knew, the Elders would lose their shit."

My mind finally begins to settle down and I'm somewhat able to comprehend this conversation. Riley isn't bad. She's actually really fucking good.

Jagger removes his arm from my shoulder and takes my hand. "Let's get you home."

"Yes. I need to shower. And eat. Then you can all fill me in on this Guardian business because I am confused as hell." I glance at Riley. "Is this why we roomed together when I got here? Did you know something was going on before we did?"

"Actually," she shares a look with the guys, "they made it happen. Thought it would be best if you stayed with someone who had a connection to them. Little did they real-ize, I hated them and I liked you."

Neo chimes in, three steps ahead of us. "Feeling's mutual."

"Yeah. Screw you," Riley retorts.

"I just..." I shake my head, finding this so hard to believe. "I just don't see you as the protective type, Ry. I'm sorry, but you're so—"

"Delicate? Girly? Weak?"

"No. Well, yeah. I guess so."

"People only see the painting you show them, Scar. They don't know what it took to create it."

Jagger once said something similar. How every student at this place is creating a beautiful picture for everyone to see while using another person's blood on their canvas.

Makes me wonder if some of us are using our own blood.

After a long walk with small talk, and Neo being an ass, we finally emerge from the tunnel.

I'm surprised to see the sun setting behind the trees, and it has me wondering what time it is.

As if he read my mind, Crew says, "Dinnertime. I'm fucking starving."

"Well," Riley hooks her arm around me, "I'd say we could all catch dinner at the dining hall, but this little moment of truth doesn't mean I like you all." She's referring to the guys, and I'm already impressed with her forwardness. It's been creeping up more and more lately and now I'm about to see just how badass my best friend really is.

"Good," Neo pulls on his helmet, lifting the visor to speak, "because, once again, we don't like you either."

Neo's the first to leave, and when I look around, I realize there are two other sleds here. "You got it back?" I ask Crew.

"Yep. All fixed. Wanna ride?"

I bite the corner of my lip, looking from him to Jagger, unsure how to respond without hurting anyone's feelings. "Go with Crew," Jagger says, patting the seat behind him. "Riley, hop on. I'll give you a ride." I toss him his keys and he catches them midair. This sweet gesture on his part makes my stomach flutter because it's obvious he's trying to be fair. Crew, on the other hand, is definitely going to take a bit before he willingly shares my time. I get it, though. Our situation isn't normal.

Fifteen minutes later, we're pulling up to the house, and I'm surprised to see that Riley is still on the back of Jagger's sled. I thought for sure he was dropping her off at the dining hall.

I question her with a look and she throws her helmet at Jagger, then jogs to me through the snow. Her arms hug her chest and her hair flaps under the hood of her sweatshirt. "Holy hell. It's cold out here."

"I'm actually super impressed you're wearing a hoodie. It's so...not you."

"It's hideous, right?"

"No," I chuckle, "it's warm." We start toward the house, and I ask, "What are you doing here, anyways? I thought you were going to the dining hall."

"Jagger thought it might be a good idea if I come back and we go over some of the stuff I learned in the past twenty-four hours. He also thought it might be good for me to check on you. Make sure you're not weirded out too much."

"Jagger is a smart guy." We head to the door as I continue to talk, "I'm definitely weirded out. It's hard to picture you as anyone but quirky Riley. Let alone, a spy."

Riley laughs. "A spy?"

"Well, yeah. That's pretty much what you are, right? A spy for the Elders?"

"I guess so. But, I'm still in training. And I've fucked up *a lot*. Wouldn't surprise me if I don't get promoted to a Guardian. In which case, my dad might disown me."

"Really? Why do you say that?"

Riley takes a serious tone, which is odd for someone so buoyant. "It's in my blood. We come from a family of Guardians."

"Don't be so hard on yourself. I'm sure you're doing the best you can."

"I'm not so sure about that. If I were doing the best I could, I would have solved this mystery by now."

"For what it's worth, we've all been trying; yet, he's still out there."

"But what kind of Guardian will I ever be if I can't even catch this stalker, who leaves traces of evidence everywhere he goes?" She shakes her head, brushing it off. "Doesn't matter. One way or another, he'll be caught. Let's get inside. It's freezing out here."

"Yeah." I look down at myself. "Yeah, I could really use a shower."

Riley chuckles. "Still can't believe you even thought I was capable of being the BCA Stalker."

I pull open the door, letting her enter first. "I still can't believe any of this."

Crew and Neo are sitting in the living room. Crew on the couch with his feet kicked up on the coffee table, and Neo lying down on the sofa with his feet dangling off the side.

"Where's Jagger?" I ask anyone who will answer me.

Of course, it's Crew that speaks up. "On the phone with his dad."

"Okay. I'm going to take a shower. You all play nice."

Turning to Riley, I whisper, "You okay if I leave you with them?"

She glances at the guys and rolls her eyes back to me. "I'll survive, but make it quick."

## CHAPTER
# TWENTY-FOUR

JAGGER

I'M PACING MY ROOM, waiting for my dad to call back. He rang a few minutes ago and said he had an update, then ended the call abruptly when Scar's dad, Kol, arrived at his house.

After a minute of anxiously waiting, my phone buzzes against my palm.

"Everything all right?" I ask immediately.

"I dunno, son. You tell me. What's this business about Scarlett digging for information on the Beckett family? I thought you said you'd keep a tight lid on what we discussed."

"I did. Never said a word. Scar, er, Scarlett's meddling has nothing to do with anything I said."

"Better not have. You boys have one job there: keep the students in line. You let the Elders and the Guardians deal with everything else."

Easier said than done, considering the shithead stalker is inserting himself into every aspect of our lives.

"Understood. Now what's this news?"

"It seems the Beckett family line continued when the

late Jeremy Beckett's mistress birthed a son seventeen years ago."

This isn't anything I don't already know, but I don't tell him that. He'll likely scold me for digging.

"Okay. Where is he now?"

"No one knows. His father was found murdered in their home over a year ago, and he hasn't been seen since. There's a missing person's report on him and a rap sheet about a mile long. He's also wanted in connection to his father's death. He's trouble, son. Kol and Sebastian have a couple contacts they're reaching out to, to start a search for this kid. I'm sure he's long gone by now, but we can never be too safe. But if anything, and I mean, *anything* suspicious happens, you need to notify me. Understood?"

*If he only knew.* "Yes, sir. And keep me updated if you hear anything else."

"How's your grades?"

"Same as always. All *A*'s."

"Good. Keep it that way and you'll be following in your old man's shoes in no time."

"Can't wait." The sarcasm in my tone is obvious, but my dad has become pretty good at only hearing what he wants to hear.

A knock on my open door has me turning my head. "I gotta go, Dad." I end the call and set my phone on the dresser. "Look at you all fresh and clean." I nuzzle up to her, burying my face in her soaked black hair.

Her wispy strands tickle my cheek as I move my mouth down to her neck. "Mmm. You smell so good." Parting her hair to the other side, I suck her skin between my teeth. "It's a shame you've got a friend over."

She giggles. "Seems she's not only my friend."

"She's certainly not ours. In fact, I barely know the girl."

"Oh, I see. So it's like a coworker sort of relationship? There's hate, but you tolerate one another?"

My fingertips dip below the waistband of her shorts and I give her ass a firm squeeze. "How mad do you think she'll be if we make her wait a couple minutes?"

"Doubt she'll even notice."

Lifting my head, I spin her around and walk her backward, both hands now beneath her shorts cupping her ass cheeks. "Has anyone ever told you how nice your ass is?"

She rolls her lips then lifts a smile. "Not recently."

"Well, it's fucking spectacular." We fall onto the bed, my body hovering over hers. Our mouths crash together and we tear into each other like wild animals. My hands move rapidly as I pull her long-sleeved tee shirt over her head and I'm not surprised to see she's braless. It's something I noticed a long time ago. Scar hates wearing bras when she's home. Doesn't matter who is here. She does not give a fuck.

With my hips raised and one arm holding me up, I unclasp my belt and tug my pants down, taking my boxers with them. Once they're hanging from my ankles, I kick them free. "God, I've missed you." I kiss her again, feeling the heat of her touch coursing through my body, going straight to my throbbing cock.

"I've missed you, too." Her soft words come out in a heady exhale, and I drag in her breath.

Lifting my head, I peer down at her. Everything about what's lying beneath me tugs at my heartstrings and makes me want to savor this moment for an eternity. Last time I was rough with Scar. It comes naturally to me. I don't know how to be anything but abrasive, but with her, I'm willing to try.

Nice and slow, my fingers drag down her stomach, raising goosebumps along the way. Scar wets her lips and arches her back when I pinch her clit, rolling it between my thumb and forefinger.

I kiss her mouth, then her lips. Moving down to her chest, I cover every inch with my mouth. My fingers move inside her and she's ready for me. Wet, warm, and tight. Her walls envelop the two fingers I'm giving her, and when I add another, curling them at her G-spot, she bucks her hips.

Pebbled nipples greet my mouth, and I graze one against my teeth before moving to the next.

"Harder." Scar whimpers and I'm glad she's a girl who knows exactly what she wants. I dig deeper, so deep that my knuckles rim her pussy and her ass lifts off the bed. I could feed her my whole hand, but I'm not sure she's there yet. Besides, this time, I want to learn her body. Memorize her expression when she gets to the height of her orgasm. Pay attention to every twitch and jolt as she comes down.

My body slides back up, my fingers delving deeper inside her, twisting and turning in a way that has her crying out. She tightens her core, squeezing my hand, and her beautiful mouth forms an O. I watch her intently. Flared nostrils, lustful eyes, and ragged breaths. "Come on my hand, baby."

And she does. Squirting her arousal all over my fingers, leaking onto my palm. Once her ass settles back on the bed, I pull them out and pop my soaked fingers in my mouth. "So sweet." I drag the same three fingers across her bottom lip, and she darts her tongue out, tasting herself before I feed her more from my tongue.

I slip down, lining my cock with her entrance, then move up, sliding in. Her arousal coats my cock, and it's fucking heaven inside her. My movements start out slow and when Scar's eyes widen, I ask, "You okay?"

She nods in response, but I have no doubt there's a sting of pain. I've always known my dick was bigger than average, and it's not an egotistical guy thing—it really is a fucking beast. Most of the time, I fuck girls through the pain, but with Scar, it's different. I never want to inflict pain on her, even if it brings me pleasure.

My movements are slow and shallow. I slide in and out, watching her the entire time. When we were together in the tunnels, I could only dream about what her face looked like as I was fucking her. Now, I can see it, and it's the most beautiful thing I've ever laid eyes on. Her drawn mouth as our bodies connect. Her blue eyes on mine. Each breath that flares her nostrils a tad. And her tits pressed against my bare chest.

Her warm hand lands on my cheek, the other pinching my shoulder, and she guides my mouth to hers. "Fuck me hard, Jagger."

I shake my head against hers. "I wanna take it slow this time. Make it last."

The next thing I know, she's pushing me back. "What are you doing?"

"Lie on your back," she demands, and her authoritative tone is sexy as hell.

My cock slips out of her, and I lie down with my back to the bed. I prop one arm under the pillow, lifting my head a few inches so I can watch her work.

She climbs on top of me, straddling my lap, and when she sits down, my cock goes in like it knows exactly where home is. Every last inch is buried inside her, my head bobbing in her stomach.

Sitting up, she arches her back, sliding back and forth, grating against my cock. "Fuck," I growl, clamping my teeth down on my bottom lip.

I sink my fingers into the flesh of her waist, guiding her movements, but when she proves she doesn't need help, I grab fistfuls of her tits, squeezing and massaging.

She's a goddamn goddess. The way she's riding my cock like it's her favorite thing in the world.

I move forward. Her arms wrap around my neck, and she bounces up and down. Her tits rising and falling. "I'm gonna —" My words are cut short when I glance over her shoulder and see Crew standing in the doorway. His arms crossed over his chest, ankles locked, as he leans into the frame. Scar senses my apprehension and slows down. "What's wrong?"

I tip my chin to where he stands, and she follows my gaze.

"Oh shit." She goes to jump off me, but Crew steps into the room.

"Don't stop," he tells her, taking us both by surprise.

He comes closer. His hands reach out, and he grabs her by the waist from behind. "Don't stop on my account."

"Crew, I…I'm sorry."

"For what? You're not doing anything wrong." He rolls her hips, and she picks up on the movement, doing it herself.

"Ride him, baby. Show him how good you are."

Scar looks at me, her eyes wide and panicked. I'm certain she thinks this is a trick, but I can assure her, it's not. For whatever reason, Crew wants her to fuck me.

"Hey," I grip her chin, "watch me."

I raise my hips and fall back down, repeating the motion as Crew holds on to her from behind.

Once she gets into the rhythm, his knees come up behind her, and he presses his chest to her back. Sweeping her hair to one side, he kisses her neck.

This isn't awkward for Crew and me because we've done this many times before. Although, this is the first time feelings have been involved. But for Scar, it's all new.

"Just keep watching me, baby," I tell her, calming her discomfort. With our eyes locked together, I squeeze her tits again while Crew smothers her shoulder in kisses, never once looking at me, while I refrain from looking at him.

Scar picks up her pace, moving faster, and when her mouth drops open, I know she's getting into it.

I put all my attention to her face, watching her as she climbs up, reaching for that orgasm. When her walls compress my cock inside her, shock waves soaring through my body, I release. Cries of pleasure surge from her mouth, and I squeeze her tits tighter, raising my hips and spilling every last drop of my cum inside her.

She's breathless by the time she stops. Our arousals mixed together in a sticky mess between us.

Crew comes forward, kisses her cheek, and whispers loud enough for me to hear, "That's my girl."

Then he gets off the bed and crosses the room to the door, closing it behind him.

Scar plops down on me, still stuffed with my cock. "What the hell was that?" She lays her head on my chest, my heart pounding against her skull.

"Don't overthink it. That's his fucked-up way of giving you his approval."

"I don't think so, Jagger. I think he's gonna be mad at me."

I shake my head, kissing the top of hers. "Nah. I

promise you, if Crew was mad, he would have yanked your body off mine and tossed you over his shoulder, then carried you out of this room. That was not Crew being upset."

Scar lifts her head, a cool breeze hitting the spot where she was resting. "You're sure?"

Lifting my head off the pillow, I kiss her lips. "Positive."

We lie there for a few more minutes, then get cleaned up and join the others in the living room.

I'm clutching the diary I found when we walk in, and all eyes land on me.

"What's that?" Neo asks, nodding toward my hand.

"I need to tell you all something."

Crew pats his lap, calling Scar over, and she takes a seat on his knee. His arm wraps around her waist, and oddly enough, I'm unaffected.

Using this time with us all together, I decide to fill everyone in on a little secret I've been keeping—including Riley. Normally, I wouldn't divulge information to her because, as far as I'm concerned, finding intel is her job. But she's here, so this could help her in her search, too.

I take a seat on the arm of the couch and hold up the diary. "I found this a couple weeks ago in the tunnels. I know we made a deal not to go back, but I'm pretty sure that deal was shot a long time ago, considering we've all been down there."

"Is this a diary?" Neo, being the ass he is, snatches it from my hand and begins flipping through it. "It's old as fuck." He shoves it in my lap, then lies back down.

"It belonged to Betty Beckett. Turns out, she was having an affair with Lionel Sunder." I glance at Scar. "Who, as we know, was one of the founding families of the Society."

"So that would have been my great-great-grandfather or something?"

"Couple greats. Not sure how many. I'm not sure of all the details on what happened, but a couple days ago, I was reading through her final entry and this is what she said." I turn to the last page and begin...

*Dear Diary,*

*It's getting worse. The war that has been waged over the land is turning deadly. I fear I will not make it out of this alive. Lionel is changing day by day. His commitment to the Blue Bloods has become obsessive, even frightening, at times. He's growing cold and angry and his frustrations are being taken out on me. What started as an affair full of love is turning to one of hate. Yesterday, I found him leaving the cabin with my late husband George's deed to the property. When I tried to take it back, he claimed it was no longer mine.*

*I'm powerless against him. Lionel took my heart to break and used my body for sex in his quest to gain control over our land.*

*If someone shall ever find this, and I've gone missing, it was at the hands of Lionel Sunder, a Blue Blood. Make them pay. Take back what is ours. Honor George's legacy.*

*Wear a mask if you shall, but whatever you do, inflict pain among them. Do not let my death be in vain. Use them if needed. Take their women and plant your seed inside them, forcing them to bear a child of half-breed. Destroy their bloodlines and never stop until we get back what is ours.*

*All for one, and one for all.*

*Signed,*

*Betty Beckett*

"Oh my god," Scar bellows. "It all makes sense now." She jumps off Crew's lap. The chills down her arm apparent. "My mom said she's convinced Jeremy Beckett killed her former roommate Kenna only days after she gave birth. What if…" I can see the wheels turning in her head, and I know exactly where she's going with this. Her eyes land on mine. "What if he used her body and impregnated her with a son, and once he got what he wanted, he killed her?"

Riley stands up, nodding in agreement. "He created a half-breed with not only a member, but a Guardian."

"A Guardian?" I question Riley's accusation.

"Yeah. Kenna Mitchell was a Guardian. About eighteen years ago, mid-school year, at the Academy, she vanished. Around seven months later, her family was notified that she committed suicide, but that was the Blue Blood way of upholding their reputation. We all know she was murdered."

Neo, who looks bored as fuck, opens one eye. "Where's her half-bred son at then?"

"No clue. I never saw anything about him in my findings."

Neo finally drags his ass up into a sitting position. His head rests back, and he closes his eyes again. "We find the son, we find the fucking creeper."

"I think Neo's right," I chime in. "It has to be Jude Beckett."

Scar sits back down on Crew's lap, looking from person to person. "But without a picture or any info, how do we find him?"

"I guess we up our game. We watch, we wait, and we attack."

"Or," Neo begins, "we toss out that slutty bitch Melody as bait. Let him get a bite out of her before we reel him in."

I shrug my shoulders, not opposed to the idea. No one

argues it, so I toss the diary onto the coffee table and get up. "Sounds like we've got a plan."

Riley yawns, stretching her arms in the air. "Can I get a ride home from one of you kind and generous guys?" Her mocking tone is evident.

I raise my hand, offering up my kind and generous services because I know no one else will. "I'll give you a ride. Lemme grab my coat and keys."

I'm at the top of the stairs when Scar comes jogging up. "That was really nice of you to offer her a ride."

I brush her hair away from her face and give her a kiss. "Do I get a reward for being so kind and generous?"

"Maybe." She smirks. "How about if I'm waiting for you in your bed tonight."

I quirk a brow. "You wanna stay the night in my room?"

When she nods, I kiss her again. "I'd say I've never been more excited to sleep."

She turns to go back downstairs and I give her a tap. When she glances over her shoulder and winks, she says, "Who said anything about sleeping?"

*Damn.* I suddenly have the urge to be a better person every day. How can I not when I get rewarded with that?

# TWENTY-FIVE

## SCAR

"Ready?" Crew asks as I swipe my messenger bag off the couch.

I step into one boot, then the other. "Yup."

Reaching for my bag, Crew holds it back. "I've got it."

I'm on my tiptoes in front of him when I press my lips to his. "Such a gentleman."

"Only with you. Mark my words, *only with you.*"

Things are still unsettled between Crew, Jagger, and me. We haven't really talked and honestly, I don't see any reason to. Whatever we're doing is working, so why fix something that isn't broken?

Three days ago, I learned of Riley's place at the Academy, and to say I was shell-shocked would be an understatement. Riley's not your typical badass girl. I recently learned that her dad, Samson Cross, is a covert investigator for the CIA. I'm sure Riley gained some of her skills from him and it wouldn't surprise me if she continues to follow in his footsteps, even if she doesn't want to.

Crew opens the door, letting me out first. It's unusually

warm right now, with only a few patches of snow, but neither of us are complaining. The downfall, we have to walk because there isn't enough snow for the sleds.

Holding Crew's hand, we cross through the yard to head onto the trail. The slamming of the front door behind us has our eyes shooting over our shoulders.

Jagger jogs toward us while Neo walks at a leisurely pace. We stand there, waiting for them, and I squeeze Crew's hand; my way of telling him I'm present for him, too.

When Jagger catches up to us, Crew hollers to Neo, "Hurry your ass up." Neo's response is a beastly growl and he continues walking slowly, and I'm sure it's just to piss us all off.

"Don't be a dick," Jagger shouts at him, but Neo just lifts his middle finger and flips him off.

Crew tugs my hand. "Let's just go."

Two minutes later, his voice comes from over my shoulder. "It's too early for this shit."

I've learned that when you ask Neo to do something, he won't do it. If you just ignore his childish behavior and act like you don't give a damn, he usually gives in.

Crew leans forward and glances at Jagger, who's on the other side of me, before tossing my bag at him. "Here, dipshit." Jagger catches it with two hands and flings the strap over his shoulder. "You're on bag duty today," Crew says. "I've got ten pounds of books in my own bag."

I glance between them, feeling a strange contentment. It makes me insanely happy when they do little shit that shows they're not bothered by this situation—Crew acknowledging Jagger is a part of my life, and Jagger acknowledging Crew is, too.

We reach the school with a good ten minutes to spare.

Seems we gave ourselves too much time for the walk and we're here early. Neo isn't pleased, but he drops on the floor in front of his locker and pops his earbuds in, pretending he's the only one who exists.

Jagger kisses me on the cheek and swings my bag over my shoulder. "I've gotta go print something in the library so I'll see you later."

When he leaves, it's just me and Crew—and the many students filling the halls, but they don't matter. Crouched down, I shuffle through my bag and pull out the books I need before stuffing my bag inside my locker and closing it.

"Gimme those." Crew takes the books from my hand and drops them to the floor in front of my locker, stacking his on top of mine. He takes my hand and pulls me down the hall while my giggles echo off the rows of lockers.

"Where are we going?"

Instead of responding, he stops walking, reaches behind me, and turns the handle to the janitor's closet, then he walks me inside.

"Crew! We can't."

His face nuzzles into the nape of my neck, and he hums. "Oh, yes, we can. Ever since I saw you riding Jagger the other day, I've been craving the same attention."

"In here?"

He grabs my waist, hoisting me up and shelving me against the far wall. My legs wrap around him, caging him in. "Damn straight."

Clutching his head, I guide his mouth toward mine and a rush of adrenaline shoots through me. There's nothing quite like the feeling of potentially getting caught. It turns me on and has me starving for his touch.

Our tongues tangle together, mouths never parting as

my legs drop to the floor. Crew takes down his pants, his belt clanking against the porcelain floor.

It's too dark to see anything, but I don't need to. I've memorized everything about Crew, and even in the dark, I know exactly where to find what I'm looking for. Moving one hand, I stretch my arm between us and get a firm hold on his erect cock. My hand glides up and down, stroking his full length.

Soft lips work their way down my collarbone, and my head falls back against the wall, eyes closed. "Take me, Crew."

With a husky voice, he croaks, "Oh, I will. I'm gonna fuck you so hard, the students passing in the hall are gonna come."

In one swift motion, Crew swoops me back up until I'm straddling him again, my skirt bunched at my waist and my legs locked behind him. With my panties pushed to the side, he adjusts himself until he's lined up with my entrance. My body drops down a tad, and he slides inside me.

"God, I've missed this."

It's only been a couple days since Crew and I have had sex, but I've missed him, too.

Holding tightly to my back, Crew guides me up and down on his cock. It's an awkward position, but it works and fuck if it doesn't feel amazing.

My arousal seeps out of me, soaking my panties, and it's sure to make for an uncomfortable day, but I don't even care. I'd trash them before I'd stop what's happening.

Wrapped in strong arms, my back grating against the wall, Crew uses all his strength to keep me up while fucking me hard, just like he promised.

Tingles of desire shoot through my veins. My core tightens, heart pounding inside my chest.

Crew grunts, grinding harder and faster, giving me every inch of his rock-hard cock.

Moans of pleasure slip through my lips, growing louder and louder until I reach the point of combustion, and I howl into the small, square space. My sounds echo off the walls, fueling Crew to thrust deeper.

"That's right, baby. Come on my cock."

And I do. I lose all control and make no attempt to silence my shrills of ecstasy. My puckered nipples pebble against the fabric of my tee shirt. My thighs tremble, lip quivering. My heart beats rapidly while Crew's does the same, pounding against my chest.

He groans with a heady breath, his head swelling as he comes inside me.

I pinch his shoulders as I come down, electricity still zapping every nerve in my body.

My head drops back, feet now on the floor. "Wow," is all I can say.

"Quick but powerful." Crew presses his lips to mine. His arm stretches up, and when he comes back down, he pulls a string, turning on the light. How he knew exactly where to find that is beyond me.

There's a roll of paper towel on the shelf, so Crew grabs it, unraveling a few sheets, then he crouches down and wipes the insides of my legs, cleaning me up. I watch him as his hand slides up my inner thigh, before moving to the other. I bite my lip, grinning, while wondering how I got so lucky.

When he's done, he balls the paper towel and tosses it to the side. Once were dressed, Crew pulls open the door and I hold my breath in anticipation of what's waiting for us out there. I'm hopeful students aren't gathered around, but anything is possible. All hope is lost when I see groups of girls passing by. Fortunately, they're none the wiser, so we step out and Crew closes the door behind us.

Crew pecks my cheek, before we go our separate ways. "See you at lunch." He winks, unleashing a swarm of butter-flies in my stomach.

# TWENTY-SIX

## SCAR

I'M DRYING my hair in my bathroom when there's a knock at my bedroom door. Wearing just a white plush robe, towel in hand, I go out and pull it open. "Hey," I say to Jagger, stepping aside. "Come on in." I close the door behind him and bring the towel back to my head, scrunching my soaked strands with it.

"Riley's downstairs. Once you get dressed, come on down. She's got news."

My eyes pop open wide. "Good news?"

"Well, I wouldn't ever say news from Riley is good, but it sounds like we're one step closer to catching this guy."

"Okay. Gimme a couple minutes." I drop the towel on the floor and untie my robe. "I just need to get dressed." Full body on display, I peel back the sleeves of my robe and let it drop to my feet. "So," I speak casually, "do we still need to use Melody as bait today?"

Jagger scratches the top of his head, his eyes dragging up and down my body. "I...um...What'd you say?" His eyes land on mine, wide and observant.

"The plan? Is it still on?" I turn around, bend over, and pick my towel back up, enticing him with my ass.

"Oh, yeah. Plan's still a go."

I rub the towel against my head again, wondering if he's going to make his move.

As I come back up, Jagger grabs me from behind. "Are you teasing me, Scarlett?"

*Lord have mercy.* The way he says my name like that does wild things to my body.

With my back to his chest, his fingers tangle gently around my neck before skating down to my breasts. His thumb and forefinger caress my nipple before clamping down with pressure and hitting a nerve that has my pussy throbbing.

"You want me to fuck you, Scarlett? Or do you just wanna suck my dick while I eat you for dinner?"

Who knew that gorgeous mouth could be so dirty?

"Fuck me." My words come out in a desperate plea. "Right here. Right now."

When his hands leave my body, I miss them already. I turn around to face him, and he's already shedding his clothes.

Once we're both completely naked, he swoops me up in his arms, cradling me like a baby. Just as I think he's going to drop me on the bed and feast on me, he flips me and bends me over the bed.

Two fingers immediately crook inside me, though it's short-lived, and I whimper when he pulls them out.

The same fingers slide up my cheeks, stopping at my asshole, and he pushes the tips inside. It's a sensation I've never felt before. Fortunately, my arousal works as lube, coating his finger. There's a twinge of pain, but there's also a longing for more.

Just as he pushes his finger deeper, his cock slides in my pussy. My body jolts, heart jumping in my throat, as he fingers my ass and fucks me at the same time.

It takes a minute to get into it, but once I do, I'm all in.

My ass rocks back and forth against him. My own fingers digging into my down comforter, balling it in my palms.

"Jagger." His name drips from my mouth in a raspy moan.

"You like that?" He pinches my waist, pumping faster, filling both my holes.

"Yes," I cry out.

"Good. Because next time, it'll be my dick in your ass. Maybe I'll invite Crew to watch. You liked that, didn't you?" He pumps faster, causing my body to ride up on the bed. "Does it turn you on when he watches us?"

My only response is an unmuddled howl of pleasure. There's something about his words that has me soaring. As if he couldn't be any sexier, then he goes and speaks like that.

With my arms bracing me against the mattress and my face down, I roll my hips, meeting him thrust for thrust.

I screech and whimper and cry out, not masking my sounds, while knowing anyone could hear me. The immense pleasure I'm feeling sets no boundaries. "Oh god!"

He pumps again, and again, feeding me all of him with his finger plugging me.

When I reach the height of my climax, my walls contract, milking his orgasm. Tingles shoot through my body while blood rushes to my head.

Once his movements stop and he's slid his finger out, I

drop my full weight onto the bed. I'm in ecstasy—unable to move.

Jagger leans over my naked body and presses his lips to my cheek, returning to the sweet guy I know and love.

We get cleaned up in my bathroom, and while I feel like I could use another shower, there's no time.

A few minutes later, we're walking into the kitchen where Riley, Crew, and Neo are sitting at the round, oak table. Leave it to Neo to speak up first. "Hope you didn't loosen her up too much for my boy Crew over here."

With a balled fist, I punch him hard in the shoulder. In the past, I wouldn't have even thought twice about doing such a thing, but Neo is learning quickly that I fight back.

He snarls at me, then returns his attention to the center of the table. I expected some more cruel words or maybe a wrist grab, but it seems things really have changed. For instance, Neo makes claims time and time again that he hates Crew and Jagger—two guys who are supposed to be his best friends. But during his jabs at me, suddenly they're his boys again. I know it to be true. Neo just has a hard shell.

"What's this big news?" I ask, pulling out a chair and sitting down between Crew and Riley.

"Riley's convinced it's a student," Crew says, pushing three or four papers into the center of the table.

"And you're not convinced?"

"A student?" Crew huffs, leaning back in his chair and stretching his arms out on either side of him. "How the hell would they get past us? We can't be that naïve."

"It would explain their access to us. Regardless, it's obvious this person knows their way around the Academy fairly well."

"No shit," Neo chimes in. "The Becketts are trained to hate us from birth. Wouldn't surprise me if they were watching last year, too." His gaze casts on me. "Probably just waiting around for Scar to make her appearance."

*Ugh.* The thought makes my skin crawl. "Or maybe he wasn't watching you all, and he was watching me back home."

"But why?" Riley asks. "That's what I can't figure out. Why you? I mean, it's no secret the Becketts hate us, but to single you out? There has to be something we don't know. Some sort of past between the Sunders and the Becketts."

I chew on my nail, racking my brain and trying to think of anything my parents may have mentioned that didn't click at the time but would now. Or even my grandparents. I remember the day my grandfather passed away. He was so sick for so long and my family gathered around his bedside, Dad holding one hand and my grandmother holding the other. With his last breath, he looked at me and said, "Scarlett, you were exactly what we didn't know we needed in our lives." I took it to mean, I might not have been planned for, but, to my family, I was a blessing. Even if my birth did cause a ripple in the family. My mom fell in love with her stepbrother and in the eyes of the Society, they sinned.

"Scar?" Riley nudges me, pulling me out of my thoughts.

"Huh?"

"I asked if you're ready?"

"Oh yeah. Sorry."

Looks like it's showtime. The guys devised a plan and had Melody leave the creep his own little note. He was instructed to meet her at the river with the assumption that she wants to help him destroy us all due to her own vendetta against the Blue Bloods. Now, we get to stand back and see if he takes the bait.

"Whoa." I take a step back, hands up in surrender, when I see Neo sticking a gun into a holster beneath his shirt. "What are you doing with that?"

"Protection. What else? You can't really think we're gonna go out there and try to bring this psychopath down without protection?"

"I suppose not." This is turning out to be much more serious than I could have ever imagined. I hope like hell it's just a scare tactic, and he doesn't intend to use it.

Jagger comes down the stairs and hands me a solid black hoodie. "Put this on." Then he pulls a similar one over his head. Crew comes down the stairs, and what do you know, black hoodie.

"I missed the memo where we all have to match," Neo says, waving his fingers between us. "Or is this some sort of cute couple shit?"

"Fuck off. It's cold," Jagger tells him. "Not to mention, we need to be inconspicuous."

"Inconspicuous would be camouflaged. Not black." Says the guy wearing a black leather jacket and black jeans that are shredded in the knees.

Once we're all ready, we head out for the long walk to the river. Even if we could use the guys' sleds, they're too loud, and we'd give ourselves away. So here we are, stuck walking with Neo. Well, he's walking behind us, but when the hood of my sweatshirt pulls down, I know he's closer than I'd like him to be.

"Quit it," I snap at him, pulling it back up.

He does it again, laughing. "Fucking with you is so fun."

I pull it up, again. "Would you grow up?"

At least he's not tripping me or shoving my face into a pile of snow. Progress has been made, but we're still far from being okay with each other.

I slow my steps, letting Crew, Jagger, and Riley go ahead, while I stay back and walk beside Neo.

Crew and Jagger both glance at me, but I say, "Keep going. I'll catch up."

Neo snarls at my side. "Pulling your hood down wasn't an invitation to talk to me."

"Too bad. I took it as one. Now, don't be a dick and hear me out."

He reaches into his pocket, taking out his earbuds, sticking one in.

"Are you kidding?" I growl at him, reaching over and tugging the damn thing out of his ear.

"Bitch. Give that back."

I clutch it in my palm, shooting daggers at him. "Call me a bitch again and I'll throw it into the woods."

"Then I'd make you search for it on your hands and knees—naked." He grabs my balled fist. "Unravel your fingers or I'll break every single one of them."

I don't. Instead, I clamp tighter, my nails bedding into my palms and threatening to pierce my skin. "Do you still think I pushed Maddie?" I ask, being as blunt as possible, so I can get away from him and back to my friends.

He doesn't answer, just keeps trying to pry my fingers apart.

"The picture in my room last week shows that this guy, Jude, or whoever it is, has been watching me for a while. Would you consider the possibility that he was watching me that day on Coy Mountain, and when I went down, he pushed Maddie?"

His hands drop from mine and his feet move again. He pops his other earbud in, and this one, I leave in place because he's still got one ear to hear me out.

"You know I wouldn't do it, Neo. You just wanted to think it was me because there was no one else to blame. But now there is."

He's humming along to whatever song is playing in his right ear, completely ignoring me. I grab him by the arm, and he jerks away, sneering at me. "Answer me, dammit."

"Fine. Yes. Okay!" he finally blurts out, stopping in his tracks and facing me. "It's possible. Doesn't mean I don't hate you anymore. Doesn't mean I'm going to apologize if I'm wrong. It just means I'll consider the possibility and eventually find out the truth." He stares into my eyes, searching for a reaction. Seeing if his words have lifted some sort of veil off me, like I suddenly feel like they've done to him. He's still Neo, and I still don't like him either, but maybe the truth can make us hate each other a little less.

I hand him back his earbud and when our fingers brush, something shifts inside him. His head tilts slightly to the left, his eyes burning into mine. It's like he's questioning himself. Or maybe he's questioning me.

Then suddenly, he pivots around and starts walking again. I stand there dumbfounded, unsure what just happened, but it was a moment in time I've never experienced with Neo. It's like he had a soul, and it's as if I could almost feel it.

Bypassing Neo, I jog to catch up to Jagger, Crew, and Riley, who are almost to the riverbank. Once I reach them, Jagger throws out an arm, stopping me. "Shh," he whispers, a finger pressed to his lips.

Neo comes stampeding up, without a care in the world,

a lit joint between his lips. Crew snatches it from his mouth. "Are you fucking stupid?" He tosses the joint to the ground, extinguishing it with the heel of his boot.

"No. But I was about to be high until your dumb ass ruined it for me."

"He'll smell it and know we're here."

"He'll also smell the entire bottle of cotton candy perfume Riley put on, but you don't see me ripping off her shirt." He gapes at the sky, tapping his chin. "Now there's an idea."

Riley and I share a look, both shaking our heads in disgust with this Neanderthal. When Riley turns back around, binoculars pressed to her eyes like a true detective, she gasps. "Oh no!" She bolts for the river and we all chase after her.

"What happened?" I ask, but no one answers me.

Riley slips, sliding on her ass before her legs get tangled underneath her, and she rolls down the small hill. "Ahhh," she whimpers, going down.

I cup my hands around my mouth and holler, "Are you okay?"

Jagger is the first to get to her, and he reaches for her hand, pulling her up. By the time I get down, she's a muddy, mad mess. It's not until she points at the river that I'm able to see what she was running after.

My hand claps over my mouth, heart dropping into the depths of my stomach. "Oh my god! Melody!"

Lying face down in the river is a body with a knife sticking out of their back.

Jagger screeches as he steps into the river, the water up to his ankles. He goes deeper, and it rides farther up his jeans. "That's my hoodie."

"The girl at the party! She's the one who had your hoodie. Maybe it's not Melody. Maybe it's her?" I begin to panic, turning around, unable to look because I can't even imagine how I'll react if this person is dead. Crew comes up and wraps his arms around me, and I curl my head against his chest, sobbing into his sweatshirt.

"It's a decoy," Jagger shouts. "It's not a person."

I look over and he's holding up a soaking wet scarecrow wearing his hoodie. We all breathe out heavy sighs of relief. "Thank God."

Jagger comes up, dragging the scarecrow with him. Once he's back up on the riverbank, he tosses it to the ground. Out of breath and shivering, he says, "There's a note."

I inhale deeply, my bones shaking. "Of course there is."

Neo crouches down and pulls the knife from the scarecrow's back that went straight through a piece of paper and Jagger's hoodie. He lifts the note, and though it's wet, it's readable. *"You think you can trust someone, then they stab you in the back."*

I look from person to person, but no one says anything, so I speak my thoughts. "It has to be referencing Melody, because we used her and tried setting him up."

"Maybe." Neo shrugs. "Or maybe it's someone else who can't be trusted." He's looking right at me as he says the words, and every bit of progress we've made feels like it's been tossed into the river.

"Doesn't matter," Riley says, "this was a bust. He knows Melody was working against him, and now we've lost all the headway we had."

"But Melody was supposed to meet him," I say. "She should have been here over twenty minutes ago. If she's not here, where is she?"

No one answers because no one knows.

"We have to find her," I tell them. "I can't stand Melody, but I don't want her or anyone else to get hurt...or die."

"I'll go look for her," Riley says, taking me by surprise once again. "You guys take Scar back and make sure she stays safe."

"You shouldn't do this alone, Ry." I look at Crew, then Jagger. "Can one of you go with her?"

"Neo and I will go," Crew says. "Jagger, you take Scar home."

Neo puts up a fight, but eventually gives in. We all head down the trail together, and when it's time to part ways, I hug Riley. "Be careful."

"You, too."

Crew's next. His arms wrap around my waist, fingers snaking up the back of my sweatshirt, and his skin feels warm and soft against mine. "Everything's gonna be all right," he assures me. "I love you." If I thought my skin was warm against his, it's nothing compared to the heat rushing inside me.

"I love you, too," I tell him, honestly. Because I do. I love Crew and I love Jagger. I also love Riley. All three of them have become family to me, and each one has a part in my life that's different from the next.

Jagger and I are walking back, hand in hand, when I ask him for a favor. "Do you think I could use your phone to make a call?" This whole thing has me thinking a lot about Maddie. I try calling her often, but each time, it's the same song and dance. I'm not on the list, so I can't get any info. Occasionally, I have one of the guys get info from Neo, but his response is always, *No change,* except the last time Crew asked him. In which he said he hadn't heard anything about her in almost a week.

"Anything. What do you need?"

"Your phone. I wanna try the home again." I lift a shoulder, holding on to hope. "You just never know. Maybe Sebastian added me back on her approved list."

Jagger reaches into his pocket, pulls out his phone, and hands it to me.

I dial the number, knowing it by heart, and it rings a few times before someone answers.

"Heartland Home. How can I help you?"

"Hi, Tammy. I'm not sure if you remember me. It's Scarlett."

"Of course, dear. How could I forget? You must be calling about Maddie?"

"I am." My eyes perk up, looking at Jagger. "Are you able to give me an update?"

"Unfortunately, I can't give you any updates on her condition, but you must not have heard. Maddie's not with us anymore."

My heart begins racing, eyes wide with trepidation. "What? She's gone?"

"No, no. She's not gone. She's just not at this home anymore. She's been moved."

"Moved? Where?"

"I wasn't here during the transfer. I wish I could say more."

"Umm. Okay. Thank you, Tammy." I end the call immediately, squeezing the phone tightly in my hand. "Maddie's been moved. Why wouldn't Neo tell me?"

"That's weird. Maybe it just slipped his mind."

We start walking again, my thoughts stuck on Maddie and where she might have been moved.

Jagger's phone rings, cutting through the silence. When he answers, I watch him.

"No shit. Well, at least we know she wasn't out causing trouble." He pulls the phone from his ear and says to me, "Melody was found tied up in her room."

I'm a bitch for smiling, but Melody is learning the hard way not to fuck with people. Something tells me she *is* learning, though.

"All right. See you in a bit." He ends the call and sticks his phone in his pocket, just as I open the front door.

Sensing my unease, he takes my hand and leads me over to the couch, boots still on. "We'll figure out where Maddie is and maybe then you'll be able to get the update you want."

I nod, swallowing down the lump in my throat. "I know. Maddie just doesn't like change, and I hope her move doesn't set her back at all."

"She's sleeping, Scar. I doubt she even knows."

She knows. Maddie might be sleeping, but her mind is awake and alert. She knows exactly what's going on around her.

Jagger holds me for a few minutes until the door flies open and Crew and Neo stagger in. I bolt up, words spilling from my mouth. "How could you not tell me Maddie was moved!" I shout at Neo.

"Calm your ass down," he barks. "Maddie wasn't moved."

"Yes, she was! I called the home and they told me she's not there anymore. Don't act like you didn't know. You're still trying to keep her from me, aren't you?"

Neo doesn't respond, just taps into his phone and lifts it to his ear, his eyes on me as he speaks. "Dad! What's going on with Maddie?"

His eyes widen, so mine do the same. My stomach twists into tight knots as the look on his face spreads to one of sheer panic. "Find her, dammit! Do whatever you have to do, but you better fucking find her!'

When he ends the call, his phone goes flying from his hand, crashing into the television on the wall. I hurry to his side because I need to hear him loud and clear.

"Tell me," I say, my voice shaking.

"Maddie's missing."

"Missing?" I gasp. "How does someone in a coma go missing?"

"Someone blackmailed an employee at the home. Signed Maddie out and took her, medical equipment and all."

Neo's expression of shock mimics mine. We all stand there silently as we grasp the information we've been given.

Finally, after minutes of internally screaming.

*Who would do this?*

*Why would anyone do this?*

*Where is Maddie?*

It hits me.

"It was him. The BCA Stalker, aka Jude Beckett. He did this."

NEO'S DAD picked him up three hours after the call. Sebastian argued that Neo needed to stay put, but he wasn't having it. He told his dad either he came to get him, or he was calling someone else for a ride. So, he came.

My thoughts have been running rampant since we learned of Maddie's disappearance.

She needs medical equipment and a trained professional to care for her. There's no way Jude Beckett, a seventeen-year-old boy, has the means to give her the proper attention she needs.

At this point, we just need to find her alive before something terrible happens.

Crew and Jagger are sleeping in my bed with me, one on each side. I shouldn't say sleeping because none of us have been able to close our eyes. It's a strange sentiment, feeling so loved, yet so lost.

Nothing will be the same until Maddie is found. And once she is, nothing will be the same again.

# EPILOGUE

## SCAR

Jagger zips up the back of my Sally costume dress while I hold my hair to one side. "It just doesn't feel right. Going to a Halloween dance while Maddie is still missing."

"Neo and Sebastian will find her. I've got no doubt in my mind."

It's been over a week since Neo left, and there is still no update. Each day that passes has me feeling less and less hopeful for Maddie's safe return, but no one is giving up yet. It's almost been that same time frame since we've heard or seen anything from the BCA Stalker.

I turn around, letting my hair fall down my back. "You really think she's okay?"

His arms snake around my neck and his forehead presses to mine. "I know she is."

"I can't take you seriously with that mask on." I chuckle, when in reality, it's creeping me out.

"Says the girl with black eyes and lips."

My shoulders bob up and down. "Touché. I suppose I probably look like a fool, too."

"Fuck no. You look hot as hell. I've always wondered what it would be like to fuck—"

"Don't." I shake my head. "Don't say it." I'm not sure if he was going to say Sally, or a dead girl, but either way, it's creepy.

Everyone ordered costumes that were delivered a few days ago. After begging and pleading with both Crew and Jagger for one of them to dress as my Jack, I lost. Crew is going as the guy from the *Scream* movies, and Jagger is going as Michael Myers. Seeing people dressed up as crazed characters is ironic, given our situation.

Skirting his fingers up my dress, he caresses my inner thigh. "Don't act like it doesn't turn you on."

"Sex with Michael Myers? Hard pass." Though, my wheels are turning now. A little roleplay could be fun. *No.* At least, not right now. "We need to get going. I told Ry we'd meet her and Elias outside the athletic center.

The dance is being held inside the gym, and with Riley being on the decorating committee, I have no doubt it's going to look amazing. Halloween has always been one of my favorite holidays, although I haven't dressed up since I was a kid. It feels nice to put a mask on—figuratively, not literally, considering my face is full of makeup.

"Let's go," Crew says from the doorway.

Jagger sighs, dropping his hands from around me. "Cockblocker." The word comes out as a mumble, but I hear him.

Crew steps in the room, his mask in hand. "We've got the bus out picking people up. Figured it was best to keep everyone off the trails tonight, even with security in place."

I round Jagger and walk to Crew. "I agree. So, are we catching the bus?"

"Hell no. We got snow. We're sledding it tonight." Crew flips the bottom of my dress that sits just below my ass. "You riding with me?"

"Yeah." I look back at Jagger, who's adjusting his mask in my mirror. "Is that okay with you?"

Once he's got it positioned to his liking, he straightens his back. "Sure. Ride with him there and ride me later." I can see his wink, even through the holes in my mask, and it makes my stomach flip-flop.

"Let's go." I grab Crew's hand, laughing as we talk down the hall. It's when we reach the top of the stairs that guilt sets in. I shouldn't be laughing. I shouldn't be having any fun.

"Hey," Crew says, squeezing my hand in his, "everything's gonna work out."

I nod in response, and once Jagger catches up, we all go downstairs and leave together.

Since we got a good six inches of snow over the last forty-eight hours, I opt for my heavy winter coat and pass on the helmet because I spent way too much time on this hair and makeup. It's not something I do often, so there's no way in hell I'm letting it be for nothing.

Ten minutes later, we're pulling up to the athletic center and the place is already hopping. All three of us walk in together, Crew on one side of me and Jagger on the other. Sure, we turn a few heads because people have been talking, but since when do I give a shit what anyone thinks of me? The way I see it, these bitches are just jealous because I have two of the three guys they all want.

This dance is more on the traditional side of our gatherings. It's put on and funded by the Academy versus our keg parties at the Ruins. While technically, we're not supposed to drink, I've already heard rumors of someone spiking the punch.

"I'm gonna look for Riley," I tell the guys, and even though they nod in agreement, they both follow me. That's what happens when you're being stalked by a psycho, and it's Halloween.

As soon as I spot her, she's full-on running toward me in a pair of four-inch heels and a formfitting red dress. "You're here." She beams, throwing her arms around me.

"And you're drunk." I wave my hand in front of my nose, sweeping away the intoxicating scent of vodka.

"Little bit. But it's Halloween." Her hands fly in the air as her eyes surf the room.

I press my hands to her shoulders, taking in her outfit. "What is this? I thought you said you were the Princess Bride?" She's got the color right, and the gold ribbon belt, but the length is all wrong.

"I'm a slutty Princess Buttercup." She points across the room, and I glance in the direction to where Elias is standing. "And over there is my Westley."

He's at the punch bowl, a cup in his hand, and when he catches us looking at him, he raises it in cheers. He actually got the costume right with the black outfit and matching eye mask.

Crew and Jagger are engaging in small talk, when a strange feeling washes over me. It's not just the feeling that someone is watching me, but that someone *actually is* watching me. Riley keeps talking and I nod in response to everything she says, as if I hear each word, but I can't help but glance at the figure to my left, who is just standing there, with his eyes on me. He's dressed up as Darth Vader and his costume is on point. Probably one of the best here. There's something alluring about him. A mystery I want to solve.

"Scar. Did you hear anything I just said?"

I look back at Riley, my stomach curling. "Don't look," I grit through my teeth, "Darth Vader to the left."

Of course, her eyes snap right to him, and when they do, he comes our way.

"Holy shit. He's coming over here." I tug Riley's arm, wanting to get away because something feels off, but the new Riley shines through, brightly and boldly.

She stands tall, arms crossed over her chest, while giving herself a cleavage boost. "Who are you?" she deadpans.

The guy lifts his hand to his mask and pulls it back slowly, revealing the one person I did not expect to see tonight.

"Neo? What are you doing back? Please tell me Maddie has been found."

He shakes his head no, washing away any sliver of hope I had in this moment. "No. But we're close. We found something out, and I think this information will lead us right to Maddie. We can't talk here, though."

I look around the room in search of Crew and Jagger. As if Neo knows exactly who I'm searching for, he says, "They're outside. Follow me."

Riley and I share a look, and I can't shake this chilling feeling. Her calm demeanor tells me she's feeling anything but. Then again, she's drunk, so I wouldn't expect her to be on high alert. Maybe that's what I need—a stiff drink.

When we reach the doors, Riley glances behind her, and I do the same. Elias is still at the punch table, watching us as we leave. Hopefully he doesn't get suspicious of Riley and me following Neo outside. The last thing we need is the student body catching wind of what's actually been going on. I'd imagine all hell would break loose and parents would be picking up their kids. In which case, we'd never catch this guy.

Neo pushes open the double doors and the cool night air slaps me in the face. As he said they'd be, Crew and Jagger are waiting outside, both leaning against their snowmobiles.

We all gather around while Neo prepares to share what he found. Reaching into his pocket, he pulls out a paper, or two, and begins unfolding them. He hands them to Jagger first. I watch his face attentively as he reads it over, flipping to the other page. Eyes wide, mouth agape, he passes them to Crew. My heart is prepared to flee from my chest. I wave my hand in the air, rushing this along. "What is it?"

Crew draws his fingers to his mouth, then passes them to me. At first glance, I'm stupefied. I can't read it fast enough, but as I do, chills break out over my entire body. I flip the page, and it's even more revealing than the last—it's a death certificate.

"Oh my god." I choke, taking in a lungful of cold air.

Riley snatches the papers from me, and we all look at her, waiting for her reaction.

"No." Her head shakes, eyes on the first page. "No. This can't be."

She turns to the next page, then peers up at me. "Elias Stanton is dead!"

Preorder Book Three, *Twisted Secrets*, and find out what happens when Neo's heart thaws, and the BCA Stalker plays a deadly game!

# Also by Rachel Leigh

**Bastards of Boulder Cove**

Book One: Savage Games

Book Two: Vicious Lies

Book Three: Twisted Secrets Coming November 2022

**Redwood Rebels Series**

Book One: Striker Book Two: Heathen

Book Three: Vandal Book Four: Reaper

**Redwood High Series**

Book One: Like Gravity Book Two: Like You

Book Three: Like Hate

**Fallen Kingdom Duet**

His Hollow Heart & Her Broken Pieces

**Black Heart Duet**

Four & Five

**Standalones**

Guarded

Ruthless Rookie

Devil Heir

All The Little Things

# Acknowledgments

Readers: Thank you so much for reading Vicious Lies!

I want to give a big thank you to everyone who helped me along the way. My alpha reader, Amanda and my beta readers, Erica and Amanda. To my amazing PA, Carolina, thank you for all you do. Thanks to Rebecca at Rebecca's Fairest Reviews and Editing for another amazing edit and proofread, as well as Rumi for proofreading. To my street team, the Rebel Readers, I love you all so much and I'm so grateful for all you do. Thanks to The Pretty Little Design Co. for this amazing cover! And to all my Ramblers, thanks for being on this journey with me.

xoxo-Rachel

# ABOUT THE AUTHOR

Rachel Leigh is a USA Today bestselling author of new adult and contemporary romance with a twist. You can expect bad boys, strong heroines, and an HEA.

Rachel lives in leggings, overuses emojis, and survives on books and coffee. Writing is her passion. Her goal is to take readers on an adventure with her words, while showing them that even on the darkest days, love conquers all.

www.rachelleighauthor.com
Rachel's Ramblers Readers Group